Also by Ray Hobbs and pι

G000140772

An Act of Kindness

Following On

A Year From Now

A Rural Diversion

A Chance Sighting

Roses and Red Herrings

Happy Even After

The Right Direction

An Ideal World

Mischief and Masquerade

Published Elsewhere

Second Wind (Spiderwize)

Lovingly Restored (New Generation Publishing)

BIG IDEAS

RAY HOBBS

Wingspan Press

Published in the United States and the United Kingdom by WingSpan Press, Livermore, CA

The WingSpan name, logo and colophon are the trademarks of WingSpan Publishing.

ISBN 978-1-63683-004-9 (pbk.)
ISBN 978-1-63683-996-7 (ebook)

First edition 2021

Printed in the United States of America

www.wingspanpress.com

1 2 3 4 5 6 7 8 9 10

This book is dedicated to the memory of the songwriters, bandleaders, musicians and singers who created the unique magic that was the Golden Age of the British Dance Band.

RH

I am indebted to my brother Chris, for acting, as ever, as a soundboard and as a regular source of ideas, as well as helping to fuel my enthusiasm throughout the writing of this book.

Author's Note Regarding Dialect

At the time at which this story is set, dialect in the West Riding, as in other regions, was much more marked than it is today. Before the emergence of television and widespread access to radio, communities were unavoidably insular and therefore inclined to preserve the familiar vernacular, to the extent that their speech would have been unintelligible to the people of today.

For that reason, I have kept dialect to a minimum and used it only to enable characterisation and regional colour. Even so, I feel that some guidance is necessary, and I have attempted to provide that below.

A Guide to Dialect Words and Phrases in this Book

Na then (accent on the second word) is, at face value, the ultimate oxymoron, being a corruption of 'now then', and if that sounds meaningless, please read on, because the phrase has several uses and meanings. It can be used as a greeting, or it can advise caution. It can precede a suggestion, e.g. 'Na then, let's....' It is used commonly to indicate understanding or agreement, as in 'In that case....', 'If that's what you want....' 'I see' or 'I take your point.' Nonsense is not always what it seems. Other words and phrases, however, are more easily translated.

Gaffer: any boss or employer.

Brass: money in any form.

Owt: anything.

Nowt: nought, nothing.

Summat: something.

(To) **Mash** (tea): to brew.

Get away (pron. 'Gerraway'): an expression of surprise or disbelief.

(To) **Bray**: to strike or beat someone or something.

Muck or nettles: instant and absolute success or failure.

Brussen: brazen, bold, self-assured.

(To) **Frame**: to tackle a task or situation.
  RH

A WEST RIDING TOWN

1935

The bath was one of the highlights of Hutch's weekend. On Saturday nights, he played alto saxophone with the Rhythm Serenaders at the Town Hall, and on Sunday mornings, he took his pair of elderly clarinets to the Wool Exchange ballroom to rehearse with the Cullington Orchestra. Before that, however, was his weekly visit to the public baths in Providence Road. At twopence a time, his mother called it an extravagance; she and his sister Phyllis used the zinc tub at home, but from Hutch's point of view, it was money well spent. For twenty minutes, he could immerse himself in carbolic-scented warmth, peace and solitude. It was a time for reflection without the risk of interruption and, during that time, the rest of the world and its cruel uncertainties ceased to exist. It was two-pennyworth of self-indulgence.

He stared idly at the green-painted boards that formed the walls of the cubicle, wondering how long he had before Willie Crowther came to turn him out. Hutch had known Willie from childhood, and he'd always been a grumpy old sod.

He hadn't long to wonder, because, as if in response to the thought, there was a knock on the door. 'Are you nearly done in there, young Hutchins? There's folk waiting, you know.'

'I'll be out in a minute, Willie.'

'I'm "Mister Crowther" to you, you cheeky young devil.'

'Right, Willie.' Hutch reached for his towel. With the initials 'W C', Willie was lucky if anyone called him by his proper name. It had long been a standing joke with the local kids, although Hutch had always felt a degree of sympathy for him. Willie had been a

1

blacksmith's striker before losing an arm in the war, and now the poor chap had the job of cleaning baths and calling time. It was better than no job at all but it was hardly a man's work.

He was almost dressed when he heard Willie's voice again. 'Time now, Jack. Get a move on.'

'All right, all right.' Hutch finished dressing, picked up his clarinet case and opened the door. He could see no-one but Willie, so he asked, 'Where are these people you've got waiting?'

'Aye well, I had to get you out of there so I could clean up afore t' next 'un comes.'

'You crafty old sod.'

'Not so much of the "old" if you don't mind, and less of the language an' all.' He leaned on his mop and asked, 'You work at Atkinson's, don't you?'

'That's right.'

'I reckon you'll be out of your indentures soon.'

'I was twenty-one last January.' Hutch was proud of being a qualified engineer.

'I've heard things are bad up there,' said Willie, apparently unimpressed. 'You might be lucky to have a job afore long.'

'Isn't anybody lucky to have a job these days?' Hutch resented that sort of talk. With the weavers on two days a week and cut-backs everywhere else, he was well aware of the situation at the mill, but he didn't want to hear about it from an outsider. He left Willie to get on with his cleaning and turned to the wall mirror to comb his hair. He'd been working hard lately at parting it on the right. He fancied that if he could get it to lie down for long enough it made him look rather like Gary Cooper. He would put something on it when he got home but just for the present, he combed it back and left it in its damp state to make its own decision. He hoped it wouldn't embarrass him. The previous Thursday night, when he was dancing at Rosie Turner's, it had suddenly defied the tragacanth gum holding it down, and had sprung up on end, forsaking the Gary Cooper look for one bearing closer resemblance to Stan Laurel. He was dancing with Rosie at the time and it made her giggle, which was unsettling because he liked her. She was amusing and she had a sense of style. She went to a posh hairdresser in Bradford and had a Marcel wave.

It was a shame he and Rosie could never be more than friends. Her father was manager of Crawley's dyeing and finishing mill, and he would never let his daughter be courted by a mere maintenance engineer. It was perhaps as well that Hutch saw his future elsewhere.

———◆◆◆———

The doorway was open in the August heat and, even when he was several houses away, he could smell the mutton stew heating on the hob. It was the remains of the one they'd had on Friday and Saturday but Hutch didn't mind. He was hungry.

'Na then, Jack,' said his mother, 'did you have a good practice?' She seemed short of breath as she often did lately, and it worried him.

'Not bad. We were short of a trombone but we made do with what we had and it didn't sound too bad.'

'You'll have to write to Norman and tell him they're missing him in the orchestra,' said Phyllis, coming in from the yard.

'You're the one who's always writing to him.'

'Only because he sends me these.' Phyllis took a picture postcard from the mantelpiece over the iron range and handed it to him. 'This one came yesterday but I've hardly seen you.'

He examined the photograph on the card with a sense of wonder. He'd seen the Empire State Building on the newsreels, and been amazed by its sheer size and presence, but even more stunning than that was the knowledge that his mate Norman had actually been to New York and seen it along with everything else that fabulous city had to offer.

'It's twelve-hundred-and-fifty feet high,' said Phyllis.

'I know. It says so here.'

'That doesn't really mean anything,' said Mrs Hutchins. 'Nobody can imagine that.'

'It's nearly a quarter of a mile,' Phyllis told her.

'About twelve times as high as Atkinson's chimney,' said Hutch, reluctant to be outdone. Phyllis was an accounts clerk and good at figures, but he was an engineer, and his pride was at stake.

'Well I never.' Mrs Hutchins greeted Norman's postcards with some reservation. She was fond of him, and because his mother had died when he was only three, she'd treated him almost as one of her family, but the idea of him working as a musician on an ocean liner was beyond the scope of her imagination and she found the whole thing frightening, especially with Hutch eager to follow his example.

'You can read it if you like,' said Phyllis.

'Thanks.' Hutch turned it over to read the message.

RMS Duchess of Lancaster
15th August, 1935.
Dear Phyllis,
Here is another photo for your collection. Hope you are keeping well. Regards to your mother. Tell Hutch to hurry up and find himself a proper job.
Yours, Norman.

'No kisses,' said Hutch. 'He hasn't sent you any kisses.'

'He never does and there's no reason why he should.' Phyllis was blushing. 'Here, give me your wet towel.'

'You shouldn't tease her like that,' his mother told him when Phyllis was out of the room. 'You know she gets embarrassed.'

'She does it to me.'

'Well, even so. Remember she's your sister.'

Hutch had never been too sure what his mother meant by that, but he tried to look suitably penitent and washed his hands at the sink while she served the stew.

Phyllis sat down with them and asked, 'Was Rosie Turner at the practice this morning, Hutch?' Her eyes twinkled because she was getting her own back. So much for not teasing her.

'No, she wasn't.'

'It's no use casting your eye over her,' said his mother. 'She's a gaffer's daughter.'

'I know that, Mother.' He saw that his sister was still smiling and it was a pleasant smile. They'd had many a disagreement when they were younger but they'd grown out of that and they were close. Phyllis was just a year older than him. She was fair-haired, like him, and pretty, and he could understand why Norman kept writing to her. He looked again at the postcard, which was where Phyllis had left it on the table. She had a collection of them in a box upstairs.

'I expect that postcard's given you ideas again,' said his mother.

'The idea's been there for a long time, Mother, and I won't always have a job at the mill.'

'But you've got one now,' she said, bridling as she always did when the matter was mentioned, 'and you're a skilled man. You've got something more than most lads have, and it's worth hanging on to.'

'I know.' Frustrated though he was, he understood his mother's anxiety about his job at the mill. She was forty-three, but widowhood, hardship and drudgery had aged her by at least another dozen years. It must have seemed the greatest luxury to have Phyllis and him each bringing home a grown-up wage. His job was the bird in the hand that she'd dreamt of since his father's death in 1916, so it was little wonder she was worried.

'Mother,' he said gently, 'I know the mill's going to close soon, maybe in the next few weeks. We notice things in our department and they all tell the same story.'

'What have you noticed?'

'All the jobs that need doing, and being told not to bother with them, and I'm not just talking about routine maintenance. There's steam escaping from rusty joints all over the place and I've been told to forget them and concentrate on what's urgent. I'm not the only one who can see what's happening. Fred knows the signs.'

His mother looked at him sharply at the mention of the Chief Engineer's name. She trusted Fred Hartley's judgement. 'What has he said?'

'The last thing he said to me was, "We'll be damping down afore long, lad. Be warned." That's all, but he meant it.'

Mrs Hutchins looked down at her plate and said quietly, 'I'd die a thousand deaths if you went away to sea, Jack. I lost your father that way and I don't want to lose you an' all.'

'I'm not going to sea, Mother. I told you before when I'd been to the Bradford Odeon.' He could tell she only half believed him. Norman had gone to sea and it followed in her mind that Hutch would do the same. 'When Billy Hey heard me,' he reminded her, 'he told me to go to London. He said I'd be sure to find work there.'

Mr Hey had actually suggested that there was work to be had there, and Hutch was aware of the difference but he had an argument to win. 'I've got to do it, Mother.' He pointed to the postcard. 'Norman's getting nine quid a week and all found on that liner, and they're paying much the same in London. More in some places.'

'Never in this wide world.'

'It's right, Mother.' Phyllis had been quiet up to then, and her support, whilst overdue, was no less welcome. 'Norman told me that too, and he doesn't tell fairy stories.'

Hutch had also never doubted it, astonishing though it sounded. The only times he earned anything approaching that sum were when the D'Oyly Carte and Carl Rosa opera companies came on tour and made up part of their respective orchestras with local musicians. Even then, they only came once a year.

Mrs Hutchins shook her head in disbelief. 'All this talk,' she said. 'Silly money, London....' She shook her head again. 'And it isn't even what you'd call proper work.'

'It's what folk want, Mother,' said Hutch. 'We all like to dance, but while we do it at Rosie Turner's to the wireless and the gramophone, the well-to-do dance to a band in a restaurant and they pay a lot of money for it.'

'Well, I don't know. It doesn't seem respectable to me. There must be a lot of folk down there with more brass than sense, and it beats me where they find it these days. There's little enough hereabouts.' She looked at Phyllis and then at Hutch, and said, 'I expect you two will be going dancing on Thursday night an' all.' It was almost an accusation. She found their carefree attitude in such difficult times hard to accept.

The evening at Rosie's would hardly be the kind of scene Hutch had just painted for her but he was looking forward to it all the same, and so was Phyllis. It was what young people did.

———◆◆◆———

The Thursday evening routine was the perfect arrangement. It was Rosie's father's lodge night, which made it a convenient time for Mrs Turner to visit her sister and her young nieces. Also, the Turners had those two most desirable luxuries: a wireless set and a gramophone. The drawing room, as they called it, of their Victorian mill house was spacious enough to accommodate the half-dozen or so couples who gathered there, and there was one more visitor that Thursday, as Hutch soon discovered.

Neville Rushworth was an immaculate young man who moved and spoke with easy confidence. His uncle was Arthur Crawley, Mr Turner's employer and a man of great influence. He also had the first three dances with Rosie, one of them a foxtrot, which was Hutch's favourite.

The odd number of dancers meant that, at any time, one girl would be without a partner and, as Rosie was currently unavailable, Hutch danced with them in turn. Soon it was his sister's turn.

Seeing Rosie once more in the newcomer's arms, and noting Hutch's resentful gaze, she squeezed his shoulder and said, 'Chin up, Hutch. You knew you couldn't hold on to her for long.'

'I know, but it's galling all the same.'

'She was never good enough for you. I've said it all along.' She wore the half-smile that told him that, whilst she was not being entirely serious, at least she was wholly sympathetic. 'It's just a pity,' she said, 'there's nobody here tonight that can take her place.'

'You're right, but I can see somebody who'd rather be in my place.' He was looking over her shoulder.

She turned quickly to glance behind her. 'Ronnie Emerson? He's a nice enough lad but I couldn't get keen on him.'

'I know just how the poor lad feels.' He also knew that as long as Phyllis was holding the torch for Norman, no one else stood a chance. He just hoped she wouldn't be hurt. Norman had been his best mate for as long as he could remember and would never knowingly do anything to upset her, but such things happened.

As the dance ended, everyone applauded the invisible band. It was a tradition at Rosie's gatherings. It was also an opportunity for Hutch to make contact with his hostess, which he did without delay.

'Hello, Hutch.' Rosie greeted him as if he'd just arrived. 'What shall we have next, do you think? A quickstep or a waltz?' She moved towards the gramophone.

'I came over to ask you to dance, Rosie.'

'All right.' She sounded casual. 'Let's have this one. "Memories of You". I like the Billy Cotton band. Don't you?'

'It's a good band,' he agreed, 'but it's not a proper dance band, not nowadays.' He recalled that 'Memories of You' had been a foxtrot until Billy Cotton had recorded it at a particularly lively tempo.

'Whatever do you mean by that?'

'It's a show band, like Jack Hylton's.' He would have preferred something more intimate for dancing with Rosie but, as he wasn't feeling particularly confident at that moment, he left the thought unspoken.

'It's still fun to dance to. Quickstep, everybody!' Rosie lowered the needle and joined Hutch in the dance. 'Have you met Neville yet?' She lowered her voice as if she were sharing a secret. 'He's a dream to dance with.'

'Is he? I haven't had the pleasure.'

Ignoring the jibe, she said, 'He went to a very good school, you know, where they do Greek as well as Latin.'

'That'll come in handy when Crawley's start exporting to Greece.' He didn't really care. It was just something to say.

'It's classical Greek, Hutch. They don't speak it nowadays.' She was impatient, even though she knew Hutch had left school at fourteen and couldn't be expected to know Greek from Hindustani. 'I have to say,' she said with grudging fairness, 'you dance one of the best foxtrots in this town.'

'Thanks. As a matter of fact, I might be leaving town soon.' As he said it, he thought it made him sound a bit like Gary Cooper.

'Oh, where are you off to?'

It wasn't the expression of dismay he'd hoped for but he carried on anyway. 'I'm going to London to try my luck with the dance bands.'

'Get away.'

'I am. I could earn good money down there.'

'Oh, Hutch,' she laughed, 'I can't see you fitting in down there. I mean to say, the Rhythm Serenaders are one thing but.... Oh dear, you've got big ideas.'

'We'll see.' He was angry and embarrassed and he could feel his cheeks burning. It was one of those moments when he wished he could simply vanish without leaving a memory.

Mercifully, the music came to its end and they broke off to applaud. 'Yes,' she said, reverting to an earlier conversation, 'I like the Billy Cotton band.' It was a new thing. Maybe Mr Rushworth preferred Billy Cotton's style too.

The dancing continued with Rosie and her new admirer permanently in each other's arms. Hutch simply wanted to get his coat quietly and leave, but he had to stay to walk Phyllis home, and he was determined not to let Rosie see how he felt, so he braced himself and continued to take part in the dancing.

He was returning from a call of nature when he saw a light in the kitchen. He was feeling dry so he decided to get a glass of water and, when he reached the doorway, he saw the reason for the light. A girl, whom he recognised as Rosie's younger sister, was putting a saucepan on the hob.

'Hello,' he said, trying to remember her name, 'do you mind if I get some water?'

'No, I'll get you some.' She opened one of the green-painted cupboards to find a tumbler, and filled it with water from the tap.

'Thanks.'

'I'm just making some drinking chocolate.'

'Oh.'

'I prefer it to cocoa.'

'It meant little to Hutch. His mother had never been able to afford such luxuries as chocolate or cocoa.

'Would you like some?'

He was about to refuse but then he thought again. He was prepared to try most things and he certainly wasn't missing much in the drawing room. 'Yes, please,' he said, taking a seat at the large deal table. 'Why not?'

She poured some more milk into the saucepan and said conversationally, 'I've been doing my homework. I'm not good at figures.'

'If it's maths, maybe I can help you.'

'Thank you. It's kind of you to offer but it's only book-keeping. I'm at the secretarial college now and I have to do shorthand, typing and book-keeping.' She added, 'I'm not really stupid, just hopeless at figures, but I think I've done it right. It's a trial balance and it really has been a trial.' She poured the warm milk into two mugs and stirred them both. She was a pleasant kid, nice to look at, with dark, bobbed hair, a clear complexion and an open, honest face; not as striking as her sister, but no one could expect that at her age, and glamour was meaningless anyway, as he had begun to realise. 'You know,' he said, 'I'm really sorry but I've forgotten your name.'

'That's all right. It's Eleanor.'

'It's a nice name.'

'Thank you. I know who you are. You're Hutch.'

'That's right.'

'Rosie keeps saying what a good dancer you are. That's how I know your name.'

'Ah well, I'm not as good as Mr Rushworth. He's a dream to dance with, and he went to a school where they learn languages that nobody uses anymore.'

'Well, I can't think what she sees in him with that moustache.' She added with a mischievous smile, 'I bet it tickles when he kisses her.'

Hutch preferred not to think about that. Instead, he tried his chocolate and found that it was really very pleasant, although it seemed odd that Eleanor should be in the kitchen drinking the stuff when she could be enjoying herself with the others.

'You could come into the drawing room now and have a dance before you go to bed,' he suggested.

'No.' She shook her head firmly.

'Don't you like dancing?' He couldn't imagine anyone not wanting to dance.

'I love dancing, but Rosie says I'm too young.'

It sounded like one of Rosie's daft ideas. 'How old do you have to be?'

'I don't know. I'm seventeen now. My birthday was last month but she still says I'm only a kid.' It was clearly an area of some conflict between them.

'It'll be all right if I take you in.'

She shook her head again unsurely. 'No, not in this dress.'

'What's wrong with it?'

'Nothing. It's just a bit, you know, ordinary.' She inclined her head towards the drawing room and said, 'They've all made an effort in there.'

It was a shame, and her hopeless acceptance of the situation made him even sorrier for her. 'It's up to you, Eleanor,' he said, 'but I think you look as nice as any of them.' Her dress was plain, dark-blue cotton, and she was wearing lisle stockings, but so were the others. Only Rosie ever wore silk stockings, and that was very occasionally.

She considered his argument and then asked, 'Are you sure?'

'Of course I'm sure.'

'All right.' She took his hand and followed him into the drawing room.

'Hutch, where've you been?' Rosie's voice met them in the doorway. She gave Eleanor a severe look and asked, 'What do you want?'

'Eleanor's my guest,' said Hutch. 'I've asked her for a dance.'

'Oh, I see.' If Rosie was surprised, she recovered quickly. 'All right then, just one dance.' Turning to Hutch, she said, 'Be a good boy and find us something to dance to. Choose something lively.'

Hutch released Eleanor's hand to look through the pile of records. 'What do you like, Eleanor? I like a slow foxtrot myself.'

'Oh, yes.'

It was clear that he'd found the kindred spirit. 'Here we are.' He pulled out "Love is the Sweetest Thing". With a little help from Al Bowlly, Ray Noble would annoy Rosie no end, and there was no telling what effect they might have on Neville Rushworth. He lowered the needle and led Eleanor on to the floor. 'Love is the Sweetest Thing' was one of his favourite songs, and it soon became evident as she moved to the gentle pulse that it was one of Eleanor's too.

'You're a good dancer for someone who doesn't get much practice,' he said after a while.

'Thank you. I usually only dance at parties – birthday parties, Christmas and that sort of thing – but this is different. It's more, well, more like the real thing.' She looked around warily for Rosie but her sister's attention was centred as usual on her new partner. 'I once went to a party in the Town Hall,' she said. 'You were playing in the band.'

'I would be. It's my regular Saturday night job.'

'How marvellous.'

'Actually, I'm going to London soon, to try my luck with the bands down there.' Rosie's reaction was still fresh in his mind but he felt safe telling Eleanor.

Her eyes opened wide. 'Are you? That's really exciting.'

She was only a kid, and kids got excited about anything, but her enthusiasm still made up in some way for her sister's mockery. He relaxed and enjoyed the rest of the number.

The dance ended and Eleanor said, 'I have to go to my room now. I mustn't be down here when my mother gets back.'

'All right.' He walked with her into the hallway.

'Thanks, Hutch. It was kind of you to ask me to dance and it was very nice too. I hope you find what you want in London.'

'Thanks, Eleanor. I'll be all right. Goodnight.'

'Goodnight.' She went upstairs, smiling.

As he and Phyllis walked home, it seemed to him that, in their opposite ways, Rosie and Eleanor had made him more determined than ever to try his luck as a musician. Of course, he would be happier with his mother's blessing but that was a problem he had to overcome.

2

The mill continued to function at the same reduced capacity, but it was plain to all that it couldn't go on much longer, and when the day finally came, Hutch was among the first to find out.

He was passing through the top weaving shed when one of the girls grabbed his arm and shouted above the din of the machinery, 'Do you know t' light's out in t' toilet?'

Hutch nodded to acknowledge that he'd heard her.

'We can't see what we're doin' in there,' she bellowed, 'or where we're doin' it, for that matter.'

'All right, I'll see to it.' He was conscious of the laughter of her workmates, who were adept at lip-reading after years of working in the shed. They were a coarse lot, but it was good that they could still laugh about something.

He reached the office as Fred returned from a meeting with the manager.

'There's a light out in the women's toilet, Fred,' he told him. It had to be changed, naturally, but Fred needed to be told because light bulbs, like most commodities, had been rationed for some weeks.

'Aye, change it.' The words came out as a sigh. 'There's nowt to be gained by penny-pinching now.'

'What do you mean?'

'Sit down, lad.'

Hutch took a seat opposite Fred's desk and waited, although he knew what was coming.

'Don't say a word to anybody, Hutch, but there'll be a notice on the gate by morning.' He added quietly, 'It's as well you've got your music to fall back on. You're going to need it.'

Hutch nodded dumbly. Like everyone else, he'd been expecting it but it was still something of a shock. 'What will you do, Fred?'

'We've saved a bit for my retirement in two years' time.' Fred managed a hint of a smile. 'I'll just have to retire a bit sooner, I suppose.'

It was a shame. The old boy was making light of it but he would need all his savings, because as long as he had anything to live on he would get nothing from the dole office. Hutch hadn't given much thought to it until then but he knew about the Means Test.

'Anyway,' said Fred, 'you'll collect your wages as usual and peg out at six o'clock. I'll stay behind to damp down the furnaces and see that the place is secure.'

Hutch went about his duties for the rest of the afternoon and left Fred alone. After almost fifty years at Atkinson's it was a huge blow and he would most likely need time to himself. Hutch thought about him as he occupied himself about the place, and then about the girls he'd just left in the weaving sheds, and about all the others who were still ignorant of their fate. Life could be a bugger sometimes.

———— ►◄ ————

His mother surprised him by taking the news more calmly than he'd anticipated. Practical as ever, she'd lost little time in formulating a new budget based on Phyllis's wage and his weekend earnings with the Rhythm Serenaders. She appeared to have forgotten about his plan to seek work in London.

Later that evening he wrote to Norman.

Dear Norm,

You'll be sorry to hear that Atkinson's closed today. I feel bad about Fred and the others and I wonder sometimes where it's all going to end. Meanwhile, I'm going down to London to look for work. Do you remember Arthur Metcalfe down our street? He's a driver with Burnett's. Anyway, he's going to London on Sunday. He'll be driving down overnight and he says he'll give me a lift. That'll save me a few bob.

Wish me luck. I'll send you my address as soon as I know what it is, and then you can let me know how you are getting on.

All the best,

Your old mate Hutch.

3

Somewhere in the eastern Atlantic Norman looked around at the goods that filled the shop's shelves. It had everything that could ever be needed on a week-long voyage. He saw cotton thread, sewing silks, needles, sewing pins, hair pins, hair grips, shoelaces, ribbon and shoe whiting. He was so fascinated by the mysterious requisites of the female world that the assistant had to attract his attention.

'Your polish.'

'Thank you.' He handed over his money, took the tin of shoe polish and was about to make a bee-line for the staircase when a voice close by said, 'Hello, you're one of the musicians, aren't you? You played awfully well last evening.'

Norman looked around and then downwards. At something generously over six feet four, he was constantly making the adjustment. 'Thanks,' he said. 'I'm glad you enjoyed it.' She had dark hair and was very attractive and, now he thought of it, he remembered seeing her on the dance floor. She seemed friendly, and Norman would chat with anyone who was friendly, just as long as he could stand near the doorway and keep an eye out for the ship's officers. Any deck that was frequented by passengers was strictly out of bounds to musicians when they weren't playing in the ballrooms, and he didn't intend to be caught.

'It's a lovely band, and I was just saying to my husband what a pity it is that the American bands in New York have all their latest songs. Don't you agree?'

'We've got 'em an' all,' he said. 'It just takes time to write the arrangements, that's all.'

She was looking at him with a kind of friendly curiosity. 'I say, that's an interesting accent you've got. Are you from the north?'

'That's right. I....' Too late, he saw one of the assistant pursers. He was looking around the shop and, within seconds, his eye fell on Norman. Norman recognised him too by the wispy beard and moustache he was trying to grow. With his thick, dark-brown hair Norman's brief experiment with a moustache had been altogether more successful, a fact that he had been quick to communicate to the officer. Unfortunately, Mr Linley was an ambitious young man and a stickler for protocol. He also lacked Norman's sense of humour.

'Excuse me, madam.' The officer touched his cap to the lady. 'Is this man being a nuisance?'

'Of course not. We were just having a little chat.'

'This deck is out of bounds to musicians, madam. Will you please excuse us?'

'If I must.' She gave Norman a sympathetic shrug.

'Come to my office, Barraclough.' Linley led the way and Norman followed him resentfully. His was a free spirit and, after three months, he was bored with endless company regulations.

They descended three decks and arrived eventually at the office the assistant pursers shared.

'Stand there,' said Mr Linley, vaguely indicating the place where Norman was already standing. He picked up a telephone and spoke briefly before returning to Norman.

'Why were you on "E" Deck, Barraclough?'

'I went to the shop to get some boot polish. Some bugger's pinched mine, and I'm telling you now, if I ever find out who it was, you're going to hear a big splash. An' don't expect me to chuck him a lifebelt either.'

Mr Linley mustered his patience. 'But "E" Deck is out of bounds.'

'I know it is,' said Norman with equal patience, 'but they don't sell boot polish anywhere else, do they?' It amused him that a ship's officer could get so excited about something so trivial.

'Don't you usually address me as "sir"?'

'No, haven't you noticed?'

'Look, Barraclough, I don't think you realise how serious this is. Not only were you caught out of bounds, you were also fraternising with a passenger, a *first-class* passenger.'

'A very nice lady,' agreed Norman, 'and we were talking about music. That was until you came and interrupted us.'

Linley struggled to control his exasperation. 'But you shouldn't have been there!'

'And I wouldn't have been if I could have bought boot polish somewhere else. That's what I've been trying to tell you.'

'Don't shout at me, Barraclough.'

'I'm not shouting. It's you that's doing the shouting, and you're going to make yourself poorly if you go on.'

There was a knock on the office door and Alberto the bandleader stepped in. His real name was Albert Bartle and he hailed from Bolton in Lancashire, but passengers preferred to think they were dancing to the music of Alberto Bartoli.

Alberto looked at Norman and then at Linley. 'What's all this about, Mr Linley?' His pencil moustache gave him the appearance of being sterner than he was.

'I caught this man fraternising with a first-class passenger on "E" Deck, Alberto, I've demanded an explanation but he insists on a pathetic story about boot polish.'

'Aye, tell him about the boot polish,' said Norman.

'You tell me about it, Norman,' said Alberto, possibly in an effort to induce calm into the situation.

'Well, you see, Albert—'

'*Alberto*. We're not in the band room now.'

'This man is insolent,' said Mr Linley, 'and I've brought you here to witness his punishment.'

'You're going to keelhaul me like they did in *Mutiny on the Bounty*, aren't you? I knew it all along. I've always thought you had a look of Charles Laughton. You've got the same thick lips and chubby cheeks....'

'Barraclough, at least try to take this seriously!'

'It would be better if you took it seriously,' advised Alberto.

Suddenly Norman became serious. 'I'm sick of this,' he said. 'As soon as we get to Liverpool tomorrow, I'm off. You're welcome to this boat and its bloody silly rules. I'll have no more to do with it.' He opened the door and then paused to say, 'I'm sorry, Alberto. It's none of your doing.'

He calmed down after a while, and once more in his quarters, he considered his next move. He would get the Bradford train from

Liverpool as far as Cullington and he would call on his old mate Hutch. It would be nice to see Phyllis again too, and Ma Hutchins. He was beginning to feel brighter already.

———◆◄———

'At least you're not going to sea. I'm thankful for that.' Mrs Hutchins embraced her son again. She'd never been very demonstrative, and her hugging made Hutch feel all the guiltier.

'I'll let you know just as soon as I find work.'

'Keep enough money by to get you home,' she said, 'just in case.' She took what looked like a folded pound note from her apron pocket and pushed it into his hand.

'Mother, I can't take this. You'll need it.' He realised that there were actually three one-pound notes folded together. They represented more than half a week's wage.

'Aye well, you might need it even more than I do. Anyway,' she said, 'I've got what I need.' She pushed the money back into his hand in a way that discouraged further argument. 'Just be careful. It seems to me that with all that money being thrown around, things are bound to be dearer than they are hereabouts.' Sometimes she could be more astute than Hutch realised.

'I'll be careful,' he said.

Tears formed in her eyelids and she looked away abruptly. She wouldn't want him to see her crying. 'You'd best go, Jack,' she said. 'You don't want to keep Arthur waiting.'

'I'll walk with him down to the corner.' Phyllis had remained quiet so far but, sensitive to her mother's predicament, she took charge. 'Are you ready, Hutch?'

'Yes. Cheerio then, Mother. I'll write soon.'

'Goodbye, Jack.' The words sounded stifled.

There was much more that Hutch wanted to say, and it wasn't that he was unable to find the words. He knew exactly what he wanted to say, but it was as if some paralysis prevented the words from forming. A private and inhibited woman, his mother had never encouraged her children to discuss their emotions. As members of the new generation, they were less reserved, and shared their feelings readily with each other, but their mother had never been able to relax her guard. Consequently, Hutch found himself unable to say what she most needed to hear. Instead, he kissed her one last time and walked out of the house.

He walked in silence for a while before saying, 'I've broken her heart, Phyllis. That's what I've done.'

'No, you haven't. Don't talk daft.' She squeezed the arm she was holding, like a mother reassuring a child. 'She's just worried for you and she doesn't really understand what it's all about. I'll talk to her and she'll be all right.'

'Are you sure?'

'As sure as I'm sure of anything.'

They arrived at the end of the street. Arthur Metcalfe lived just around the corner.

Hutch put down his suitcase, his instrument cases and the haversack containing his sandwiches and Thermos flask of tea, and said, 'You understand why I'm doing this, don't you?'

"Course I do. I told you, I'll explain it to her.'

'Thanks, Phyllis. I think sometimes that most of the understanding in this world goes on between thee and me.'

'That's as maybe, but you really will break her heart if she hears you say "thee".'

'I know.' Their mother's objection to the rough vernacular was a family joke but they couldn't laugh. Instead, they both smiled weakly and then Hutch took her in his arms and hugged her. "Bye, Phyllis. I'll write.'

'You'd better.'

'Everybody should have a sister like you.'

'Aye, but think of the bother you'd have telling us apart.'

'I'll always know which one's my sister.'

'Get away.' She wiped her eyes with her sleeve. 'Go on, Arthur'll be waiting.'

"Bye, Phyllis.' He kissed her.

"Bye, Hutch. Show 'em how it's done.'

4

Norman stopped for a moment outside the house in Albert Terrace, where he'd lived most of his life. Just two years had passed since his father's death, and the place naturally had mixed memories for him. His father had been gassed in 1915, and his disability had allowed him to work only intermittently. Their life together had never been easy and they both owed a great deal to Mrs Hutchins and her rugged kindness.

His eye took in the familiar details: the granite setts, the worn flagstones, the uniform cellar grates, the bare clothes lines that criss-crossed the street and the row of scrubbed and stoned doorsteps that contrasted with the blackened walls. He was thankful he'd been able to break away from the life he'd known there, although thanks to his impulsive nature, his future was now less certain than it had been a few days earlier.

The door was open when he arrived at the Hutchins' house so, removing the unfamiliar trilby, he stepped across the threshold and called, 'Are you there, Ma?' He'd called her that for as long as he could remember.

Mrs Hutchins stopped laying the table and looked up in surprise. 'Norman, whatever are you doing here? You'll stay for tea, won't you?'

'As a matter of fact I was wondering if you could put me up. It's just for a night or two.'

'You're welcome any time. You know that. We weren't expecting you though, so you'll have to take us as you find us.'

'Thanks, Ma. How are you keeping?'

She sighed hard. 'Well, it's hard to say. Did you get our Jack's letter?'

'It was waiting for me in Liverpool. I read it on the train.'

'Well then.'

'He'll be all right, Ma. I'll go and see him when I know where he's staying.'

Her expression brightened. 'Oh, will you really, Norman? Have you got time to do that?'

'I daresay.'

'It'll cost you a fortune.'

'That's all right, Ma. I've allowed for it.'

'Ah, well then, it'll be really nice if you do that.' She took the boiling kettle from the hob and filled the familiar brown teapot. 'So, are you on holiday?'

'It's a sort of holiday.' There would be time later to own up to his folly.

'That's nice.' She sat beside him on the sofa, waiting for the tea to brew. 'That's a lovely suit you've got on,' she said. 'Did you get it in America?'

'No, I had it made in Liverpool. The cloth's local though.' He offered her his sleeve so that she could feel the quality of the dark-blue worsted cloth. 'It's from Atkinson's.'

'Very nice too. You never know, it could be one of the last pieces they made.'

'Aye, it's a shame.'

'And just when our Jack was doing all right there. Goodness knows what'll happen to him now.'

'I told you, Ma, he'll be all right. He's a good sax player.'

'I just don't know what to think.'

'That tea should have mashed by now.' He said it to change the subject but, now he thought of it, he was ready for a cup of tea.

'And I'm sat here talking.' She stood up to pour the tea. 'You'll be parched after your journey. Do you still have milk in it?'

'That's right, Ma, but no sugar, thanks. Just think of it,' he said, taking the tea from her, 'I've steamed three-and-a-half thousand miles for a brew at your house.'

'Well I never.'

It never took much to make Mrs Hutchins say that, and Norman kept it up with stories of his travels while she prepared the meal. He was a natural storyteller and she was so engrossed in his description of a life she could never have imagined that for a short time she took her eye off the clock.

'Look at the time,' she said eventually. 'It's a quarter-past six already. Our Phyllis will be here soon, and I haven't got the potatoes on. It's all your fault, Norman Barraclough, coming here with your tales from over the sea.'

'All right,' he said, 'I'll leave you to get on while I go and meet Phyllis.'

'That's a good idea. She'll be right glad to see you.'

He knew roughly where he would find her, knowing that she would scorn the tram and walk the whole way. It was almost a half-hour walk from Rimmington's, the department store where she worked, and the journey was mainly uphill, but Phyllis was as thrifty as her mother. He set off down Bentley Road and within ten minutes, he caught sight of her on the railway bridge. She was wearing a green cloche hat that cast a shadow across her face, but he recognised her easily enough, and she recognised him.

She stared for a moment and then hurried towards him, making no attempt to disguise the delight she obviously felt. 'Norman, what are you doing here?'

'That's what your mother said. I'm beginning to wonder if I'm still popular here.'

'Of course you are, you daft thing. We weren't expecting you, that's all.' She eyed his suit with special interest and said, 'You look like a gentleman, dressed like that.'

'I *am* a gentleman.' He transferred his folded mackintosh to his right hand and asked grandly, 'May I offer you my arm?'

She looked up at him, smiling with undisguised pleasure. 'You're as daft as ever, but it really is a nice surprise having you home again.' She squeezed his arm eagerly. 'How long have you got?'

'I'm going down to London to see Hutch when he sends his address, but not before I've had a few days with you and Ma.'

'That's nice. She's told you about Hutch then?'

'He wrote and told me, and I've had a chat with her about it.'

'She's worried daft about him, you know.'

'I know. I've been trying to take her mind off things but I can only do that for so long.'

Back home, they managed to keep up the distraction for a while longer and, after they'd eaten, Norman opened his case.

'These are for you, Ma,' he said, handing her a brown paper parcel.

'Well I never.' She opened the parcel and wrapping tissue to find a pair of tan kid gloves.

'I hope they're the right size,' he said, watching her put them on.

'They're a lovely fit.' She viewed her gloved hands from several angles. 'But Norman, you shouldn't spend your money on me. These must have cost a fortune.'

'Not really.' All Norman cared about was that he'd seen her wear the same worn-out gloves for as long as he could remember, summer and winter, and he was glad he was able to replace them. 'You're to wear 'em, mind. They'll do no good in a drawer.'

'Well, thank you, but I still say you shouldn't have.'

He handed another parcel to Phyllis. 'I hope these are all right, Phyllis. Female clothing's a mystery to me.' He caught an enquiring look from Mrs Hutchins and smiled at her innocently.

'Norman!' Phyllis removed the wrapping and held up a box containing silk stockings. 'They're lovely,' she gasped, 'and don't think I'm not grateful, because I am, but when am I going to wear these? You know what folk are like round here.'

'We'll just have to go somewhere where you can wear them. As a matter of fact, I thought you and I could go dancing tomorrow night. That's if it's all right with Ma, but before that, I wondered if you'd both like to go to the pictures tonight.' He glanced over at Mrs Hutchins, who seemed satisfied that the gift of stockings was decent and proper, but who possibly shared some of her daughter's concern. Neighbours' reactions had to be considered.

'Yes,' she said, 'you'll cause a stir with them on.'

'So is it all right for me to take Phyllis dancing, Ma?'

'Of course it's all right if it's what you want to do, but do you really want me to come to the pictures with you? I'm sure you'd be happier if it was just the two of you.'

'That's what we want, Ma.'

'That's right, we want you to come.' Now recovered from her surprise, Phyllis reassured her.

'I got an *Intelligencer* at the station this afternoon.' Norman got up to retrieve it from his coat pocket. 'They'd none left, but the lass in the kiosk let me have hers. She always had a soft spot for me.' He opened the paper at the listings page at the back. 'Here we are. At the ABC there's *Here is My Heart*, starring Bing Crosby; the Picture Palace is showing *Sanders of the River* with Paul Robeson and Leslie Banks; the Pavilion's got Jack Buchanan in *Brewster's Millions*....' He broke off when he heard a joint murmur of approval. 'I take it it's Jack Buchanan, then?'

'Oh yes,' said Mrs Hutchins.

'If that's all right with you,' said Phyllis.

'I wouldn't want to see anything else.'

Mrs Hutchins looked thoughtful for a moment and said, 'It's a shame our Jack isn't here.'

———— ►◄ ————

It had seemed only good manners to stay awake while Arthur was driving, and Hutch was feeling the effects of his sleepless night. His eyelids felt dry and swollen and there was an awful stale taste in his mouth that not even strong tea could shift.

Arthur pulled into the side of Regent Street and pointed to the left along Beak Street. 'The place you're looking for is through there. I've no doubt somebody'll give you directions.'

'Thanks, Arthur. I'm obliged to you.' He knew that Arthur had made a detour to get him closer to his destination. For that and the journey itself, he was indebted to him.

'You're welcome, lad. I hope it works out for you, but you know where to write if you need a lift back.'

'Thanks again, Arthur.' They shook hands and Hutch climbed down, lifting his luggage down after him. It was a lot to carry but he hoped it wouldn't be for long.

He waved briefly as he watched Arthur go, and with him his last contact with home, at least for the time being. Two hundred miles was a long way for someone who'd never travelled further than Ilkley Moor on a Sunday school outing. He put the thought behind him and took out the list of addresses the Union secretary had given him. The first one was in Marshall Street, and he could just about make out the name on the fold of his map. It was an old map that Arthur had given him and it was quite worn where it had been repeatedly folded, but it looked like the third street on the left. He crossed the first two with care, aware that the traffic in London was heavier than any he'd seen. Arthur had pointed out some of the new road crossings on the way in, with their flashing beacons, so Hutch imagined he wasn't the only one who was concerned about crossing the hectic streets of London.

He found Marshall Street and the number he was seeking, but there the quest ended with a notice in a downstairs window that read *No Vacancies*. Still, it was only the first address on the list. He consulted it again and saw that the next one was in Warwick Street, which wasn't far away.

Unfortunately, he found the same sign in the window of the house in Warwick Street, and a similar one at the address in Bridle Lane.

Putting his cases down again to rest his arms, he consulted the list and Arthur's map. The next address was in Rumbold Street, so he picked up his belongings and set off again.

He found the street quite easily and went straight to number twenty-six, one of several three-storied Victorian houses. Thankfully, there was no sign in either of the front windows, so he knocked on the door and waited.

The woman who opened the door wore a clean pinafore, but the clothes it protected were not those of a servant. Hutch imagined she must be the lady of the house.

He asked, 'Are you Mrs Wheeler?'

'Yes. What can I do for you?'

'I'm looking for lodgings. I got your name and address from the Musicians' Union.'

'I see. Do you want to come in?' She had a pleasant way of speaking that was like neither the cockney nor the refined accents Hutch had heard on people's wireless sets. She stood aside to let him in. 'You can put your cases in here for now,' she said, opening the door to a sitting room.

'Thank you.' He put his cases and haversack down gratefully.

'Have you travelled far?'

'Yes, I came down from Yorkshire last night.'

'I thought you must be from the north.' She nodded, as if confirming it to herself. 'There's a room available. I'll show it to you in a minute. It's two pounds ten a week including meals or, if you prefer to feed yourself, it's twelve shillings a week. Either way, I'll need two weeks' rent in advance.'

Hutch swallowed hard. Two pounds ten shillings was expensive, and twice that was out of the question. He asked, 'Why do you need two weeks in advance?'

'It's a bond, a deposit, in case you damage something.'

'I see.' He wondered for a moment about trying elsewhere, but came to the conclusion that there was no guarantee that he would find anywhere, let alone a place that was less expensive. He had to make a decision. 'I'll feed myself,' he said, 'if that's all right.' Twenty-four shillings was a lot out of his meagre savings but the alternative was beyond his means.

'Perfectly. I'll show you the room. By the way, what's your name?'

'Jack Hutchins.'

'I'm pleased to meet you, Mr Hutchins.'

'Likewise, Mrs Wheeler.' As he shook her hand, he wondered for a moment if there was still a Mr Wheeler. There was a wedding photograph on a sideboard. It seemed that the young Mrs Wheeler, then rather pretty, had married a soldier, and he wondered if she might be a war widow. There was certainly no shortage of them.

'I've got three other gentlemen staying here,' she said as they climbed the Lincrusta-lined stairs, 'so I've got another room vacant. If you hear of anyone looking for somewhere to stay, you might let them know.'

'Yes, I will.' So far, he knew no one in London, but that would change.

She opened a door on the second landing and beckoned him in to look around. At first sight, the room looked inviting, with a brown linoleum-covered floor and floral-patterned wallpaper that didn't look very old, and he was quick to notice the light switch by the door. He'd only been used to electric light at the mill and at Rosie's house. Most people's homes he'd been in were lit by gas.

There was the usual bedroom furniture, a small table with two dining chairs, and under the window was an earthenware sink and a low cupboard that supported a double gas ring. Everything showed signs of frequent use, but that was only to be expected.

'You'll have to put money in the meters for electric light and gas,' she said, pointing to the two meters behind the door. 'Laundry's collected every Thursday morning and delivered the next day. You'll find a laundry list downstairs on the hall table. You can leave your money with me but it's up to you to have your things ready for collection. My husband's an invalid and my time is precious.'

'I'm sorry to hear that.'

'Another thing I should mention is that I make it a rule that there are to be no ladies in gentlemen's rooms and *vice versa* after ten p.m.'

'Of course not.'

She gave a nod of acknowledgement and said, 'The bathroom's on the first floor. I'll show you.'

Hutch followed her downstairs, wondering what else might turn out to be extra. The list was growing all the time. A bathroom, though, would be a marvellous thing.

'This is the bathroom,' she said, opening a door at the end of the landing, 'and there's a second lavatory at the end of the second-floor landing.'

The bathroom seemed to Hutch to be the pinnacle of luxury. An inside lavatory was a refinement, a second one was a bonus, but here was a bath as well as a hand basin, and each was supplied with hot water by a geyser. He'd helped install one in the mill manager's house when he was an apprentice but he'd never imagined himself using one.

'You'll need to let me know when you want a bath,' said Mrs Wheeler.

'Why's that?'

'Because it's sixpence extra for the gas.'

Suddenly the price of a bath had increased threefold, but at least he wouldn't have Willie Crowther banging on the door, and it was probably worth the extra fourpence for that alone.

'If you're satisfied with everything I'll find you a rent book and leave you to move your things in.'

They went downstairs, where she relieved him of twenty-four shillings, and when he'd unpacked his bags he set off on the next stage of his adventure, which was to find a job.

The best way to do that, he'd been advised, was to go to Archer

Street, where the Musicians' Union had its headquarters. There, he was told, he would find a kind of open-air labour exchange, and Monday afternoon was reckoned to be the best time to be there. It seemed to Hutch that London was full of new ideas.

His first impressions were mixed. London was no cleaner than Cullington, Bradford or anywhere else he knew, and he'd already encountered heavy traffic. On the other hand he was looking forward to seeing the illuminated advertisements in Piccadilly Circus, and he knew from the newsreels that there was much more that he should see once he'd found a job.

He located Archer Street quite easily. It was much shorter and narrower than he'd imagined – no more than a couple of hundred yards long and wide enough for just two vehicles – but a crowd of twenty or so had gathered there and more were arriving. He pushed his way through into the office and showed his membership card.

'All right,' a bored young man at the desk said, 'just hang around outside with the rest of 'em.' It was almost eleven-thirty and people were still arriving.

With no shortage of company, he had the opportunity to speak with numerous others during the course of the day, and he learned a great deal about the music business, imagining that the knowledge might soon be useful. Unfortunately, however, success was to prove elusive on that first day. Several jobs for alto sax players came available but all of them went to men who were well-known in the business and, when the office closed, he had nothing to show for the six wearying hours he'd spent there.

Accordingly, he took a cold meat pie back to his room and wrote a letter.

Dear Mother and Phyllis,

I hope you are both well. Everything is fine here. The room is nice, the bed is comfortable and there are two inside toilets like the one at Rosie Turner's. There's a bathroom with everything in it, including hot-water geysers. There's even electric light. The landlady is very friendly and helpful.

She wasn't all that friendly but there was no point in telling his mother that.

I made some useful contacts today so I hope to find a job soon.
Your loving son and brother,
Jack.

He took the letter to the post box so that it would be delivered the next morning and then returned to his room to fall into bed, exhausted.

———— ▸◂ ————

By Wednesday, Hutch was feeling more miserable than he'd ever thought possible. The crowd outside the Union office had grown to a hundred or so, enough to crush the spirits of the most ardent optimist.

A voice next to him asked, 'What sort of work are you looking for?' The man had a curious accent that made 'you' sound like 'yeow', and he wore the expression of a permanently disillusioned man.

'Dance bands,' Hutch told him. 'I play clarinet and alto sax.'

'You and a thousand others.'

'What?'

'I'm saying you've got competition.'

Hutch looked at the crowd around him and had to admit, albeit to himself, that the man was right.

'It's all right if they know you,' the man went on. 'If they know how good you are, then you've got a chance. Otherwise you might as well give up before you start.'

Hutch controlled his impatience and asked, 'What about you then? Do they know you?'

'Oh yes, they know me all right. They know me too bloody well.' He seemed disinclined to elaborate further.

'Where are you from?'

'Wolverhampton. You're from up north, aren't you?'

'That's right.'

'Thought so. You look as if you haven't a bloody clue.'

'I've been around more than you think.'

For a moment the man allowed his expression to relax slightly, as if he were about to break a lifelong habit and smile. 'Have you now? Ah well, I'm going to get some chips. You coming?'

Hutch shook his head, hungry though he was. He was conserving his money for one meal a day, and he wasn't thrilled with the man's company anyway.

From time to time, a name was called, and when its owner was found a message was handed over. Sometimes several names were called in quick succession and Hutch's spirits sank yet further. No one was going to call his name, because no one outside Cullington had heard of him. It was looking more and more likely that Rosie Turner would be proved right and he would have to return home to join the dole queue, a figure of fun with big ideas. And after he'd caused his mother so much upset.

After a while, he tried telling himself that three days was a very short time, and that things could change in another week or so, but his experience so far told him otherwise, and it would be an awful gamble with what little money he had. He decided to give it the rest of the week, and then if nothing happened, at least he'd given it a fair try.

With that decision made, he relaxed a little and took more notice of his neighbours. Snatches of conversation told him that some of them already knew one another. He heard them speak of places where they'd worked and some of the musicians they'd worked with. Their accents were varied and sometimes they were difficult to follow but he managed to get the gist of what they were saying. At first he felt guilty at eavesdropping, but it was difficult not to.

It was during an interesting discussion about a well-known bandleader that he found himself eye to eye with a man of around his own age. His dark hair was carelessly combed and his clothes showed signs of wear but they were of good quality, and he looked a good deal more confident than Hutch was currently feeling.

He asked, 'Have you been here before?'

'Monday was my first day,' Hutch admitted. 'Have you done this before?'

'Frequently.'

'What sort of work are you looking for?'

'My background's classical,' the young man told him. 'I've been depping until now but suddenly that's thin on the ground. To be honest, I'll take anything that comes along.'

'What's depping?'

'Deputising. You know, standing in for chaps who are ill or away somewhere.' He looked surprised to be asked. 'Where are you from?'

'Cullington.'

'Where's that?'

'Yorkshire.'

'You've come a long way.' He held out his hand. 'I'm Clive Penfold.'

'Jack Hutchins. Everybody calls me "Hutch." '

'Glad to meet you, Hutch. What's your line?'

'Dance music.' It sounded strange on his own lips and, as he said it, he decided to come clean. 'I've played with a band, but not in London, so no one here's heard of me.'

'Is that what you've always done, dance music?'

'It was only part-time,' Hutch admitted. 'I was an engineer 'til the mill closed.'

'Bad luck, but at least you're trained to do more than one thing. I've done nothing but play the fiddle since I left the Academy.'

'What's that?'

'The Royal Academy of Music. You needn't be impressed. It certainly hasn't kept me in work, and that's what really matters.'

'It sounds very grand.'

'I suppose it does but, as I said, a name doesn't pay the rent. What's your instrument?'

'Clarinet and alto sax.'

Clive nodded. 'If I were you, Hutch, I'd keep my options open. If you can pick up some kind of work – anything for now – you never know what might turn up later. That's what I'm doing.'

'It sounds like a good idea.' So far, he'd been so single-minded in his ambition that he'd never considered it.

'Tell you what, shall we go and get a cup of tea?'

'Where?'

'At the *café* round the corner in Great Windmill Street. We'll hear if anything comes up.'

'All right.' All Hutch knew about Great Windmill Street was that it was the home of the famous Windmill Theatre, where girls posed in the nude. He'd wondered, sometimes, what it must be like, to go into a theatre and see something like that. On this occasion, however, he had other priorities.

They wove their way through the crowd and, as the pavement began to clear, Hutch saw the *café*. In his desire to conserve his cash and his anxiety not to miss opportunities, he'd never noticed it before, but now it seemed to radiate a welcome. Clive pushed his way through the smoke-laden parlour to reach the counter. The man who was serving looked up in response to his wave.

'All right, I've seen you. Don't panic.'

'Two cups of tea, please.' He turned to Hutch and asked, 'Milk and sugar?'

'Milk and two, please.' Hutch hardly ever had sugar in his tea. For most of his life, it had been carefully rationed, but now he felt the need of it to stave off his hunger.

The *café* proprietor poured two mugs of tea from a large urn and dispensed milk into them. 'In or out?'

'In,' Clive told him, spooning sugar from a baking bowl and carefully avoiding the brown lumps left by the wet spoon.

'That's fourpence then.'

Hutch put his twopence on the counter beside Clive's.

'If you take it outside, he charges a deposit of sixpence on each mug, and you can buy four for sixpence in Petticoat Lane,' said Clive. As they left the counter he said, 'He's one chap who's making a fortune out of music.'

'How did you come to be at the Royal Academy of Music?' Now that he'd heard of it, Hutch was intrigued.

'I won a scholarship.'

'Like the County Minor?' He and Phyllis had sat that one, even though their mother couldn't afford to send them to the grammar school.

'I don't know. I haven't heard of that one. It was an open scholarship that paid my fees. My guv'nor was against it from the start—'

'Who?'

33

'My father.'

'I see.'

'Mother persuaded him to go on paying me an allowance whilst I was at the Academy – I think he hoped I'd lose interest quite early – but after four years, he said I had to make my own way or come to my senses and find a proper job. He's the most awful philistine.'

'Is he?' The combination of blighted ambition, a posh academy and a stern father called a 'guv'nor', who was also a philistine, was like a fairy story to Hutch.

It was Clive's turn to be curious. 'How did you get started? On the clarinet, I mean.'

'Oh, Mr Wilkins from the Prudential taught me, and then later on I joined a local band, the Rhythm Serenaders, and the town orchestra, and then I got an alto sax. It's quite easy to play the sax when you can play the clarinet.'

'I'll take your word for it. It looks difficult enough to me.'

'It's the same with most instruments, I suppose. The violin can't be all that easy.'

'No, I can't disagree.'

They finished their tea and went out on to the pavement, which was considerably emptier than when they'd left it.

'It's nearly half-past five,' said Clive, looking at his watch. 'The office will be closing soon.'

'Time to go home then.' The cloud that had hung over Hutch for most of the day began to return.

'Not on your life. I've done this before, remember. The fewer there are here the better your chance is if something comes up. Let's hang around for a while.' The crowd was dwindling as he spoke and it seemed good advice, so Hutch stayed.

In fact, it was almost six o'clock and time for the office to close, when a short, slight man in a shapeless checked jacket and cloth cap arrived at the doorway. He spoke without removing the cigarette that dangled from his lips.

'Typical,' he said. 'First chance I get to come down here and everyone's buggered off.' He looked around at the few who remained. 'I'm looking for a second fiddle.'

'Here.' Clive's hand went up instantly.

Cautious relief showed on the man's face. 'What have you been doing, mate?'

'Depping with the Queen's Hall Light Orchestra.'

The man rolled his eyes. 'You'll be coming down in the world but I don't suppose you'll mind that. It's the Farringdon Empire. Are you interested?'

'I certainly am.'

'I thought you might be.'

Clive pointed to Hutch and asked, 'Do you need a clarinet and sax, by any chance?'

The man stared incredulously at Clive before saying to no one in particular, 'Amazing. Not only is this bloke the last fiddle player on the street, he's a mind reader as well.' Turning to Hutch he asked, 'Do you play the clarinet, mate?'

'Yes.' Hutch's pulse was beginning to race.

'You got a pair?'

'Yes.' Playing with the Rhythm Serenaders only called for the B flat clarinet, but the longer 'A' instrument coped more easily with certain keys encountered in other kinds of music. 'I've got an alto sax as well,' he said.

'We need a second reed. Done any pit work?'

Hutch could scarcely believe it. 'Yes,' he said, 'I've played with the Carl Rosa and the D'Oyly Carte when they came on tour.'

'Bleedin' 'ell, what a pair. Be at the theatre at eleven o'clock sharp tomorrow morning so Mr Levy can hear you both.'

5

The man in the checked jacket greeted them at the stage door in much the same spirit as before.

'They've turned up an' all. It's Fritz Kreisler an' Jimmy Dorsey. The band room's down the passage, lads, first on the right. You'll find Mr Levy there or in the pit. Mind your heads as you go through.'

They thanked him for his directions and found the low door that led beneath the stage to a low-ceilinged and dimly-lit area that appeared to be the band room, although the only clues were a few wooden chairs and a battered wooden violin case that had been left to gather dust.

'Let's try the pit,' said Clive. As he spoke, the door opened and a man peered into the room.

'Hello, you must be the new boys. I'm Joe Levy.' He had dark, wavy hair and a neat, short beard and moustache. He offered his hand and they introduced themselves.

'Clive Penfold.'

'Jack Hutchins. "Hutch", that is.'

'All right, boys, get set up and I'll find something for you to play.'

They took out their instruments and tuned to the piano in the pit.

'Right,' said Joe, placing a sheet of manuscript on a stand. 'You first, Clive. Let's hear you play that.'

Clive glanced through the music and then played it confidently. Hutch didn't recognise it, and he realised that it was most likely a second violin part.

When Clive had finished, Joe smiled approvingly. 'Very good, my boy. Now it's your turn, Hutch.' He produced another sheet of manuscript and put it on a stand for him.

As soon as Hutch looked at the scribbled manuscript, his heart sank. He lowered his clarinet and tried to make sense of the hieroglyphics.

'Is something the matter?'

'This is terrible stuff to read, and it's all in thick pencil.'

Joe half-smiled. 'You were expecting neon, maybe?'

'No, I'll manage.' Hutch looked at it again and suddenly he recognised the piece, which was simple enough now that he could make some of it out. It was Mendelssohn's 'Spring Song' arranged for solo clarinet. With a huge sense of relief, he lifted his instrument again and began to play, confident that if he found himself struggling to make out some of the awful scrawl, at least he could busk the thing as he remembered it.

When he came to the end, Joe was smiling.

'Well done,' he said. 'The turns bring their own band parts, or "books", as they call them, so you have to be able to read anything in this business, but I think you'll survive.' He picked up the manuscript and said, 'All right, boys, you can start tonight. We play to two houses, six-fifteen and eight-thirty, Monday to Saturday. Band call is at ten o'clock on Mondays, we pay five guineas a week and if you can't come in for any reason, it's up to you to find a deputy. Is there anything else you need to know?'

Elated though he was, with money uppermost in his mind Hutch had one important question. 'Will you be keeping us a week in hand?'

Joe frowned. 'What is this "week in hand"?'

'Where I come from,' Hutch explained, 'they don't pay a new man until he's worked two weeks, and then when he leaves, they pay him the extra week. I don't know why, but that's what they do, and I just wondered if you did the same.'

'They should rob a man of his wages, already?' Joe shook his head in disbelief at such a notion. 'Not at this theatre, I hope. Be here at a quarter to six, boys. Don't be late.'

They celebrated by eating at a place they'd seen near the bus stop. As it was still only mid-morning and neither had eaten breakfast, they ordered bacon, eggs and fried bread, which went down like a royal feast. It was the first time Hutch had eaten in a *café*.

When he was back at his lodgings, he took up his pen again.

Thursday 29th August, 1935.
Dear Mother,
I told you I'd get a job soon. It's at the Empire Theatre in Farringdon, just a short bus ride from here.

He thought it wise not to mention the fact that the theatre was a music hall. His mother was unlikely to approve.

It pays five guineas a week. That's a pound more than I got at the mill. I'll send some money as soon as I can but I'll draw less than three pounds this week as I only started today. At least they are not going to keep me a week in hand like they did at the mill.

He was actually surprised that the job didn't pay more than it did, but Clive explained that the pay was good for music hall musicians, who often had a day job as well.

I met a violinist called Clive. He went to the Royal Academy of Music and he knows how things are done down here. The conductor is called Joe. I'm not sure how to spell his surname because it is Jewish, like some of the names you see on the wool merchants' plates. Joe seems very friendly. I think he will be all right to work for.
I hope you are both keeping well. I'll write again soon. Love to Phyllis.
Your loving son,
Jack.

He considered writing to Norman, and then decided to leave it until later. He had some shopping to do and, on his travels, he might also find a picture postcard to send to Phyllis. It wouldn't be the same as one from Norman but she might find it interesting all the same.

His final choice turned out to be a view of Piccadilly Circus, because it was close to where he lived and he thought Phyllis might like to know that. It had crossed his mind while he was out that he might send one to Rosie Turner as well, just to make his point, but although he was relieved to be in work again, he still hadn't found his ideal job, so he saved that idea for later when it might have greater impact.

———◆◄◆———

'I've brought a different partner tonight, Rosie.' Phyllis lingered on the doorstep for a moment to observe her reaction.

Rosie's eyes opened wide. 'Good heavens, it's Norman. What are you doing back here? Come in, both of you, and let me take your coats.' Rosie took Phyllis's hat and coat and waited for Norman's.

They exchanged greetings and went through to the drawing room, where they found several couples dancing to a record that was nearing its end.

'I'll put something livelier on now,' said Rosie. 'I don't know who chose that one. By the way, Norman, have you met Neville?' She looked around and saw that Norman had moved on and was enjoying a reunion with some of his old friends. She shrugged and picked out a record, calling out, 'Quickstep, everybody!'

Norman and Phyllis took to the floor to 'All I Do is Dream of You.'

'Rosie prefers lively numbers nowadays,' said Phyllis. 'I think it's got something to do with Mr Rushworth.'

'Is he the soppy-looking object she's dancing with?'

Phyllis turned her head to look. 'That's him.'

'They're probably right for each other.'

'Yes, I can't think what Hutch saw in her, but he knows the truth about her now. She wasn't very nice to him on his last night here.'

Norman nodded sympathetically and stood aside when Neville Rushworth asked Phyllis for the next dance, when it seemed only good manners to dance with Rosie. Once on the floor he found her in an inquisitive mood.

'It must be nice for you,' she said, 'seeing Phyllis again.'

'It's always nice to see Phyllis. She's one of my best friends.'

'I know that, but I've wondered if there might be something more than that between you.' There was a familiar twinkle of mischief in her eye, that he'd always found irritating.

'Have you now?' It was almost too easy to put Rosie on the spot, but she asked for it.

'Well, yes.'

'I see.'

Clearly uncertain, she said, 'Look, I only said I'd wondered now and again.'

'You know, Rosie, it seems to me you haven't got enough to think about. I'd take up a hobby if I were you. You could try knitting, or maybe collecting cigarette cards.'

Suddenly the twinkle was back. 'Norman, you're a tease.'

'And you, Rosie, are a nosey parker.' Nodding in the direction of the gramophone, he said, 'That Billy Cotton knows how to shovel the coal on. He'll kill us all off at this tempo.'

'Neville and I like the lively ones best.'

'Aye, but it's the slow ones that take skill. Now, my mate Hutch dances the best slow foxtrot I've ever seen. He's a treat to behold.'

'He's very good,' she agreed. 'Actually, I thought he'd be here tonight. Do you know what's happened to him?'

'Aye, he's gone down to London. He went last weekend.'

'Did he?' She sounded incredulous. 'So he really meant it?'

Norman nodded. 'He usually means what he says.'

'Oh dear.'

'What's up?'

'Nothing.'

She was quiet for the remainder of the number, but when the record ended she said, 'You know, I teased Hutch when he told me about going to London. I told him he was getting big ideas.'

'Oh, he's got them all right.' He joined in the applause along with everyone else. 'I suppose we all have, but that's ambition. If we didn't have that we'd never achieve anything.'

'Well, all right, but the thing is, he seemed to take offence when I said it. But I never thought he meant it, about going to London.'

'I shouldn't worry, Rosie. It'll take more than a daft remark from you to blow Hutch's light out. You can depend on it.' He could see Neville Rushworth approaching so he took his leave of her and rejoined Phyllis.

'That Neville Rushworth is a stuck-up twerp,' she told him.

Norman looked at her sharply. 'What's he said to you?'

'Calm down, he didn't insult me. Well, not really. He asked me where I worked. I mean to say, that's the last thing we talk about when we come here. Most of us want to forget about work.'

'Well, he hasn't a clue, has he? I don't suppose he's done a hand's turn in his life.'

'I'm sure he hasn't, but that wasn't all. When I said I worked at Rimmington's he told me he was a shareholder.' She snorted. 'He just had to let me know how important he is.'

'So he really is as daft as he looks. I wondered, because it can't be easy.'

'Anyway, how did you get on with Rosie?'

'About the same as usual, really, but I'll bet you anything it won't be long before she puts a slow foxtrot on.'

Phyllis shook her head confidently. 'She won't do that.'

'Don't be so sure. I told her it was the one that took the most skill, and she'll be dying to show off Useless Eustace again before the evening's out.'

'Norman, you're wicked.'

'Aye, and I told her Hutch was the best I'd seen. Mind you, to give her credit, she spoke well of him.'

'So she should after what she said to him.' She added thoughtfully, 'And considering what he's taken on. Not everybody would dare to do what he's doing.'

'You're worried about him, aren't you?'

'I can't help it.'

'He'll be all right, Phyllis. He's got talent to sell, and he won't be on his own after tomorrow. It'll be him and me, just as it's always been.'

Phyllis rolled her eyes upwards. 'I know. Fighting Blackshirts and getting into all sorts of trouble. Tell me I was dreaming when you said you'd walked out on your job, Norman. I can't believe you'd do something as daft as that.'

'No,' he said, trying to look more contrite than he felt, 'you weren't dreaming.'

It was fortunate that at that moment, Rosie provided a distraction by announcing a slow foxtrot, and he was able to lead Phyllis on to the floor.

———◆I◆———

The baritone who had done so well in first house came on again to his tab music 'My Song Goes Round the World.'

'Good evening, ladies and gentlemen. I should like to sing that old favourite, "On the Road to Mandalay." There was polite applause in anticipation, which seemed only right to Hutch, but the barrackers at the bar immediately singled out the singer as their target.

'Don't feel you 'ave to!'

'Bring on the dancing girls!'

'You ain't in your baftub nah!' They rewarded themselves with loud, coarse laughter. Wally Martin on first reed nudged Hutch and said, 'Dancing girls are about their weight. That lot are drunk already.'

It was all the same to Joe, who started the intro. The song went well and there were no interruptions until the singer announced his second number, 'The Floral Dance.' Then the onslaught was resumed.

'Put a sock in it!'

'Let's 'ave a bit o' jugglin'!'

'Sing somefink we know!'

'Yeah, somefink we can understand!'

'I'm sorry, gentlemen, I haven't come here to sing nursery rhymes.' It was clear that the singer had dealt with rough audiences before. He nodded to Joe and the intro began.

Hutch had started the evening with some apprehension. Everything had happened very quickly and he was still coming to terms with the fact that he was now employed as a musician in the nation's capital, when only ten hours earlier he'd been an unemployed engineer. With a successful first house behind him, however, his anxiety had receded and he was now enjoying the programme, at least as far as concentration allowed. He was pleased that when the baritone came to the end of his turn, the applause matched his performance. The group at the bar were strangely and gratifyingly quiet, and Hutch heard later that one of them had been thrown out for making a lewd proposition to one of the ice cream sellers.

6

On Saturday afternoon, Hutch was trying to mend a hole in one of the pockets of his evening dress trousers. He'd bought a reel of white cotton thread, a packet of needles and a pair of scissors, and had set about the job, imagining that it would be straightforward. However, having pricked himself repeatedly and finding that the thread had mysteriously knotted itself like a conjuror's rope, he decided to admit defeat and use a safety pin, and he was about to go out and buy one when Mrs Wheeler called to him from downstairs.

'Mr Hutchins?'

He threw the trousers, needle and thread down and opened the door. 'Yes, Mrs Wheeler?'

'There's a man down here to see you. He says he's a friend of yours.'

'Oh, right. Will you send him up, please?' He couldn't imagine why Clive should be calling on him at four o'clock but maybe he'd be able to offer some advice about sewing. He'd lived away from home for some years, so it was likely.

But it wasn't Clive who hurried upstairs to greet him. Hutch stared in amazement, but it was the visitor who spoke first.

'Hutch, you old bugger!'

'Norm, you old sod, what are you doing here?'

'Everybody's been asking me that lately.' Norman shook his hand enthusiastically. 'I've come here to keep an eye on you. I told your mother I would.'

'So that's how you knew where I was.'

'That's right.' He followed Hutch into the room and put down his suitcase and then his trombone case. 'I'm seeking a job an' all.'

'What happened to the job you had?'

'I've decided the steamship life's not for me.' He took the dining chair that Hutch offered him. 'I fancy something on dry land for a change. And speaking of dry things, are you going to put the kettle on? That underground railway's a fine thing when you get the hang of it, but it's as hot as hell down there and I'm fair parched.' He felt in his coat pocket and took out two envelopes. 'I've brought you some letters an' all, to save stamps.'

'Thanks.' Hutch looked at them and recognised Phyllis's and his mother's handwriting. 'I'll read them later,' he said, dropping them on the bed. 'I'll tell you what, Norm, it's good to see you.'

'Aye, and it's good to see you, but it seems I can't let you out of my sight for two minutes. What the hell have you been doing?' Norman pointed to the blood-spotted lining of the trousers Hutch had thrown on the bed.

'There's a hole in one of the pockets and I've been trying to mend the bloody thing, but it's harder than I thought.'

'Give 'em here. I'll do it while you get the kettle on. Is it this hip pocket?'

'Aye, but it isn't as easy as it looks.'

'Give over. I've been doing it for years. Don't forget I'd no mother and sister to sew things for me.' He set about unpicking the knotted thread. 'Although, to be honest, when the job got technical I usually brought it round to your house.'

'I remember. How were my mother and Phyllis when you left them?'

'Right as rain. I had the best part of a week with them before I came down, and they were fine.' Suddenly he smiled with amusement.

'What's the joke?'

'You should have heard Rosie on Thursday night, Hutch. I took your Phyllis round there.'

'What did she say?'

Norman shook his head at the thought. 'You know, we've been going round to Rosie's for years now and we're forever talking about her. We shouldn't really.'

'No, we shouldn't.' Hutch remembered defending her on several occasions.

'But she does play the lady of the manor, you have to admit.'

'Go on then. What did she say?' Hutch was still sufficiently interested to keep Norman from straying off the subject.

'She's worried because she poked fun at you about coming down here. She thought she might have hurt your feelings. I set her straight though. I told her that by this time you'd have got yourself a job in a posh establishment and you'd be surrounded by adoring society women.'

'Get away.'

'No, I told her straight.'

'And what did she say?'

'Not much. That daft article Neville Rushworth got her up to dance. Honestly, I'd forget about her if I were you, Hutch. I don't think she'll be in the window much longer.'

'I have really.' He poured boiling water into the teapot and found two cups and saucers.

'Good lad. You'll find plenty more in the big city.' He looked around the room appreciatively and said, 'This is a nice enough place you've got here.'

Hutch nodded. 'It's a bit pricey but it's all right.'

'How much?'

'I feed myself, so it's twelve bob a week. Mrs Wheeler took two weeks' rent in advance and that was a bit of a shock, but now I'm in work it doesn't seem so bad.'

'It sounds all right to me. I wonder if she's got a room free.'

'I believe she has. I'll ask her in a minute.' He poured out the tea and handed Norman his. 'It'd be all right if we got rooms in the same house, wouldn't it?'

'It would that.' He threw the trousers back to Hutch.

'Thanks, Norm.'

'That's all right. Another time I'll show you how, and then you can do your own.' He sipped his tea and gave it his cautious approval. 'Now, tell us about this job of yours.'

———— ◆►◄ ————

Having spoken with Mrs Wheeler and secured the remaining room, Norman accompanied Hutch and Clive to the theatre, where Hutch introduced him to Joe and he learned that there was no vacancy for a trombonist. Still, he'd made a contact, and he proceeded to watch the show from the front stalls, where he was able to draw the conclusion that Joe did need a trombonist, although preferably not the one he had.

As they got off the bus, Hutch and Norman surprised Clive by insisting on walking into Piccadilly Circus.

'What is so special,' he asked, 'about Piccadilly Circus?'

'We've never seen it,' said Norman. 'That's what's special about it. I expect it's commonplace enough for you, and I've no doubt one day we'll get used to it, but give us a chance to see it first.'

'All right.' Clive was growing used to Norman's direct manner. 'It's not far.'

As they reached the end of Shaftesbury Avenue, Clive stopped them and said, 'There's an excellent music shop here if you need reeds and that kind of thing.'

'Half a minute, Clive,' said Norman. 'Let's look at this lot first.' The lights of Piccadilly Circus had seized his attention, and anything else was of secondary importance. He walked closer, mesmerised by the neon ballet being performed before him.

'Look at that baby,' said Norman. 'He's drinking milk.'

'And the dog,' said Hutch, equally entranced.

'He's smoking.'

'You're right.'

'Bugger me.'

They continued to watch the moving lights until Hutch read, '"Gordon's Gin is the Heart of Every Good Cocktail". I might see the point of it if I knew what a cocktail was.'

'It's a mixed drink,' said Clive, 'enjoyed by people on grander incomes than ours.'

'If that stuff I had in the theatre is anything to go by they haven't even learned how to brew ale down here.' There were still aspects of London that had yet to win Norman's approval.

Hutch asked, 'Who's the little bloke with the bow and arrow?'

'That's Eros, the Greek god of passionate and physical desire,' said Clive.

'It sounds like a nice job. I wonder how he wangled that.'

'Family connections. His mother was Aphrodite, Goddess of Love, and his father was Ares, God of War, hence the bow. Cupid's arrows made people fall in love, but it seems he didn't choose his targets very carefully and he caused a lot of unpleasantness.'

'Aye,' said Norman, 'we've met a few of that sort, youngsters with more power than sense.'

Hutch was still studying the statue. Finally, he asked, 'How do you come to know all this, Clive?'

Clive shrugged. 'I learned it at school. I was hopeless at physics and chemistry so I chose classics. It was more interesting as well.'

'And did you have to learn languages that nobody uses anymore?' The absurdity of it still surprised Hutch.

'Latin and Greek? Yes, but it's not true that they're not used anymore. They're not spoken, it's true, but people still use them to study the great civilisations.'

'Is there much call for that these days?' With the reflection of the Nestlés baby flickering across his face Norman's expression was difficult to make out but the question sounded serious enough.

'Yes, there is. We can learn a lot from the Greeks and Romans. Almost any situation you can think of has its parallel in the ancient world.'

'Get away.'

'It's true. They experienced the whole lot: war, famine, rebellion—'

Norman was still sceptical. 'What about this slump we're going through?'

Clive nodded. 'Money was a constant problem in those days too.'

'So how did they solve it? I reckon this government would give a lot to know the answer to that one.'

'Ah well, it usually involved invading another country. Slave labour helped as well.'

Norman grunted, obviously unimpressed.

'They had some good ideas too. For instance, do you know who invented democracy?'

Norman considered the question briefly and said, 'No, you've got me there.'

'It was Plato in the fourth century BC.'

'Well, bugger me.'

'It's his favourite word,' said Hutch, sounding like a parent who has long since given up hope. 'It has been since we were about five.'

It was Clive's turn to be surprised. 'Have you two known each other as long as that?'

'More or less,' agreed Norman. 'It was after my mother had died in the 'flu epidemic and Hutch's mother looked after me. That's when we got to be mates.'

Clive nodded. 'You must both have a lot of catching up to do, and I've got things to do tomorrow as well, so I think I'll leave you to it.'

—▶◀—

Norman watched Hutch perform the morning ritual with his hair. It was Sunday and there was no hurry.

'I wouldn't bother with that tragacanth stuff if I were you,' he said. 'Brilliantine makes it shine and that's what lasses like.'

'This is to hold it down,' said Hutch, forcing his hair flat with his comb.

'You're wasting your time, you know. You don't look at all like Gary Cooper.'

'Don't I?' Taken aback momentarily, Hutch stopped combing and turned to face him.

'No, you look more like... the other one.'

'Who?'

'It'll come to me in a minute.'

'Randolph Scott?'

'No, not him.'

'Ronald Colman?'

'No, not Ronald Colman. The other one.'

Hutch felt his patience slipping. 'What other one?'

Norman snapped his fingers triumphantly. 'I knew it would come to me.'

'Who, then?'

'Charlie Chaplin.' Moving sideways to dodge the pillow that Hutch threw at him, he asked, 'Have you had any thoughts about where we could go today? You've been here longer than me so you know your way around better than I do.'

'I've only been here a week, Norm. I haven't had time to see any of the sights.'

'All right, have you got your map handy? I wouldn't mind having a look at the Tower of London.'

Hutch delved into the pocket of his mackintosh and retrieved Arthur's map, which he opened out carefully on the table. 'The Tower of London isn't on this map,' he said presently. 'I think it must have been where one of these holes is now.'

Norman studied it for a minute before coming to a decision. 'In that case, if we walk down Piccadilly we'll come to Hyde Park Corner. Then we can have a look at the park, or we can maybe walk along Park Lane to the Grosvenor House Hotel, where Jack Harris and his band do their broadcasts, just to say we've seen it.'

'From the outside, you mean.' Hutch folded the map and put it back into his pocket. 'That's all we can do.'

'We won't always be outside looking in, Hutch. I'm confident of that.'

'Happen not, but you've got to get a job first.'

'Oh, I'll get a job all right.'

'I hope so. It's not as easy as that.' Hutch opened the door and beckoned him out. 'Come on, Norm. We're wasting sunshine.' He knew better than anyone that Norman would only ever learn the hard way.

They made their way in the September sunlight towards Shaftesbury Avenue, where Hutch bought a *Sunday Pictorial* from a street vendor.

'It's official,' he announced on finding the page he wanted. 'Nobody can overtake us now. The County Championship's ours again.'

'I never doubted it.'

'Well, it's official now.' Hutch read on. 'It says here that Hedley Verity's taken a hundred and ninety-nine wickets this season. Bill Bowes hasn't done too badly either.'

'I'm pleased to hear it, Hutch, but can we move on? We're blocking the thoroughfare.'

Hutch looked up and down the street. There was no one near them. 'I realise cricket's not your game, Norm,' he said, 'but this means a lot to me, particularly since Lancashire made off with the Championship last season.'

'All right, I'll buy you a pint later on to celebrate. You're right, though, it isn't my favourite sport. I prefer a bit of action.'

Hutch nodded. 'And violence.' They walked on.

'Not deliberate violence. That's got no place in sport.'

'Right enough.'

'But every now and again somebody tries it on and you can't let them get away with it.' He broke off to comment on the traffic in Shaftesbury Avenue. 'Just look at this lot. Even on a Sunday morning, they're in a hurry. They're wrong in their heads, Hutch.'

'It's just a different way of living, I suppose.'

'Aye.' Norman was thoughtful for a moment, and then he returned to the original subject. 'When I played with St Martin's Football Club,' he said, 'I remember the Reverend Forster saying to me, "Norman lad, you must always remember that when you're as big as you are, and let's face it, you're built like a brick shithouse—" '

'I bet he didn't say that.'

'Not in so many words. I can't remember just how he put it. I was.... What's that thing we did in Miss Morley's class when you repeat something in your own words?'

'Paraphrasing.'

'That's right, I was paraphrasing. Anyway, he said that a big lad like me has a responsibility not to throw his weight about unless he has good reason to. I've always remembered that.'

'It was good advice.'

'He was a fair man and full of good advice.'

They came to Piccadilly Circus and stopped again, remembering the previous evening. It seemed very drab in daylight except for the knowledge that the lights that had seemed so magical were still there and only waiting to be switched on.

After a while, Hutch asked, 'What made you go over to St Martin's? We had a football team at Bradford Road Wesleyans.'

'St Martin's treats were better. We even went to Bolton Abbey one year.'

'Get away.'

'We did. We had a picnic down by the river.' He paused to recall it with obvious pleasure. 'It was a heck of a day. The sun was cracking the flags and the river was as clear as glass. You could see the fish swimming round in it. Of course, we weren't allowed to catch any.'

'Why not?'

'It was private land. All the fish belonged to the landlord.'

'Like the mill dam at Atkinson's, I suppose.'

'Aye, but this belonged to some duke or other.' After a little more thought he said, 'We played cricket before tea and I was bowled out for a duck but it was worth it for the rest of the trip.'

'You usually went for a duck. Do you remember when we played at school and you used to shut your eyes every time you took a swipe at the ball?'

Norman looked uncomfortable. 'Aye well, we've already agreed that it's not my game.'

'Sorry, Norm. I couldn't resist that.'

'Aye well, I suppose it's each to his own, and you never broke any records at football, did you?'

'That's true.'

'You see, we're different, you and me. Where I'm good at controlling the ball and kicking and heading and that sort of thing, you're good at swinging things.'

It was Hutch's turn to feel slighted. 'There's a lot more to cricket than swinging the bat,' he said.

'That's not what I meant. When you bowl you can swing the ball, and you can make clever strokes an' all. That's what I'm saying. There's a lot of skill in those things.'

'That's true enough.'

'Blow me down, Hutch, look at this lot.' Norman was staring at the bustling prospect that was Hyde Park Corner. 'London must have emptied itself into this place.'

'I doubt it, Norm, but it's evidently the place to be. Most of them seem to be heading for the park.' He watched the stream of pedestrians passing through the park gates and said, 'It's a big enough place. Do you reckon we should join 'em?'

'Aye, let's do that.'

They crossed Park Lane and merged with the others. As they passed through the gateway Hutch said, 'You know, it feels wrong, somehow, strolling along like this on a Sunday morning. I feel as if I should be doing something useful.'

'What do you have in mind?'

'Well, I'd normally be practising with the orchestra at the Wool Exchange at about this time. It's been part of my life for so long that it feels strange not to be there.'

'It was part of mine an' all before I went to sea, but you soon get used to a different way of life.' He seemed to lose interest in the subject when he noticed a Walls ice cream vendor. 'Hutch,' he asked, 'do you fancy an ice cream? I haven't had one for years.'

'Neither have I.' Hutch put his hand into his pocket but Norman stopped him. 'Have this one on me,' he said. Walking over to the vendor, he asked for two cornets.

The vendor filled two cones with ice cream and handed them over. 'That'll be fourpence,' he said.

Hutch watched Norman hand over the money and took one of them. 'Thanks, Norm,' he said, feeling a trifle awkward. In spite of three day's pay, he still had to be careful, but at the same time he was mindful that Norman was out of work, and whilst that didn't seem to worry Norman, it was nevertheless something to be borne in mind.

'Lovely.' Norman savoured his first lick. 'It's just the job on a day like this.'

'Mm.' Hutch let the ice cream melt on his tongue and then asked a question he'd had in mind since Norman's arrival. 'What's it like, being at sea, Norm? I've never even seen it.'

'It's surprising how you get used to it. I spent a fair amount of time at first, looking out to sea – we had a little bit of deck that we were allowed on – but, after a while, it was just so much water. It looks very much as it does in the pictures, and it's just as grey sometimes but, on a nice day, it's blue and cheerful. One thing I have to say, though, is that it's always changing. One day it's so calm that you don't know you're at sea, and the next you're steaming through Atlantic rollers as big as houses. It's not so good then.'

Hutch absorbed that information as far as he could. 'All the same,' he said, 'I'd like to see it for myself some time.'

As they were so near to the bandstand, Hutch walked over to read the notice that was pinned to it. 'There's a band coming this afternoon,' he said, 'at two o'clock, a military band.'

'Aye well, military band music's all right if you like that sort of thing but I'm inclined to give it a miss. I don't know about you.'

'Me too. We could just have a stroll round the park. There's plenty to see.' He'd already seen several girls, some of whom were quite pretty. It was a pleasant prospect, but then another idea came to him. 'I know what we could do.' He'd noticed the sign earlier when Norman was buying the ice creams. 'If we carry on up this way it'll take us to Speakers' Corner.'

'Aye, I've heard of that. It could be interesting.'

They continued along the path, each taking a lively interest in anything they found unusual, and presently Norman drew Hutch's attention to a young woman with a dog. Remarkably, he was more interested in the dog than in the young woman.

'That's one of them French poodles, isn't it?

'I believe so. Hutch had only seen them at the pictures.

Norman raised his hat to the young woman as she passed by, and waited until she was out of earshot. 'I imagine she paid somebody to cut its hair like that,' he said, 'but I wouldn't have paid good money for it.'

'No, I can't say I'd be in a hurry to put my hand in my pocket either.'

After a little thought, Norman said, 'I know we all talk about poodle-faking, but I've never been able to work out where poodles come into it exactly.'

Hutch was watching a dog chase a large branch. It was a large black and tan dog with a curly coat, and whilst it was obviously no weakling it was finding the branch quite a challenge. Nevertheless, the dog retrieved it, dropping it neatly at its owner's feet, and it was at that point that the owner decided that enough was enough, because he clipped the dog's lead on to its collar and led it away.

'I think,' said Hutch, who had been giving some consideration to Norman's remark, 'the trick was to take almost any kind of dog and give it a daft haircut so that a lass would stop and stroke it, and it gave the lad the opportunity to get to know her.' He picked up the branch that the dog had left behind and used it to practise a drive to deep mid-wicket.

'What a bloody silly thing to do. What sort of a crackpot would go in for a performance like that?'

'They were society lads, Norm. They didn't know any better.'

'I don't suppose they had our advantages, Hutch.'

'Aye, you can't buy common sense.'

They made their way along Broad Walk, noting various musical venues in Park Lane that they knew only by name, until they became aware of sounds of excitement ahead.

'It sounds like a set-to, Norm,' said Hutch, listening to the yells and jeers.

'Aye, and on a peaceful Sunday morning. I wonder who it could be.'

The irony in Norman's tone wasn't lost on Hutch. 'Maybe it's our old sparring partners, Norm.'

'Aye, I believe I can see one or two black shirts up there. Mind you, it is only one or two and I can't imagine why. There's usually a plague of the buggers.'

'It looks like most of 'em are moving off up that way,' said Hutch, pointing towards Lancaster Gate, and true enough, the noise from Speakers' Corner had diminished rapidly.

'Well, good riddance. Let's see the rest of 'em off.'

They ran the last two hundred yards to where a Blackshirt was holding a man by his arms whilst another hit him repeatedly. The victim was almost senseless by the time Norman reached them.

'Leave him alone, you buggers!'

The one who had been administering the beating gave Norman an insolent stare before looking around for any support that might remain.

'Did you say something?'

'I told you to leave him alone. Are you deaf as well as daft?'

Using his right to block an attempted hook, Norman drove his left into the Blackshirt's solar plexus, causing him to double up, wheezing like a locomotive at the end of a long journey. He followed his first blow with a right hook that caused his antagonist to close his eyes and lose interest in the proceedings. The other relinquished his hold on the victim and came at Hutch.

Hutch moved his stick from hand to hand, watching his opponent's eyes as they followed it to and fro. Then, using both hands, he swung it hard and his victim lay on the ground, clutching his middle.

'I... can't... breath!'

Hutch looked down at him without pity. 'I could try standing on your throat,' he suggested. 'That might help.' He raised his foot and the man wriggled frantically out of his way.

Norman's antagonist merely lay still.

Nodding towards a large litter bin that stood nearby, Hutch asked, 'Are you thinking what I'm thinking, Norm?'

'Good idea. Bring it over, Hutch.' He dragged the now half-conscious Blackshirt to his feet and nudged the other with the toecap of his shoe. 'On your feet, you bugger. Come on, both of you, back to back, arms down by your sides.' When he was satisfied, he nodded to Hutch, who pushed the bin down over their heads and shoulders, finally striking it with his stick and demanding, 'Can you hear me in there?'

There was a muffled yell.

'Right,' said Hutch, 'We've got a message for your boss. Are you listening?'

The two whimpered in duet.

'Good. You can tell Sir Oswald-bloody-Moseley that if he comes here we'll shove him in the bin an' all, because that's where he belongs, him and the rest of you.' He gave them a shove to send them stumbling in no particular direction.

Hutch knelt beside the Blackshirts' victim, a slight, grey-haired man who might have been smartly dressed when he set out for the park, but his grey suit was torn and stained with blood from his nose and mouth. His face was developing into one massive bruise but, surprisingly, he was still conscious.

'Are you all right, mate?' Hutch knew it was a silly question. Under the circumstances, though, it was difficult to know what else to say.

'I'll... I'll be all right. It could have been much worse.' His lips were split and bleeding, making speech difficult. 'I'm very grateful to you both.'

'Not a bit of it,' said Norman. 'A bit of a skirmish with a couple of Moseley's apes has just set the day up nicely, hasn't it, Hutch?'

'That's right.' Turning to the injured man again, Hutch asked, 'What had you done to upset them?'

'I was making a speech.'

Hutch looked at the overturned wooden crate and broken placard and nodded.

'I wasn't the only one.' The man touched his swollen lips gingerly. 'I was just too slow in getting away.' He paused for a second to catch his breath and said, 'Also, I don't think they were at all keen on my choice of topic.' He made a couple of attempts to get up, finally allowing Hutch and Norman to assist him.

Norman eyed him critically. 'Would you like us to see you home?'

'Thank you, but you've been too kind already. I'll be all right if I can get a taxi.'

'We'll get you one.'

They helped him to the gates, supporting him on either side. Hutch kept glancing in the direction of Lancaster Gate.

'I don't think them two have found their mates yet,' he said.

'I don't think they will either.' Norman pointed across the park and, when Hutch followed his finger, he saw the pair, still trapped inside the bin and stumbling toward the Serpentine to the undisguised amusement of passers-by.

Hutch asked, 'What was it about your speech that upset them? Your board was so badly smashed I couldn't read what it said.'

'It was about Mussolini.'

'Oh aye?' Like many others, Norman had never given Mussolini much thought.

'Everyone seems to regard him as a joke but his troops have been threatening Abyssinia for a year now. He must be stopped before he mounts an invasion.'

'I can see now how you came to upset them,' said Hutch, 'but I really don't see how making a speech in Hyde Park is going to stop Mussolini. As I see it, the League of Nations should be doing something about it. Isn't that the sort of thing they're paid to do?'

'Ah, if only they could.' Having reached the gates he turned to face them, now supporting himself. 'But I shan't bore you with it any longer. You gentlemen have been very kind to me and I don't even know your names.'

'I'm Jack Hutchins, and the bloke hailing the taxi is Norman Barraclough.'

'I'm delighted to meet you both. My name is Arthur Normanton.' Having shaken them both by the hand he searched painfully in his waistcoat pocket and produced a card, which he handed to Hutch. 'If I can be of service to either of you in any way, please let me know.'

'We'll do that,' said Norman, 'but your taxi's arrived.'

As the cab came to a stop beside them, the driver caught sight of Mr Normanton and winced.

'Blackshirts,' explained Hutch.

'Bastards,' said the driver.

As they watched the taxi disappear Norman said, 'Well, Hutch, we've made our mark. I think I'm going to enjoy living here.'

'You might,' said Hutch, 'once you've found yourself a job.'

———— ►◄ ————

It seemed that trombonists were plentiful, because Norman was still jobless after a week. He was, however, a man of stubborn resolve, and when Monday came around again he took his place as usual in Archer Street, determined to be there from the start. His persistence was rewarded when one of the staff called from the office doorway, 'Norman Barracloth?'

Norman looked up in surprise. He couldn't think of anyone, apart from Hutch, who knew he was there. 'Barra*clough*, yes, that's me.'

'Telephone call for you. It's the Farringdon Empire.'

That made sense. He followed the woman into the office, wondering what Hutch could possibly want. He took the receiver from her – it was one of the modern telephones he'd seen in the films, with the mouthpiece and earpiece all in one unit – and asked, 'What's up, Hutch?'

'Only your lucky break. Can you grab your trombone and come over here straight away?'

———◈———

When Norman arrived at the theatre, he found that band call was still in progress. Hutch caught sight of him and winked. Joe Levy merely told him to take his place in the pit.

Joe spent the next forty-five minutes or so taking the orchestra through any passages in the artistes' band parts that might otherwise cause problems later, and then he was free to speak to Norman. 'The job's yours if you want it,' he said. 'I expect Hutch has told you about the pay and conditions.'

'Yes, he has.'

'All right, be back here at a quarter to six.'

'Thanks, Joe. I'll be here.'

Hutch joined him as soon as Joe was gone. 'I bet you never expected that,' he said.

'No.' Norman was beaming. 'It's a stroke of luck all right. What happened to the other bloke?'

'He's gone. Joe's had trouble with him before, turning up the worse for drink and letting everybody down at the last minute. He telephoned this morning, saying he was under the weather. It wasn't the first Monday morning he'd done that, and Joe knew just what the problem was, so he sacked him on the spot.'

'He wasn't much of a trombonist either. I don't know how he lasted as long as he did.'

'Well, let's hope you'll last a bit longer. Do you fancy a celebration?'

'What sort of celebration?'

'Bacon and eggs. It's what Clive and I had after Joe set us on.'

Still beaming, Norman said, 'Lead the way.'

———◈———

Norman chose a postcard with a picture of Piccadilly Circus.

Dear Phyllis, he wrote, *I'm now in the same orchestra as Hutch. I told you we'd both get jobs, and this will do nicely for a start. I thought you'd like this picture, although it's not as good as the real thing. I hope you and Ma are keeping well. It was grand seeing you both. Take care.*
Yours, Norman.

Hutch's letter was more informative.

Dear Mother and Phyllis,
In case this reaches you before Norman's postcard, I'd better tell you that he's now got a job in the theatre orchestra as well, so you can both stop worrying. I can't tell you how grand it feels to be earning a living as a musician. Just fancy – being able to work at the thing you like best! When we've done a few weeks, we'll see about finding a deputy apiece so that we can come home for a weekend.
I'm learning a lot from Norman about cooking, and it's just as well really. I suppose looking after his dad meant he had to be able to turn his hand to most things. Even so, it must have been a great luxury for him to come and eat with us.
Look after yourselves and don't spend the enclosed postal order all at once!
Your loving son and brother,
Jack.

7

The Farringdon Empire's Christmas pantomime was 'Cinderella.' It ran from Friday 20th December until Saturday 3rd January, closing only on Sundays, Christmas Eve, Christmas Day and Boxing Day. Thus, Hutch and Norman were able to travel to Yorkshire on the 24th to return late on the 26th. They had little enough time and they filled it with enjoyment. They had both sent money beforehand to pay for extra food, including, for the first time in Hutchins history, a turkey. According to Phyllis, Mrs Hutchins had viewed its size with alarm when her daughter bore it into the house, and called it scandalous that anyone should spend so much on meat, Christmas or no Christmas. Even so, she enjoyed it as much as any of them, just as she enjoyed having her boys at home, albeit for two days.

Presents were strictly of the token kind; they cost little but came with a wealth of affection and goodwill. It was Christmas as it had always been, but with rather more to eat and much to celebrate.

Another tradition, at least for Phyllis, Hutch and Norman, was the Boxing Day visit to Rosie Turner's. Her parents always went visiting in the morning, and that was when Rosie greeted her friends.

Norman took Phyllis aside and asked if she still had the silk stockings from his previous visit.

'Of course I have,' she said. 'I've only worn them once.'

'Well you'd best get them on again,' he advised her. 'I don't want Rosie running away with the idea she's the only one round here with a sense of style.'

'It's not Rosie's stockings I'm worried about. I just wonder how Hutch is going to feel when he sees what she's wearing on her left hand.'

When they arrived at the Turners' house, Rosie welcomed them and lost no time in showing her engagement ring to Hutch and Norman. Mr Rushworth was also present so they congratulated the couple politely because, whatever they thought of them, good manners had to be observed. Even so, Rosie was still fair game for leg-pulling.

'Norman's been telling me about the place where you work,' she told Hutch. 'It sounds really posh.'

'It is, but we don't use the word "posh" down there.'

'Don't you?'

'No, it's considered common. The word of the moment is "exclusive".'

'Ah.'

Hutch wondered how long it would be before Rosie managed to work the word into everyday conversation. He wasn't naturally facetious but the thought amused him. He could accept her engagement to Mr Rushworth but he was already tired of her artificial ways and her insistence on showing off her diamond ring at every opportunity. It was as if he were seeing her at last for the vain and empty creature she was.

'I suppose you meet lots of society people in your work.'

'Lots,' he agreed. They weren't quite the society Rosie had in mind but there was no need for her to know that. 'Actually,' he told her, leaning forward confidentially, 'only last week, I danced with a girl who'd danced with a man, who'd danced with a girl....'

'Who'd danced with the Prince of Wales?' Rosie's eyes shone with excitement.

'Let me finish, Rosie. He'd danced with a girl who turned the Prince of Wales down. She had a headache at the time and he's a hopeless dancer anyway. He hasn't a clue about the foxtrot.'

'Hutch,' she pouted, 'you're a tease.'

'So are you, Rosie, but hopefully that'll be a thing of the past, now you're spoken for.' He looked around the room and asked, 'Where's Eleanor?'

'Oh, she's around somewhere.'

'I hope you're not still shutting her out. You treat the poor lass like Cinderella.'

Rosie pouted again, giving Hutch the impression that she'd been practising, maybe for Mr Rushworth's benefit. 'If that's what you think,' she said tartly, 'I'll call her and you can see for yourself.' She left the room and went to the foot of the staircase. 'Eleanor,' she called, 'come down to the drawing room. Hutch has a glass slipper for you to try on.' She swept in again, ignoring Hutch, and said, 'I'm putting a record on. Quickstep, everybody!'

Through the open door, Hutch saw Eleanor reach the foot of the stairs and turn towards the drawing room. She was wearing a dark-blue pinafore dress with a cream blouse and she stopped when she saw Hutch in the doorway.

'Merry Christmas, Eleanor.'

'Merry Christmas, Hutch.' Her grin broadened. 'It's really nice to see you again. Rosie said you wanted to see me.'

'Of course I do. I'm not going to stand by and see you left out in the cold again.'

'I'm not really left out. It's just... they're Rosie's friends, not mine.'

'I hope I'm your friend,' he said, trying not to sound too hurt.

'Oh, you are.' She flushed guiltily and asked, 'Did you find what you wanted in London?'

'We're getting there.' It was easy to tell Rosie a load of nonsense but her sister was a different matter. 'We've got jobs as musicians,' he told her, 'and better things lie ahead, I'm sure.' He had to raise his voice towards the end of the sentence because of a vigorous *forte* offering from Billy Cotton and his band in the drawing room.

'She still likes her music fast and loud,' said Eleanor.

'Aye, well, good taste isn't given to us all. I'll tell you what though.'
'What?'

'If you think that crowd in there are just Rosie's friends, I'll introduce you to Norman and my sister Phyllis. They'll change your mind.'

She was about to reply, when the Cotton band reached the end of the number and someone called out, 'Put something seasonal on, Rosie.'

'I wish she would,' said Eleanor.

A few moments later, her wish was granted as Guy Lombardo and his Royal Canadians filled the air with 'Winter Wonderland.'

Hutch asked, 'Shall we dance?'

'Oh, yes.'

They danced in the spacious entrance hall. It was a private moment, and it seemed to Hutch, a special one, as Eleanor seemed to find pleasure in every beat of the music and, for that brief spell at least, her pleasure was his.

As they stood apart at the end of the number, he saw her raise her eyes to the ceiling and he followed her gaze up to a bough of mistletoe that hung from the glass lampshade.

'Happy Christmas, Eleanor.' Before bashfulness could seize him, he kissed her.

'Oh, happy Christmas, Hutch.' She was clearly delighted.

'Now,' said Hutch, a little self-consciously after the kiss, 'come and meet some genuine people.'

8

Since the death of King George the Fifth on the 20th of January, conversation had been about little else. It was expected that many places of work in London would be closed on the day of the funeral because of the large number of people who wanted to pay their respects as the *cortège* made its way through the streets. For the musicians at the Farringdon Empire, however, closure came early when an electrical fault led to a fire backstage, and urgent repairs became necessary. The theatre was duly closed after first house on Saturday 25th and was scheduled to reopen on Thursday 30th after extensive rewiring.

'They're not exactly generous with their wages,' Norman complained, 'and to dock us three days' pay is going too far.' It was the morning of Wednesday the 29th, the day after the funeral, and they were clearing up after breakfast.

'Aye,' said Hutch, 'It's time we found something better. I'm not looking forward to standing in Archer Street again but it seems to be the only way.'

Norman folded his towel and draped it over the side of the sink. 'While we've got a bit of time off,' he said, 'I think we ought to make the most of it.'

'What have you got in mind?'

'Well, according to Eva in the box office, the new Fred Astaire picture's worth a bob of anybody's money.'

'What's it called?'

'*Top Hat.*'

'Is Ginger Rogers in it?'

'Of course she is.'

'That settles it. Where's it on?'

'I'll tell you in a minute.' Norman picked up his copy of the *Daily Sketch* and leafed through it until he came to the listings page. 'Here it is,' he said, 'The Marble Arch Pavilion at one-twenty, three fifty-five, six-thirty and ten-past nine.'

'If we go this afternoon,' said Hutch, 'we can go dancing tonight.'

'Good idea, Hutch. Who's playing at Hammersmith Palais?'

'As far as I know it's Oscar Rabin.'

And so they made the most of their remaining free time, and the incomparable partnership of Fred Astaire and Ginger Rogers followed by an evening of dancing put them in good heart for the time they would have to spend waiting patiently in Archer Street for someone to call for a trombonist and a saxophonist.

———◆❙◆———

They spent Thursday, Friday, Saturday morning and Monday afternoon in Archer Street but without success. Norman was becoming increasingly impatient, whereas Hutch was inclined to be philosophical.

'Four days,' he reasoned, 'are neither here nor there in job hunting terms. We were both lucky to get jobs at the Empire as quick as we did, but you can't expect it to happen like that every time.'

Norman was predictably unimpressed, but it was a familiar difference and one with which they'd coped on many occasions, and so they spent the next day in Archer Street amiably divided in outlook but still agreed on their objective.

It was beginning to look like another fruitless day until half-an-hour before they were due to leave, when they heard a call for a clarinet and alto sax, a trumpet and a trombone. Within seconds, Norman had pushed his way through the dwindling crowd, claimed the official's attention and was beckoning, quite unnecessarily, to Hutch to join him.

'It's Felix Beaumont's band at Arturo's Club in Soho,' the young man told them. His announcement prompted unexpected laughter from some of those remaining but Hutch and Norman paid no heed to it. Their luck was apparently in.

9

The auditions were surprisingly brief, but Hutch and Norman were hired immediately as they were unable to work out a week's notice at a theatre that was currently closed. Accordingly, and with some regret, they phoned their resignations to Joe Levy, mindful that working under his direction had been the pleasantest part of the job.

They were as yet undecided about Felix Beaumont, who'd so far had little to say to them beyond a somewhat off-hand offer of employment at eight pounds ten shillings per week, which was nevertheless a considerable improvement on their earnings at the theatre. They learned rather more at Tuesday morning's band call, when Mr Beaumont stepped on to the band stand and nodded to them generally by way of a greeting. He was a tall, slightly-built man with dark, slicked-back hair and a pencil moustache, whose matinee idol looks were only marred by the appearance of dark shadows beneath his eyes. Whether they were caused by lack of sleep or by some physical disorder, Hutch had no idea, and he quickly dismissed the thought as the bandleader announced the first number.

'We'll begin with "About a Quarter to Nine". I imagine the new chaps are familiar with it?' He looked in turn at Hutch, Norman and Alex Thompson, the new trumpet player.

'Yes, sir.' In truth, Hutch had never played it, but sight reading had never been a problem.

' "Felix," ' he prompted.

Norman and Alex both assured him that they knew the number.

'Right. A-one, a-two, a-one-two-three-four....' As it was scored as a dance number there was no verse, but a short introduction led into the chorus, which began with the melody in the reeds; at least that was according to the score.

'Stop, stop!' Felix was staring fiercely at the tenor sax player. 'Daniel, it has obviously escaped your notice that you're *tacet* for the first four bars of the chorus.'

Daniel looked puzzled. 'That's news to me, Felix.'

'Well, it bloody-well shouldn't be. I was marking those bloody parts up at four o' clock this morning.' He flinched when the outer kitchen door slammed. 'If I take the trouble to do that, the least you can do is read what I've bloody-well written!'

'I agree, Felix. There's no argument about that, but there's nothing in my part to say I'm *tacet*.' He held up the tenor sax part to show him.

'Oh, for...! Well, I don't know how that happened. The melody in the first four bars is with the alto sax and clarinet.'

'Presumably, I'm in on the fifth bar, Felix.'

'Of course you are. Trumpet and trombone are in at bar twenty. Okay?' He was about to count them in when the kitchen door slammed loudly again, prompting a torrent of invective from the frustrated bandleader. He was interrupted in mid-flow when a woman in a pinafore and a headscarf wrapped like a turban appeared beside the bandstand.

'It was the wind what done it,' she said. 'I've propped the door open so it won't 'appen again.'

'Good. See that it doesn't.'

The cleaner departed muttering something about some people needing a lesson in manners, and the band call was resumed.

They took a break at ten-thirty and Hutch, who had recently developed the taste for coffee, a luxury hitherto unknown in his life, took his readily. Norman lost no time in engaging Daniel in conversation.

'I'll tell you what, Daniel,' he said, 'if Felix spoke to me the way he spoke to you this morning, the two of us would have serious words.'

'He can be sharp,' agreed Daniel, 'but he's an excellent musician and he's all right when you get to know him. Give him a chance.'

Feeling drawn into the conversation, Hutch asked, 'How long have you known him?'

'Almost two years, longer than anyone else in this band.'

'You must know him quite well, then.'

'After all this time? I should hope so.'

'Well,' said Norman, 'you're certainly loyal.'

Daniel shrugged. 'Why not? He's been loyal to me.'

'What do you mean?'

'When times are difficult and competition is keen it's not always easy for men of my race to find work, but Felix took me on without hesitation, simply because I'm a good tenor sax player.'

Norman looked puzzled, and then Daniel smiled and said, 'My surname is Rosenthal. Does that suggest anything to you?'

'Oh, you're a....'

'A Jew, yes.' He laughed at their awkwardness. 'We must be thin on the ground where you boys come from.'

'Not really,' said Hutch, 'but most of them are wool merchants and we were mill engineers. We didn't move in the same circles.'

'Of course and, as everyone says, we keep ourselves to ourselves.'

'They say that,' agreed Hutch, 'and they may be right, but we don't give a bugger what nationality anyone is, do we, Norm? There are Belgians living up our way who came over in nineteen-fourteen and they're just the same as us. There's too much attention paid to where folk come from.'

Daniel half-nodded in agreement. 'You're right about that, but my family's lived in London for a long time now. The problem is of a different kind.'

'Not as far as we're concerned,' Norman assured him. 'You're a musician. That's all we know, and it's all that matters.'

'In that case,' said Daniel, offering his hand, 'I'm pleased to meet you both.'

———◆◄———

In the following week, Hutch and Norman came to agree that Felix was an excellent, if occasionally absent-minded, arranger. His only real failing seemed to be his quick and violent temper, for which he was well known within the dance band world, and it wasn't long before Hutch received a taste of it. They were rehearsing 'Red Sails in the Sunset' at the time.

'Stop.' Felix tapped the score on his music stand. 'Hutch, have you decided to take the morning off?'

'No, Felix. What's the problem?'

'The problem,' said Felix, sounding like someone explaining a simple concept to an idiot, 'is that you should have been in at bar one.'

Hutch looked at his part and shrugged. 'According to this, I'm *tacet* for the first four bars.'

'What the hell do you mean?'

'Look.' Hutch passed his part to him.

Felix examined it, closing his eyes in exasperation. 'You've got the First Alto Sax part, not the Second.' Turning to Ed Miller on First Sax, he demanded, 'What have you got there, Ed?'

'I'm in at bar nine, Felix.'

'No, you're bloody not.' He held out his hand impatiently. 'Give me your part.'

Ed handed over his band part, and Felix compared it with Hutch's. Finally, realisation dawned.

'You've got each other's part.'

Hutch frowned. 'But it says—'

'Never mind what it damn-well says. Swap parts, cross out "First", "Second" or whichever one isn't yours, and write over it what it bloody-well should be.' He raised his eyes to the ceiling in a gesture of hopelessness and said, 'Maybe then we can get on with this rehearsal.'

'That's all very well,' objected Ed, 'but I take a dim view of us getting the blame all the time for your mistakes.'

Felix seemed about to explode. 'Oh, you do, do you? Well, maybe you'd find another band more to your liking.'

'There's no "maybe" about it.' Ed began dismantling his saxophone. 'I've had as much as I'm prepared to take of your foul temper. As far as I'm concerned, you can take that baton of yours and stick it up your arse.' Fastening the clips on his sax case, he added, 'At least you won't be able to blame anyone else for that.'

Livid, Felix watched him go, wincing when the door slammed. 'Hutch,' he said, 'take over as First Sax. I'll sort out the money with you after the rehearsal.'

'Okay, Felix.' Hutch moved to the seat that had been Ed's and waited.

'Right, "Red Sails in the Sunset" from the top. A-one, a-two, a-one, two, three, four....'

The rehearsal continued almost without incident, the only interruption coming when someone outside started a motor bike. As the two-stroke engine stuttered into life, Felix lowered his head and grasped his music desk so violently that his knuckles shone white. He remained in that position for at least a minute while the musicians looked at each other in helpless silence.

Eventually, Felix raised his head and said, 'They should ban bloody motor bikes.' He mopped his forehead. 'We'll leave it there. I'll see you all this evening. Thank you.'

As they left the club, Hutch said, 'At least he thanked us. That was rare but welcome.'

'Aye,' said Norman. 'He's bad with his nerves, right enough.'

They suspected they knew the cause of it. It was something suffered by many but was seldom mentioned. Hutch was given a reminder, however, that Saturday morning.

———◄►———

Through chatting with other musicians, Hutch gained the impression that he and Norman had been lucky to find 26 Rumbold Street. The rent was apparently reasonable for the area and the facilities were superior to those in most places. They were also fortunate in Mrs Wheeler, who ran the house very efficiently despite having to care for her invalid husband. Hutch had thought her brusque at first but he quickly formed the conclusion that her off-hand manner was probably down to her having so much on her mind. He imagined her husband must be seriously disabled, because in all the time he'd lived there he'd never seen him about the house. They did meet eventually, however, in remarkable circumstances.

Norman had gone to catch the morning post and Hutch had just left their laundry in the passage, when he heard voices coming from one of the ground floor rooms. One was a man's voice, gasping and indistinct; the other was Mrs Wheeler's and it sounded as if she were engaged in something strenuous but at the same time trying to sound reassuring. He tapped on the door and asked, 'Mrs Wheeler, are you all right? It's me, Jack Hutchins.'

'Just a minute.' She said something to the man before coming to the door and opening it just a few inches.

'You sound to be struggling,' said Hutch. 'I wondered if you needed help.'

'It's kind of you to ask.' She was breathless and seemed anxious. 'I'm trying to move my husband. It's his lungs, you see. He has no strength left.'

'Well, said Hutch, 'I'm a strong lad. I should be able to lift him.' He added, 'That's if you want me to.'

'Would you mind? It's not very pleasant, I'm afraid. His lungs are in an awful state.'

Don't worry, Mrs Wheeler, I've dealt with this kind of thing before.' He followed her into the room, where a man in pyjamas lay gasping on the bed. The fluid in his lungs bubbled horribly as he fought to breathe, but it was a familiar scene for Hutch. He asked, 'Was he gassed in the war?'

Mrs Wheeler nodded. 'I have to get him across the bed.'

'I know.' Have you a chamber pot handy?'

'Yes.' She reached beneath the bed and pulled one out, seemingly divided between anxiety and embarrassment.

'Come on then, Mr Wheeler.' Hutch slid an arm beneath his upper body and lifted him. 'Mrs Wheeler, can you shove a couple of pillows under his middle?'

'Yes, of course.' She dragged two pillows from the top of the bed and laid them beneath her husband's body as Hutch lowered him so that his head hung over the side of the bed. Having done that, he proceeded to pat his back rhythmically, stopping after a while to massage, and then patting again. All the while, Mr Wheeler coughed repeatedly, spitting copious amounts of phlegm into the chamber pot.

Mrs Wheeler watched him and asked, 'How did you learn to do that, Mr Hutchins?'

'Norman's dad was gassed in the war. He was in a shocking state sometimes, and we had to do this for him regularly. He was a big man, like Norman is now, and it took both of us to shift him when we were kids.'

'Had he no wife?'

'No, Norman's mother died of the flu at the end of the war.'

'Poor boy. Was your father in the army as well?'

'No, he was in the Navy.'

'He was lucky, then.'

'Not so as you'd notice. His ship was blown up at the Battle of Jutland.'

'I'm sorry, Mr Hutchins. I spoke without thinking.'

'I reckon we all do that sometimes.' He gave Mr Wheeler's back a final pat and said, 'There now, Mr Wheeler, let's get you the right way up. Pillows, please, Mrs Wheeler.' He grasped the patient under his arms, lifted him and lowered him gently so that his head lay on the repositioned pillows.

'Thank ... you. You're ... very kind.' Mr Wheeler was still breathless but the congestion was much less audible. His hair was completely grey, and that surprised Hutch because he didn't look that old. Mrs Wheeler, he reckoned, might be forty at the most, and the two had looked very much of an age in the wedding photograph.

'Thank you, Mr Hutchins. I'm very grateful.' Mrs Wheeler pulled the bedclothes over her husband. 'He's not always as bad as this but he suffers with nerves as well. The doctor's very good with him. He was in the Medical Corps in the war, but there's a limit to what even he can do.'

'Shell shock?'

'Yes.'

'I'm sorry, Mrs Wheeler. Send for me or Norman if you need help with him any time. We'll be glad to help.'

She smiled for what seemed the first time. 'I will.'

It was good to see her smile. It made for a pleasanter atmosphere, and Hutch was a friendly soul who expected others to be as friendly. He imagined that the ten minutes he'd spent helping Mrs Wheeler would make life at number 26 much more agreeable. He also thought he knew the reason for Felix's behaviour.

10

Rehearsals continued to be turbulent, so that most of the musicians came to accept Felix's tantrums as an unpleasant but inescapable fact of their existence, and so things went on until one morning in February, when he rounded on Hutch over a missed entry.

'Hutch, have you forgotten how to count?'

'No, Felix.'

'Where were you, then, at bar thirty-six?'

'Still *tacet* according to this.' Hutch handed his part to the fuming bandleader.

'Well, you bloody-well shouldn't be. Play the first clarinet cue,' he told him, handing the part back.

Hutch did as he was instructed, and the rehearsal continued with only two more incidents, neither of which included him, but when they broke for the day, he made a point of asking Felix for a word in private.

'What do you want?'

'Tell me to mind my own business if you will, but I was just wondering, Felix, if you're getting any treatment for your nerves.'

Felix looked at him sharply. For a moment, Hutch expected another explosion, but the bandleader seemed to crumple. He sat down and stared at the floor.

Hutch said, 'That's shellshock you're suffering from, isn't it?'

Felix continued to stare.

'Norman's dad was gassed and shellshocked. That's what made me realise it.'

It was as if Felix's thoughts had been far away. Suddenly, he asked, 'Where?'

'Hey, Norm,' said Hutch. 'Was it Loos where your dad was gassed?'

'That's right.' Norman joined them, possibly wondering how his father's disability had come under discussion. 'Loos,' he confirmed, 'nineteen-fifteen.'

'I was at Neuve-Chapelle,' said Felix quietly. 'It was a bloody hell hole.' He seemed to consider Hutch's original question, because he said, 'Doctors? What do they know? They weren't there.'

'Some of them were, Felix. Our landlady's husband has shellshock as well as being gassed, and his doctor was in the Medical Corps. He knows what it's about.'

Felix closed his eyes, and it was impossible to imagine what was happening inside his mind.

'If you like,' offered Hutch, 'I'll get his name and address for you. Mrs Wheeler, our landlady, speaks well of him.'

———— ►◄ ————

Felix was grateful enough for Hutch's offer, and he consulted the Wheelers' doctor, although the improvement through medication took a while to become apparent. Evenings at the club were successful, however, and both Hutch and Norman felt that the move had been, on the whole, worthwhile. Otherwise, normal life, with its inevitable distractions, went on.

One such event took place after Hutch and Norman had left the club, and Norman realised he'd left his cigarettes behind. Hutch, who didn't smoke, was unable to help him, so Norman returned to the club, hoping that there might still be someone there. Arturo, or Arthur, to give him his real name, was often the last to leave.

Hutch continued to Rumbold Street and his bed.

He had no idea at first how long he'd been asleep, when the knocking on his door woke him.

'Mr Hutchins, Mr Hutchins.' The voice was Mrs Wheeler's. 'Mr Barraclough is on the telephone. He says it's very important.'

'All right, Mrs Wheeler, I'm coming.' Bleary-eyed, Hutch struggled into his clothes and joined her in the hallway by the telephone.

'Norm, it's Hutch,' he said. 'What's up?'

'I'm at Savile Row Police Station, Hutch.'

'What the heck are you doing there?'

'I've been arrested, you daft bugger. What do you think?'

'What for?'

'Brayin' two Blackshirts' ear'oles for 'em. Apparently, it's against the law down here.'

'What do you want me to do?'

'How should I know? All I know is I'm allowed to make one telephone call, and this is it.'

Hutch thought quickly. 'I'll come over.'

'Right. You'll have to excuse me if I don't put the kettle on for you. I'm a bit restricted in what I can do.'

Hutch put the telephone down. 'I'm sorry you've been disturbed, Mrs Wheeler,' he said. 'He's been arrested, but it's bound to be a mistake or a misunderstanding. He's a law-abiding chap.' Even so, Hutch wasn't surprised that the charge had something to do with physical violence.

'Oh dear.'

'You go back to bed and I'll sort this out.' He hoped Norman hadn't already made things worse for himself. There was always a danger of that.

He got a taxi to the police station and was there within a few minutes.

A bored-looking sergeant on the desk asked, 'What can I do for you?' He didn't seem all that keen to be helpful, but Hutch remained polite.

'I've come to see Norman Barraclough. He says he's under arrest.'

The sergeant consulted a large book and found Norman's name. 'Yes, Norman Alfred Barraclough,' he said, 'charged with affray. Are you his solicitor?'

'No, they come a bit expensive, I've heard.'

'They're not cheap,' agreed the sergeant. 'You'll have to sign the book, all the same.'

'What book?'

'This one.' The sergeant opened another massive tome and found the next empty space.

Hutch printed his name, as requested, filled in his address and the name of the prisoner he'd come to see. When he came to 'Capacity', he consulted earlier entries and wrote, 'Friend'.

'I'll get someone to take you to see him,' said the sergeant. He put his head round a door marked *Duty Room* and issued a sharp order. A young constable emerged.

'Take this man to the Interview Room,' he said, 'and get that chap we brought in half-an-hour ago for affray.' By explanation, he added, 'He's a mate of his.'

The constable led Hutch down a drab and cheerless passage, and opened a door for him. 'Wait in here,' he said.

Hutch entered the room and looked around him at the dowdy walls, which were distempered in something between cream and brown, although the colour might have been affected over the years by tobacco smoke. The whole place reeked of it. By contrast, the door and skirting boards were the same colour as the cubicles at the public baths in Cullington. There was no window, and the only furniture consisted of a bare table and three wooden chairs.

Presently, the constable reappeared with Norman, who, far from humble, looked simply affronted. The constable said, 'Knock on the door when you're ready to leave.'

'Right.' Hutch waited until he was outside before speaking to Norman. 'What happened, Norm?'

Norman sighed heavily. 'I went back to the club and picked up my cigarettes, and I was looking for a taxi, when I heard a scuffle. Well, I looked where the noise was coming from and I found two of Moseley's gorillas laying into Daniel and calling him all the names under the sun because he's a Jew.'

'Our Daniel?'

'The tenor sax player, yes, and the poor bugger didn't stand a chance, so I lent him a pound of muscle.'

It was a familiar story. 'How did the police get involved?'

'They were passing and they heard the.... I was going to say "struggle", but there was no struggle, only one of 'em gasping for breath. I'd knocked the other one out cold.' He sighed again. 'They arrested me and charged me with causing an affray, as if it were my fault.' He shook his head at the injustice of it.

'What happened to Daniel?'

'They brought him in an' all. Then, when they realised he were the innocent victim, they patched him up and sent him home.'

'Do you know when you'll be up for trial?'

'Aye, tomorrow morning at Westminster Magistrates' Court.'

Hutch thought. 'I'll ask at the desk if they'll let me speak up for you in court,' he said. 'If I do, don't say a word.'

'What, just keep quiet?'

'Yes, Norm. Leave the talking to me.' He knocked on the door for the constable. 'I'll see you tomorrow, Norm. Remember, not a word.'

The constable brought him back to the desk, where the sergeant was still on duty.

'Have you seen him?'

'Yes.'

'He's a big lad. I wouldn't want to get on the wrong side of him.'

'You'd be as safe as houses,' Hutch told him. 'He only hits bullies and thugs.' Suddenly reminded of something, he asked, 'What happened to the Blackshirts?'

'They're still in the cells, moaning about their bruises and the unfairness of life. Your mate walloped 'em good and proper.' He gave an apologetic shrug and said, 'It still doesn't make it right, though, what he did.'

'What about what *they* did? That's not right either.'

'They'll go before the beak as well. Don't you worry.'

Hutch asked, 'Will they let me speak up for my mate?'

'I don't see why not. Ask the Clerk of the Court when you get there, and he'll arrange it.'

Hutch had plenty to think about on the way home, and it was some time before he was able to sleep. He lay in bed, planning what he was going to say on Norman's behalf, although a great deal depended on his friend's ability to curb his resentment, and Norman was not known for keeping his opinions and feelings to himself.

———◆◄———

The Clerk of the Court was frustratingly elusive, and it was some time before Hutch was able to speak to him.

The official peered at his list for the day and said, 'Norman Alfred Barraclough, ten-thirty. What is your name?'

'Jack Hutchins.'

'Take a seat in the court when it opens, Mr Hutchins, and then you'll be called when the time comes. Address the magistrate as "Your Honour".' It was obvious that Hutch was a newcomer to court proceedings, so he said, 'You'll get a chance to speak to your friend when he arrives.'

It turned out to be a fleeting chance, and Hutch only had time to give the advice, 'Plead guilty, and then leave it to me.'

'Guilty?'

'Yes, you *are* guilty, but I'm going to appeal to the magistrate's sense of... well, his sense of justice, I suppose.'

Norman was led away, growling, and Hutch still feared the worst, which was inevitable if his friend insisted on speaking for himself. He was cheered somewhat, though, when one of the policemen who'd brought Norman to court said, 'Your mate could be luckier than he thinks. He's drawn Mr Prentice, the Stipendiary Magistrate.'

'Is that good?'

'He's one of the few who have no time for Moseley and his Blackshirts.'

At length, the court was opened, Hutch found a seat, and the proceedings commenced with a case of drunk and incapable. The magistrate seemed very severe, although it wasn't surprising in the circumstances.

His next two cases were of vagrancy, and Hutch suspected that such occurrences were common. They were dealt with very quickly, although with little mercy, and then the Clerk read out Norman's name.

Norman was brought, incongruous in evening dress, into the dock, the particulars of the case were read out and the Clerk of the Court asked him how he pleaded. To Hutch's relief, he entered his plea of 'guilty' quietly and without additional comment. The two police officers involved gave their evidence.

Eventually, the magistrate asked, 'Has this man anyone to speak in his defence?'

The Clerk of the Court consulted his notes and said, 'Mr Jack Hutchins, a colleague, I believe, Your Honour.'

'Is Mr Hutchins in court?'

Hutch rose diffidently to his feet. He'd never spoken in public, and he found the surroundings particularly intimidating.

'Well, Mr Hutchins?'

Hutch cleared his throat nervously and made his submission. 'Your honour,' he said, 'Norman Barraclough and I have known each other since we were five years old. In all that time, he has only ever hit anybody in self-defence or when he had to defend somebody else. There were times when we were at school, when he had to deal with a bully, but he would never fight for any other reason, and he was never a bully himself.'

Norman grasped the front of the dock and opened his mouth to speak.

'Leave it to me, Norman,' said Hutch.

'I were only—'

'No, leave it to me.'

'That's probably good advice,' said the magistrate. 'You have asked Mr Hutchins to speak for you. Kindly allow him to do so.'

Norman shrugged and stood back.

'Last night, Your Honour,' said Hutch, 'it was just as I've been saying. The victim was a workmate of ours, a quiet and peaceful man. All the Blackshirts had against him was that he was Jewish. Norman heard the scuffle and, seeing our fellow-musician being attacked, he defended him. That was all. He hadn't gone looking for trouble. He simply felt that he had to defend an innocent victim against two thugs. He has never been in trouble with the police, and this experience has been very difficult for him.' Hutch could see the magistrate nodding impatiently, so he decided to end his speech there.

'Thank you, Mr Hutchins. You may be seated.' Turning his attention then to the Clerk of the court, the magistrate asked, 'Is the victim of the attack in court?'

'If you'll give me one moment, Your Honour, I shall find out.'

Raising his voice somewhat unnecessarily, he asked, 'Is Daniel Rosenthal in court?'

Somewhere behind Hutch, a voice said, 'I'm here, Your Honour.'

Hutch turned and saw Daniel. His face was bruised and his lower lip was cut so badly that it was clear he wouldn't be playing his saxophone for a while.

'Mr Rosenthal, do you agree with the account Mr Hutchins has given to the court?'

Speaking with difficulty, Daniel said, 'Yes, Your Honour. That's what happened.'

'Thank you, Mr Rosenthal.' Finally, he addressed Norman. 'Norman Alfred Barraclough, your friend and colleague Mr Hutchins has spoken quite eloquently on your behalf. It is true that the victim in this case was assaulted criminally, and I understand that you went to his defence with the best of motives, but I cannot let it go at that. The fact is that you broke the law in attacking the two ruffians, and you have quite rightly pleaded guilty to that charge. I am therefore binding you over for one year, in the sum of five pounds, to keep the peace. Do you understand what that means?'

Norman mumbled, 'I'm not sure,' hastily adding, 'Your Honour.'

'It means that, instead of going to prison, you will agree to refrain from fighting or otherwise inflicting injury on others, for a period of one year. A payment of five pounds to the court will be necessary, and if, within the next twelve months, you are convicted of a similar offence, you will be sent to prison. Is that clear now?'

'Yes, Your Honour. Thank you, Your Honour.'

'Are you in a position to pay the five pounds?'

'Yes, Your Honour, but I don't think I have it on me this minute.' Norman felt in his pocket and took out two one-pound notes.

Hutch raised his hand.

'Yes, Mr Hutchins?'

'I'll make up the five pounds, Your Honour.'

'Thank you, Mr Hutchins. As far as Norman Barraclough is concerned, you are evidently a friend indeed.' His observation prompted polite laughter among the court officials, although Hutch couldn't see anything funny in what he'd said.

The rest was routine. The magistrate stood, and everyone bowed as he left the court. Hutch stayed behind to watch the next hearing, which involved the Blackshirts.

The magistrate returned, and the Blackshirts were led, bruised and bloodied into court. Hutch heard the indictments read, and the defendants were asked how they pleaded. Incredibly, they stood up proudly to plead guilty.

'Have you anything,' asked the magistrate, 'to say for yourselves?'

Instead of speaking, both men gave the fascist salute.

'You will both apologise for that or I shall hold you in contempt of court,' said the magistrate.

No apology was forthcoming, so Hutch had the satisfaction of seeing them sentenced to a total of three months each for assault and battery, and the further offence of contempt of court.

Hutch and Norman stayed for a word with Daniel, who was understandably grateful for Norman's intervention and embarrassed that his champion had endured a night in a cell. The two then returned to Rumbold Street to change before going out for a celebratory breakfast. Mrs Wheeler was waiting to hear the news.

'A misunderstanding, Mrs Wheeler. That's all it was.'

'Oh, what a relief. I've been on tenterhooks all morning.'

Later, changed and refreshed, Norman said, 'I'll tell you what, Hutch. It were worth a fiver to see them two buggers being led away to be locked up.'

'It was my fiver, Norm,' Hutch reminded him. 'At least, three quid of it was.'

'I'll give it to you now, Hutch.'

'Aye, well, just remember, you've got to keep your fists to yourself for twelve months.'

In a more sober tone, Norman said, 'I'll behave myself. Thanks, Hutch. I won't forget it.'

11

Daniel returned to the band after a week, and things continued almost as before, with rehearsals punctuated by outbursts of anger from Felix, alternating with evenings of sheer enjoyment as the band simply played. Hutch never found out whether Felix had become a permanent patient of the Wheelers' doctor, or whether he was avoiding any situation in which he was required to talk about his problem. He was seldom to be found in an approachable mood, so well-wishers could only wonder.

The club hosted a special celebration on St Valentine's night, which turned out to be a great success, and band members went home reminded in the best possible way of why they'd chosen that way of life. That, as much as anything, contributed to the shock that came the following morning.

The band were gathered in the band room, waiting for Felix, who, for all his failings, was usually punctual. Being a poor sleeper made him so, and they were convinced that something unpleasant had happened to him. Their suspicion was confirmed when Arthur, the proprietor called for their attention. He seemed unusually deflated.

'Boys,' he said, 'it's bad news. Felix's landlady found him unconscious this morning. He'd taken an overdose of a sedative or a sleeping draught.' He swallowed hard. 'He died shortly after reaching hospital.'

There was a few desultory and almost whispered remarks from the stunned musicians, and then Arthur spoke again.

'Out of respect for Felix, the club will be closed tonight. I'm paying you all up to last night plus a week's severance pay, and then I have to find another band.'

Someone asked, 'Why can't we carry on? One of us can stand in front.'

'I'm sorry,' said Arthur. 'The contract is with the bandleader, and we no longer have one.' He raised his hands against the swell of protest. 'I'm sorry, boys, but that's the way it is.'

Hutch asked, 'How can we find out about the funeral?'

'There won't be one. Suicides don't get a Christian funeral or burial.'

'That's disgusting.'

'It's the law, Hutch.'

Daniel was thumbing through his diary.

Norman said, 'I don't think you'll find any gigs in there, Daniel.'

'I'm looking for a telephone number. I'm going to give Bert Ambrose a ring and see if he knows of anyone who's hiring sax players.'

'Why Ambrose?'

'Because I know him, and because we have something in common.' He saw Norman's puzzled expression and enlightened him. 'I'm not the only four-by-two in the dance band world,' he explained.

'Good luck, Daniel.'

When they were alone, Hutch asked, 'What kind of a bloody country is this, Norm? The poor bugger can't have a decent funeral, and all because he couldn't face life any longer.'

'I know, mate.' Norman steered his friend towards the nearest café. 'It's hypocrisy. That's what it is.'

They bought tea for Norman and coffee for Hutch.

'We're back where we started, Hutch,' said Norman. 'I suppose it's back to Archer Street for us.'

———— ◆◄◆ ————

They spent Monday, Tuesday and Wednesday morning in Archer Street with no success, but later in the day, Hutch overheard part of a conversation that set him wondering. He drew Norman out of general earshot and said, 'There's a new club opening in Mayfair and they're recruiting a band from scratch.

I don't know the name of the bandleader, but he's an American chap, a sax player who played with the Dorsey Brothers until they split up.'

'Was he there when they fell out? That must have been quite a set-to.'

'I don't know, but the bloke who owns the club is called Normanton. Now, does that ring any bells?'

Norman put his head on one side, as he often did when he was thinking, but it gave him no assistance. 'No,' he said, 'I can't say it does.'

'Cast your mind back,' Hutch told him impatiently, 'to that day in Hyde Park when we caught some Blackshirts laying into a bloke because he'd made a speech about Mussolini. His name was Normanton. I've still got his card back at the digs.'

'That's right.' Norman's memory was functioning again. 'He said if there was anything he could do for us we'd only to ask.'

'Yes, well, I'd feel a bit awkward about taking advantage of that, but we'd only be asking him to get the bandleader to listen to us.'

'That's if he's the same bloke.'

'Right enough, but how many Normantons can there be in London?'

'I don't know, Hutch. It's a big place.'

'Well, there's only one way to find out. I'll ring him up tonight.'

It made sense to spend the rest of the day in Archer Street, which they did, but still without success.

———◂▸◂———

When Hutch eventually made the call, he was relieved to find Mr Normanton at home.

'Mr Normanton,' he said, 'this is Jack Hutchins.'

'Oh, and how can I help you?'

'Maybe you don't remember me. We met in Hyde Park. You'd made a speech about Mussolini and you were set on by Mosley's thugs.'

'I beg your pardon, Mr Hutchins. Of course I remember you now. You and your friend probably saved my life.'

'Well, maybe it wasn't as bad as that but it must have felt like it.'

'I assure you, it did. Now, how may I be of assistance?'

'Well, I don't know if we told you when we met, but we're musicians, and I'm ringing to ask if you're the owner of the club called The Golden Slipper, that's opening in Mayfair.'

'No, I'm afraid not.' Mr Normanton chuckled. 'Night clubs are not my line of business at all. I imagine you heard that the proprietor's name is the same as mine?'

'That's right, Mr Normanton. I'm sorry to be a nuisance.' He was about to end the conversation and hang up the earpiece, when Mr Normanton said, 'Wait a moment, Mr Hutchins, after what you and your friend did for me, the last thing I'd call you is a nuisance. I know the proprietor of The Golden Slipper rather well; in fact, he's my nephew, and his name is Fred Normanton. If you're looking for work I should be delighted to speak to him for you.'

'Could you, Mr Normanton? All we're asking is for the bandleader to give us an audition. Then it'll be up to him to decide if he wants us.'

'Of course it will. Now, I'd like you both to come and see me. Could you come around to my office in Charing Cross Road tomorrow morning?'

'Yes, I'm sure we could.'

'In that case, shall we say ten o'clock? I shall have dealt with my post by then and I shall be able to give you my full attention. The shop is called "Technical and Scientific Books".'

Hutch wrote down the full address and thanked him before returning the earpiece to its cradle and giving Norman the gist of his conversation with Mr Normanton.

———— ◆►◄ ————

The shop was surprisingly large, considering its specialised nature, but they found an assistant, who reported their arrival to Mr Normanton and directed them to his office. He seemed genuinely pleased to see them and asked his secretary to make coffee.

Hutch looked around the office, which was surprisingly

cluttered with items of stock, and he scanned the titles of the books that occupied Mr Normanton's desk.

'I see you've got George Hesketh's *Economical Steam Distribution*,' he observed.

Mr Normanton picked up the book. 'Oh, do you know it?'

'Yes, we were engineers before we left Yorkshire, you see, and George Hesketh was Chief Engineer at Isaac Singleton's, one of our competitors.'

'Fascinating. Actually, my father's family hailed originally from the West Riding. How long have you been in London?'

'I think Hutch had been here a couple of weeks when we met you. I'd only just arrived,' said Norman.

'And you're dance band musicians now, I believe?'

'That's right. Hutch plays the clarinet and alto saxophone and I play the trombone.'

Mr Normanton's secretary came into the office with a tray loaded with coffee things and proceeded to pour and hand coffee to the guests.

'Fred, my nephew,' said Mr Normanton, 'was just ten years old and away at prep school when his parents were lost at sea.'

Hutch wondered idly what a prep school was, but forbore to ask. For the moment, he and Norman merely nodded sympathetically, not wishing to interrupt.

'Naturally, my wife and I became responsible for him and we brought him up as our own.' He smiled and said, 'I know what you're both thinking. You're wondering how the nephew of a dealer in technical literature came to be the proprietor of a night club. Well, I agree that the two interests hardly go hand in hand but the fact is that we always gave Fred a great deal of latitude. Some would say we spoiled him, although I would disagree. At all events, he grew up with all the interests of a normal young man, and when the time came to choose a career he used the money left to him to invest in those interests. 'The Golden Slipper' is his latest venture, and I wish him well in it.'

'Do you think,' asked Hutch, 'there's any chance of an audition?'

'I think there's every chance. I shall speak to him very soon. Now, how can he get in touch with you?'

Hutch gave him the telephone number at 26 Rumbold Street, and Mr Normanton brought the meeting to its end. They left with his very best wishes and the assurance that his nephew would feel similarly well-disposed toward them.

As they left the shop, Norman asked, 'What do you reckon a prep school is, Hutch?'

'I've no idea, Norm. Maybe it's a place like the one Rosie Turner's *fiancée* went to.'

'Well, they can't all be as daft as him, can they?'

———◆◀———

It was three days later, on Friday morning, that Mrs Wheeler called upstairs, 'Mr Hutchins, you're wanted on the telephone.' As Hutch reached the foot of the stairs, she said in an awed tone, 'The caller sounds like an American.' She lingered in the hall while Hutch picked up the phone and answered it.

'Jack Hutchins.'

'Hello, Mr Hutchins.' Mrs Wheeler was right about the caller's accent. 'This is Carl Duverne, bandleader at the Golden Slipper; at least, I will be when the operation gets off the ground. I hear you and your friend want to come over and do an audition. Is that right?'

'Yes, if that's all right.'

'It sure is all right. You guys have friends in high places. I got the tap on the shoulder this morning from Fred, and that's fine just so long as you understand that I have the final word, okay?'

'Of course.' Hutch could hear his own heart beating.

'You're trombone and alto sax, right?'

'That's right. I play clarinet and alto sax.'

'I see. I need someone on alto and tenor sax, ideally, but we'll talk about that when you come over. Can you make it for two o'clock this afternoon? I'll give you the address.'

———◆◀———

Mr Duverne met them at the door. He was maybe thirty or a little older, tall and slim, with dark, well-trimmed hair and he wore a grey, single-breasted suit with a waistcoat and a maroon paisley tie. A pencil moustache and a welcoming smile complemented the ensemble.

'Come in, boys,' he said. 'Be careful not to fall over the stuff the builders have left behind.' He led them through a short, dark passage and into what was obviously going to be the main part of the club, because at one end, a dance floor was being laid. At various places around the room, men were either painting the woodwork wine-red or hanging cream, embossed wallpaper.

'Now, I know one of you is Jack Hutchins.'

'That's me.' Hutch offered his hand. 'This is Norman Barraclough.'

'Delighted to make your acquaintance.' He shook hands with them. 'I'm going to leave you to warm up for a few minutes while I make a phone call.'

'Well, Hutch,' said Norman, taking his trombone from its case, 'it'll be muck or nettles in a minute.'

Hutch was too preoccupied to say anything. As well as being naturally nervous about the audition, he was concerned about Mr Duverne's earlier reference to the tenor saxophone. If the outcome depended on that, he hadn't a chance.

They were ready to play by the time the bandleader returned from the office, and he decided to hear Norman first. Hutch already knew what Norman was going to play. He'd chosen 'I'm in the Mood for Love' because it was new, it showed he was up to date with dance band repertoire and it was full of sustained notes that would demonstrate the quality of his tone. He picked up his trombone and went straight into the chorus, playing it straight the first time, and then repeating it with discrete improvisation. It was a fine performance.

Mr Duverne smiled and asked, 'Where have you played in the past, Norman?'

'On the *RMS Duchess of Lancaster* and before that with a band at home called The Rhythm Serenaders. Oh, and we were both at Arturo's with Felix Beaumont until just lately.'

'Yes, that was very sad. Okay, Norman, take a break while I listen to Jack.' He turned irritably to the men laying the dance floor and asked, 'Can you guys give us five minutes?' The hammering stopped and, still anxious, Hutch put his saxophone to his lips and played two choruses of 'I'll String Along with You.'

'Okay, Jack,' said Mr Duverne, 'do you have a tenor sax?'

Hutch shook his head dumbly. 'I've played one,' he said, 'but I'm afraid I haven't got one.'

'Never mind. Give me two minutes and I'll get mine. It's in the office.' He disappeared again, leaving Hutch to question the point of continuing. Even if his playing came up to scratch, he knew he could never afford such an expensive instrument.

'Here, Jack.' Mr Duverne handed him a tenor sax already assembled. 'Take a minute to warm up.'

Hutch slipped the cord around his neck and went through the process, still wondering why he was doing it. Eventually, he gave a nod and started Ray Noble's 'The Very Thought of You.' By the time he came to the end of the second phrase, he realised he was playing an instrument of quality. It had a lovely tone and he played on, simply enjoying the exquisite song and the instrument itself.

'That's one of my all-time favourite numbers,' Mr Duverne told him when he'd finished, 'and you played it very well.'

'Thanks, Mr Duverne, but it's no good. I can't afford a tenor sax.'

'What do you reckon you'd have to pay for one over here?'

'About thirty pounds, I should think, at the very least. I can't find that, Mr Duverne.'

'Call me "Carl". It's not my real name. I'm called Sam Green, but who wants to hear *his* band?' He took the instrument from Hutch and said, 'I still need to hire another sax player, so the question of whether he plays tenor or you do is up in the air for now. If I decide to give you the tenor parts, you can use mine until you get one. How does that sound?'

Hutch stared at him. 'Do you mean we've got the jobs?'

'Yes, you're both hired.'

'Thanks, Carl. I mean *thank you*. It's... it's too good to be true.'

'It's true all right. I want you both, and I want your sax playing enough to make you that offer, Jack. You'll both be on one month's trial at ten pounds per week. After that it'll rise to twelve, at least for the time being, and you'll get one pound per hour extra when we're recording.' Reading their stunned expressions, he said, 'Be assured, this band's going places.' He shook hands with them again and asked, 'Is there anything else we need to deal with?'

'Just one thing, Carl,' said Hutch. 'It's my name. Everybody calls me "Hutch".'

Carl smiled. 'Okay. "Hutch" it is. There's no copyright where names are concerned, so even if "Hutch" Hutchinson gets to hear about it he can't complain.'

Hutch didn't care how the singer might feel about sharing his name. As far as he and Norman were concerned, the world was suddenly a rosier place.

12

The Golden Slipper opened on Saturday 29th February. As 1936 was a leap year, it was considered a suitably romantic date on which to open, refitting and decoration having delayed the event beyond St Valentine's Day, and the club's inaugural members and their guests enjoyed the romantic night they were promised. Carl had appointed a vocalist, a talented and self-assured young man with Latin good looks, called Miles Wendover, who was instantly popular, at least with the female guests. For the rest, champagne abounded, the band played some of the great romantic numbers of the age, and the influential press were much in evidence.

It was a glorious night, too, for Hutch and Norman, who were once more playing the music of their choice and enjoying every note. The regime was strict; Carl expected the highest standards from his musicians in performance, appearance and behaviour, but no one minded because it was in their interest for the club to be successful. The musicians had taken part in publicity photo shoots and most of them had made liberal use of the official picture postcards of the club and the band. Norman sent one to Phyllis and another to Fourth Officer Percival Linley, c/o *RMS Duchess of Lancaster*, as he told Hutch, 'Just to show the bugger.'

Hutch wrote a letter to his mother and Phyllis, and then sent two postcards to the Turner household: one to Rosie and the other to Eleanor, because he knew Rosie would never share hers with her sister.

He was surprised when, a few days later, a letter arrived, addressed to him at the club. It had a Cullington postmark.

As soon as he had a moment to spare, he opened it and found it was from Eleanor Turner.

Dear Hutch,

Thank you for your postcard, which I found very exciting. I knew you would be successful, and I'm very pleased. Good luck for the future.

Yours truly and with all good wishes,
Eleanor Turner.

It was little more than a polite 'thank you', but it was a damned sight more than he could expect from Rosie, and he appreciated the gesture because it was clearly genuine.

————◆⬩◆————

Despite their new-found affluence, Hutch and Norman were still very conscious of the way of life they'd left behind in Yorkshire, and incidents occurred from time to time that reminded them of the unhappiness that existed elsewhere in the country. One such event took place shortly after the club opened, when the two were making their way to work.

It was a particularly cold evening, one of those times when the temperature makes senses and awareness seem keener, and, through the noise of the late evening traffic and the hurried footsteps of frozen pedestrians, Hutch caught the faint sound of voices in harmony. He stopped for a second to listen.

Norman stopped two paces ahead of him and asked, 'What's up, Hutch?'

'Listen, Norm.'

'What is it?'

'Somebody's singing.'

Norman listened. 'Aye it's coming from ahead of us.'

They walked on, and the singing grew louder, until they came to a line of pinched and frozen men. To say they were ill-clad for winter weather did their plight no justice. There were seven in all, of whom three wore thin, shabby raincoats; the others had no coats at all but were dressed in threadbare jackets and trousers, and their boots were so worn as to be of scant protection against the wet tarmac. They walked in single file beside the pavement edge and, as they walked, they sang in a language that meant nothing to Hutch or Norman, but their music had a tragic and compelling beauty.

As the song reached its end, Hutch drew level with the man at the head of the line and asked, 'What was that song called?'

'It's called "*Myfanwy*", sir. Would you like to hear another?' The man took off his cloth cap hopefully.

'I could listen to you all night,' said Hutch, dropping a half-crown piece into the cap, 'but don't call me "sir". We're working men, same as you. We've been luckier, that's all.'

'We could use a bit of luck, I'll not deny it.' The man looked down at the coin in his cap and said, 'This kind of luck, by choice, and we thank you for it.'

'Where are you from?'

'We're from Wales, mun. We're all miners but there's nothing for us there so, as we're members of the colliery male voice choir, we're trying to earn a bob by singing. It's patchy though.'

Never slow to come to the point, Norman asked him, 'When did you last have a square meal?'

'Last night, it was, although I'd hardly describe the meal as square, if you get my meaning.' He turned to speak to the young man behind him. 'It was last night, wasn't it, *bach*? You lose all track of time with this carry-on.'

'That's right, Dad.'

'He's my son,' explained the man, somewhat unnecessarily. 'I'm Dai Edwards and so is he, so I'm Dai and he's Dai *Bach* 'cause he's a youngster, see?'

It was more than Hutch could bear. He asked, 'Do you like fish and chips?'

Dai rolled his eyes at the thought. 'Any food's popular when you're starving, mun.'

'All right. Come with us.'

'It'll be all right, will it? We have to walk in the gutter when we're singing, see, or they'll have the English law on us.'

'You'll be all right with us,' Norman told him. 'If the law wants to know, we're your visible means of support.'

'Thank you, lads, and I mean that.' He and the others fell in step with them. 'What do you fellows do for a crust, then?'

'We're musicians. I play the trombone and Hutch plays the sax. We work in a night club.'

Possibly unable to imagine such opulence, Dai merely nodded and asked, 'Would you like to hear a song as we go?'

'Yes,' said Hutch, 'if it's anything like the last one.'

'Fair enough. This one's called "*Bugeilio'r Gwenith Gwyn*". It means "Watching the White Wheat".' He glanced behind him by way of a signal and led his choir into the song.

As they walked, Norman whispered, 'I take it we're heading for Lee Kwan Yan's chip shop?' The Chinatown restaurant had been open only a short time, and its proprietor was keen to attract business, hence the English addition to the menu.

'That's right.' The two men fell silent again, listening to the singing, while passers-by viewed them with curiosity and wonder.

Hutch led them into Little Newport Street and stopped outside an empty restaurant with a 'Closed' sign on the door. At six o'clock in the evening it was too early for normal business. He tapped on the window.

Dai and the others looked at him in surprise. 'Eating in a *café*, is it now?'

A man in a white dinner jacket opened the door and Hutch asked, 'Do you think you could manage cod and chips seven times for these lads, Mr Lee? They've come a long way.' He took out his wallet.

'Okay, Hutch.'

As far as Mr Lee was concerned it was welcome business, and it was no problem for Hutch and Norman, but they all knew that when the meal was over the seven men would return to the streets, dependent once more on the compassion of London's pedestrian public.

Carl had been busy again and hired a female vocalist called Penny Merry. She was pretty, talented and, at twenty-one, drawn naturally to band members of her own age, although she seemed a little in awe of Norman, possibly because of his forthright manner. She had no such reservation about Hutch and chatted with him regularly to the apparent annoyance of her male vocal counterpart.

'He's scowling at me again,' she told Hutch during a break from rehearsal.

Hutch studied her fair, bobbed hair, her smiling blue eyes and creamy complexion as he so often did, at a loss to see why anyone might scowl at her.

'He only does it when I'm talking to you.'

'Maybe he doesn't like musicians,' suggested Hutch. 'We're not all that carried away with him.'

'Why not?' Her half-smile suggested she already knew the answer.

'Because he's so cocky. He's well and truly in love with himself.'

'He told me he's never nervous when he sings, and I can't understand that because I feel sick sometimes, I'm so scared. Do you get nervous, Hutch?'

'Yes, I do, and it's not such a bad thing. You heard Miles throw that song away this morning, didn't you?'

'Which one?'

' "Dancing Cheek to Cheek". It's a great song and he just went through the motions because there was no audience for him to show off to. A little bit of nervous tension might make all the difference.'

'It makes a big difference to me,' she said gloomily.

'You need to find a way of concentrating so hard on the words and the music that you forget about nerves.'

'How can I do that?'

He looked at his new wristwatch and saw that they would have to return to work in a few minutes. 'When I came here and played for Carl,' he told her, 'I reckoned I hadn't a chance. I was in the wrong frame of mind altogether, but he lent me his tenor sax, the one I'm using now, and when I started playing, all I could think about was the glorious sound the instrument was making and the beautiful song I was playing, and that was what got me through the audition.'

'We have to go back now,' she said, torn between duty and the conversation they were having, 'but let's talk about it later.'

He agreed readily. Talking with her about music was easy enough, much easier than finding the nerve to ask her to go out with him, which was what he really wanted.

———◆◆———

Another thwarted lover was Norman, although the object of his desire had no connection with the band. Had a benevolent genii offered him a hundred pretty female vocalists, he would have turned them all down without hesitation. That was how constant he was, and yet in all the time he'd been aware of his feelings he'd never disclosed the identity of his fancy to those closest to him. Constrained by circumstances, he'd said nothing to Hutch or to Mrs Hutchins or, most importantly, to Phyllis, because she was the girl in question.

———◆◆———

Fate was initially kinder to Hutch. When a man is inexperienced, shy and tongue-tied, he needs an event that will spur him into action, and such an incident took place after a band rehearsal two mornings later, when he was returning Carl's tenor saxophone. To reach the office it was necessary to pass the dressing rooms and, as he returned that way, he heard raised voices in Penny's room. One of them was hers and she was telling someone urgently to keep his hands to himself. He couldn't make out what the man was saying but he'd heard enough. When he opened the door, he saw that Miles had Penny trapped against the wall, struggling to free herself. That was until Hutch grabbed him by the upper arm to turn him round, and then hit him with a right hook that caused him to fall semi-conscious to the floor. A few seconds later, Carl arrived, demanding to know what the noise was about.

'He was forcing himself on Penny,' Hutch told him, nursing his bruised knuckles.

'That's right,' said Penny hotly, 'the bugger was trying to touch me up. I don't know what might have happened if Hutch hadn't come when 'e did.'

It was the first time Hutch had heard her swear or use a coarse expression, and both came as quite a surprise, but it was difficult to blame her in the circumstances.

Carl looked down at Miles, who was now properly conscious and massaging his jaw, and said, 'You're fired.'

When he and Penny were alone, Hutch asked, 'Are you all right?'

'Yes, I'm fine.' She touched his arm affectionately. 'Thanks, Hutch.'

'The pleasure was all mine.' It was the kind of thing one of Gary Cooper's characters might say and it made him feel unusually confident. 'What you need now,' he told her, 'is something to take your mind off what's happened. They're showing *The Ghost Goes West* round the corner. Have you seen it?' He'd been keeping an eye on the listings for the local cinemas ever since Penny's arrival at the club.

'No, I haven't, and I like Robert Donat.'

'Would you like... you know...?'

'Yes, I'd like to, but do you think we could eat first. I'm bleedin' starving.'

'Okay, we could go to the Corner House.' Suddenly he was feeling generous.

———— ▸◂ ————

Lunch at the Corner House was pricey by Hutch's standards but he didn't mind. It was a first date and therefore an important one. They both enjoyed the film but Hutch was somewhat surprised when, during the main feature, Penny suddenly reached across and took his hand in hers. He'd never known a girl take the initiative like that but he imagined it must be normal behaviour in London. Similarly, when he left her at her lodgings at the opposite end of Rumbold Street to his, she inclined her face and waited for him to kiss her. It was nice, but he knew he had much to learn about the big city way of life.

13

Hutch and Penny continued to spend time together over the next two weeks, during which he learned more about her. He discovered that her family home was in Romford in Essex and that prior to becoming a band singer she had worked as a shorthand typist for a firm that made collar and shirt studs.

Another development was that the routine chaste kiss outside her lodgings soon gave way to one that grew daily in intensity, a source of excitement and wonder for Hutch, whose previous liaisons had been altogether more restrained. It was at such times that Penny frequently emerged from their embrace to say fretfully, 'I wish she'd go out once in a while.' The person in question was her landlady, who had so far failed in that requirement. Unfortunately, Mrs Wheeler was no more accommodating, as her shopping trips were necessarily brief.

The day came, however, when Penny arrived for the morning's rehearsal and said to him with more than a hint of eagerness, 'Come round to my place afterwards. She's going to be out all day.' Her summons could mean only one thing, and Hutch was caught in a dilemma.

Apart from an isolated and one-sided encounter when he was an apprentice, he was without sexual experience. The incident had occurred during the first week of his employment at Atkinson's mill, when part of his unofficial induction was an 'inspection' by three of the girls in the top weaving shed during their breakfast break. He had arrived in his fourteen-year-old innocence, not knowing what to expect, and had been bundled with good-natured laughter into a dark corner of the shed, where two of the girls held him while the other burrowed expertly into his overalls. He had been horrified at first, before experiencing, somewhat guiltily, a degree of arousal that increased until the moment when the girl keeping watch reported the approach of the overlooker. Hutch's embarrassment at the laughter of the electricians waiting for him outside was in some way assuaged when he learned subsequently that his assessor had declared him 'a champion grower.'

His feelings, therefore, regarding Penny's invitation were confused. He found her utterly desirable; their late afternoon embraces, however blissful, always left him craving more, and she made no secret of her need. On the other hand, he had behind him twenty-one years of coy, northern, working-class upbringing and, always lurking at the back of his mind, the conviction that, whilst men occasionally gave in to temptation, nice girls simply didn't do that kind of thing.

Willpower enabled him to concentrate on the rehearsal, which was over all too soon. Carl dismissed the band and, after much inner turmoil, Hutch's decision was dictated by the one element that was not negotiable: he was simply unable to refuse her. Accordingly, he shelved his plans for the afternoon and accompanied her to her room.

When they arrived at the house, she led him upstairs and across a landing with a creaking floorboard. There was no one in the house to hear it but it nevertheless increased Hutch's already loaded anxiety.

He was surprised to find that her room was even smaller and untidier than his. Penny seemed not to care about the state of her room, however, as she closed the door and launched herself immediately into his arms.

'I thought she'd never go out,' she said, releasing him to unfasten his coat buttons. 'Put your clothes on that chair.' She indicated the only chair in the room, which was already draped with various items of feminine underwear.

As he removed his overcoat, he said, 'Look, I wasn't expecting... you know, and I haven't been to the barber's.'

'Your 'air looks short enough to me.' She took off her shoes and sat on the bed to unfasten her stockings.

'No, I mean I haven't got... anything to, you know... use.'

She laughed as she rolled down her stockings and lowered her skirt. 'I know what you meant. I was pullin' your leg.' She lifted her jumper carelessly over her head and let it fall to the floor. 'You don't need anything. I've got a cap.' Then, seeing his baffled expression, she explained, 'I don't mean a cap to wear on me head, silly. It's to stop me gettin' pregnant. I dealt with that before we left the club. Come on, get your clothes off.' She threw her blouse on top of her jumper and removed her petticoat and brassiere.

Hutch tried not to gape. He'd only ever seen monochrome images of breasts when a workmate once showed him a copy of 'Health and Efficiency' magazine, but now he was looking at real ones and they were exquisite.

'Get a move on, Hutch.' She stood up and removed the rest of her underclothes in one deft movement. Then, in a moment of realisation, she turned to face him and said matter-of-factly, 'You've never done it before, have you?'

Startled though he was by her total nudity, he was about to protest his lack of innocence but, as usual, decided to tell the truth. 'No,' he admitted.

'What, never?'

'Never.' He shook his head, completely deflated.

'Is it against the law where you come from, then?'

'No, I just....' He wondered how much worse it could get. 'I was working twelve-hour shifts, six days a week, and with everything else I had to do I never managed to fit it in.'

Suddenly she smiled. 'Come and sit down,' she said, sitting on the bed again. She drew him towards her and kissed him softly. 'You're allowed to touch me,' she told him. 'I'm not fragile.' She put her arm around his shoulders and said, 'There's nothing to worry about. I'll tell you exactly what to do. It'll be really nice, I promise.'

If her reassurance had done much to convince him, the silky feel of her naked body did the rest, and he was unfastening his shoes when he heard the downstairs door being opened and then closed.

Penny stiffened. 'Hell,' she whispered. 'Get behind the bed and lie flat.'

Sharing her alarm, he obeyed her instantly and adopted the

prone position on the cold linoleum floor behind her bed. As he did so, he heard footsteps on the stairs. A woman's voice asked, 'Are you back, Penny?' Hutch heard the floorboard on the landing creak. Peering from beneath the bed, he could see Penny's feet and ankles and the hem of her dressing gown as she donned it hurriedly. She opened the door a few inches.

'Are you all right?' The landlady's question was no doubt prompted by seeing Penny undressed at midday.

'No, I've got an awful headache. I was just lying down for an hour.'

'Oh, I'm sorry to disturb you. I only came to let you know I was back. Can I get you anything?'

'No thanks, I've taken an aspirin.'

'Good girl. Well, I hope you feel better soon.'

Hutch saw the door close, heard the floorboard creak and the footsteps descend the stairs, and then he breathed normally again.

'That was a close thing,' said Penny. 'Just think, if you'd been a bit quicker off the mark she might 'ave caught us at it.'

Only one problem remained. 'How,' asked Hutch, 'am I going to get out of the house?'

'That's easy.' Penny looked as if she'd just remembered something. 'I was supposed to get matches for her on me way back but I forgot. She can't light the gas stove without 'em, so she'll have to go out again. Then you can sneak out.' Idly, she picked up her underclothes. 'If you don't mind,' she said, 'I'll make myself decent again.'

'No, go ahead. I couldn't....'

'You'd be a good 'un if you could after a fright like that.' She shook her head at the hopelessness of the situation and said, 'I'm just thankful I don't have to live here much longer.'

'Where are you going?' It was Hutch's first intimation that she was moving.

'I've got a place in Warwick Street. It's over a restaurant, and I can't see the chap who owns it worrying too much about who I bring home.'

Big Ideas

Penny moved into her new bedsitter ten days later and lost little time in offering Hutch her hospitality, so that, under her patient and expert tutelage, he was finally able to leave innocence behind him whilst retaining only a residual sense of guilt.

14

The Golden Slipper and its band had lost none of their appeal; Penny was as popular as ever, and now Carl had taken over from Miles. He had an appealing voice that blended easily with Penny's, a quality that was soon to be heard by a much wider audience.

Several of the musicians had noticed a man seated alone and paying particular attention to the band, and each had his own theory. One thought the man might have been scouting poachable talent for another band, and that seemed a likely theory. Another floated the possibility that he'd simply taken a fancy to Penny. After all, he reasoned, who wouldn't? They were both wrong, however, as they learned at their next rehearsal.

'You're possibly wondering who the lone guy was at Table Four a few nights ago,' said Carl. 'He was from the BBC, and I can tell you now that because of the impression he took away with him we're going to get our turn in the National Programme's late night spot from eleven-fifteen until midnight. You can tell your folks to keep an eye on their *Radio Times*.'

'I'm pleased at the way things are going,' he told Hutch and Norman after the rehearsal. 'If we do a few nights on the National Programme it shouldn't be long before we get a recording contract. I've spoken to a few people out there and they tell me there's interest already.'

'I just can't get over it,' said Hutch.

'What can't you get over?'

'How quickly everything happens in this business.'

'It doesn't always happen as quickly as this,' said Carl. 'Some bands will always struggle, but we've got something going for us here. We've got a new club, a new band, good musicians and a reputation.'

'What reputation?'

'Mine. Before I came over here I worked with the best guys in the business, and the studios here know that.' If anyone else had said that, it would have sounded like a boast but they knew that Carl was simply stating a fact.

'It must be different for you here,' said Norman. 'I didn't spend much time in New York; we only had less than a day there each time we docked, but it seemed to me there was always a lot of noise and bustle. Everything was exciting.'

Carl smiled at his description. 'Not every town's like New York,' he said. 'I was born and raised in a sleepy little place in New Hampshire, but I know what you mean. It takes a lot to get you guys excited, and the music's different as well.'

Norman frowned. 'We play all the same numbers, don't we?'

'Sure we do, but we don't play them the same way. The American sound is bright, but the British style is more what you'd call mellow and understated, like the British character. D' you know what I mean?'

They knew what he meant, but the topic for the rest of the day was the forthcoming broadcast, whenever that might be. Hutch and Norman discussed it that Sunday evening in Hutch's room. They'd both decided that the pub was too noisy for civilised conversation, and the draught beer was of questionable quality, so they bought a crate of bottled Bass and took it back to Rumbold Street.

'Do you know the best thing about being on the National Programme, Norm?'

'Everything about it is good.' Norman opened two bottles of beer and handed one to Hutch. 'We get an extra quid for the broadcast, suddenly we're famous, and.... I don't know what else, but it all looks champion to me.' He poured his beer deftly into a glass. 'What have you in mind?'

'It's the thought of people at home, those who have wireless sets, hearing the band, and being told by someone else, just out of the blue, that us two are part of it.'

'Now word's got around, there'll be a few up yonder talking about how they knew us before we were famous.'

'That's right. There's my mother and our Phyllis too, now they've got a wireless set of their own.' That small luxury was the result of a recent transaction between Hutch and Phyllis.

'Aye.' Norman finished his beer and took two more bottles from the crate. 'I can just see them tuning in, with your mother as proud as a new hat and trying not to show it.'

'Phyllis will be proud for both of us, Norm.' He'd been waiting for an opportunity to bring the conversation round to her.

'Have you heard from her lately?' Norman tried not to appear too eager for news but he was a hopeless actor.

'I had a letter from her this morning.' It was Hutch's turn to feign detachment, and he thought he did it rather better than Norman.

'Is she keeping well?' Norman handed him a bottle.

'Well enough. I thought you might have heard from her.'

'Not since last Wednesday.'

'Oh.' Hutch poured his beer slowly and carefully, trying at the same time to read Norman's features. 'In that case you won't have heard about Ronnie Emerson.'

Suddenly, Norman's casual façade crumpled. 'Ronnie Emerson? What's he been up to?'

'Well, you know he's keen on our Phyllis.'

'Yes, I know that, but what could she possibly see in him?'

Hutch put his glass down slowly. 'He pays attention to her. Lasses like attention, you know.'

'But he's not right for her.'

'In that case, somebody needs to tell her, don't they?'

'Haven't you told her?' Norman was almost truculent.

'It's not for me to tell her, Norm.'

'You're her brother, aren't you?'

'That's true, but she doesn't like me interfering in such matters. No, it really needs to come from somebody else.'

'Well, I don't know what to say.' In his confusion, Norman drained his glass and took two more bottles from the crate. 'Has there been some kind of development, or what?'

'I don't know if you could call it a development, exactly.' Hutch drank slowly and put his glass down again before elaborating. 'Ronnie's always at Rosie's on Thursday nights, as you know, and he never lets Phyllis out of his sight, but now that he's a man of leisure, he's taken to walking her home from work most days. He's being very attentive.' He nodded to make his point. 'I said lasses like attention, didn't I?'

'Right enough, but not from weedy Emerson, blast it.'

'Yes, and you'd think he'd have some competition, wouldn't you? Mind you, being on the dole drives that kind of thing out of most blokes' minds. Ronnie must be very keen on her to be able to concentrate like that.'

'But what can a man on the dole offer her?'

'Na then, Norm, you know our Phyllis better than that. If you asked her to choose between a rich man she didn't like and a poor man she liked, you know what her answer would be.' He looked across at Norman's almost-empty glass and said, 'You're putting the lotion away a bit sharpish, aren't you?'

'Well, it's enough to drive a man to drink. I don't know how you can fashion to let your sister throw herself away on a twerp like that.' He was clearly agitated, a state of mind that Hutch's casual manner did nothing to ease.

'I think,' said Hutch, 'the advice should come from a bloke who's known her for some time, a chap she can trust.'

'Damn it, Hutch....' Frustration had deprived Norman of coherent speech.

'More than that, though, he needs to be as keen on her as Ronnie is.'

'Why, for heaven's sake?

'Because the more he cares about her the more determined he'll be to persuade her.' Affecting a thoughtful pose, he said, 'I can only think of one bloke who could do it.'

'Oh?' Norman made no effort to hide his alarm. 'Who's that?'

'You, you chump. You've been smitten with her for years.'

Norman closed his eyes tightly, as if to dispel the embarrassment that was making him blush like a girl. Eventually he asked, 'How did you know?'

'Everybody knows.'

'Everybody?'

'Except our Phyllis, of course.'

'Doesn't she know?' There was relief as well as incredulity in his voice.

'She hasn't a clue,' confirmed Hutch. 'She's the only one you've managed to kid.' It seemed to him that neither of them had an inkling about the other's feelings. Maybe that was what people meant when they said love was blind.

'Oh hell.'

'Chin up, Norm.' Hutch's amusement was only exceeded by his relief at having finally raised a delicate matter.

'And you want me to tell her Ronnie Emerson's not right for her?'

'That's right, and when she gets shirty about it and tells you it's none of your business, that's when you can tell her you've been daft about her for years, so it really is your business.' He summoned his thoughtful pose again to say, 'Mind you, it beats me why you've kept it a secret for so long.'

'Oh hell, Hutch.' It seemed that shock had deprived Norman of the greater part of his vocabulary, albeit temporarily, and he had to collect himself before attempting an explanation. 'It's been difficult,' he said eventually. 'I've known Phyllis as long as I've known you and your mother. I even call your mother "Ma", for goodness' sake. I feel like one of the family.'

'That's true,' said Hutch. 'You're almost a member of the family, but when all's said and done you're not related to our Phyllis so I really don't see what's been holding you back.'

'I just didn't want it to look as if I was taking advantage... of being so close, I mean.'

'Well, now the time's come to take advantage. It'll soon be Easter and we'll have Good Friday and Easter Monday off. That's when you'll be able to... you know, press your suit, as they say.'

'I'll have pressed my suit before then, Hutch. I'm not going to turn up at your house looking like a ragamuffin.'

'I'm not talking about clothes, you nitwit. I mean you'll be able to tell her what's what between the two of you, hopefully before Ronnie Emerson makes any more headway.'

Norman was looking worried again. 'He's got time to make a lot of that before Easter,' he said.

Hutch thought quickly. 'Write to her – tomorrow, when you're sober – and tell her you want to talk to her at Easter about an important matter that affects you both.' That, and the letter Hutch would write, would surely keep Ronnie Emerson at bay until Norman could a-wooing go.

15

Norman and Hutch caught the earliest train to Leeds on Good Friday. Norman, normally the very model of self-confidence, was suddenly assailed by nerves.

'You've known our Phyllis long enough,' said Hutch. 'Why are you suddenly shaking in your boots?'

'I'm just not used to this kind of thing, Hutch. I've never gone in for soft talk with lasses.'

'How do you usually talk to them?'

'Just normal, like.'

'Well, then.' Hutch shrugged, as if the answer were obvious. 'She knows you as well as I do. You don't need to act like Rudolph Valentino.'

'I wish I could. He didn't need to say anything.'

'There wouldn't have been any point in him saying anything, Norm. All his pictures were silent ones.'

'That's what I mean. It were easy enough for him.'

The argument continued as far as Leeds, when Norman lapsed into a worried silence, which he maintained for the duration of the onward train journey into Cullington.

They arrived at the house to find, predictably, a warm welcome and the kettle on the hob, although Norman had to rely on Hutch to keep the conversation flowing.

Eventually, Hutch put his cup down and said, 'Come on, Mother, get your hat and coat on. It's so nice out there, we should go for walk in the park.'

'Just us, Jack?'

'Yes, I've something I want to talk to you about, and Norman and Phyllis want to talk an' all.'

Expressionless as ever, she reached her hat and coat from the hooks behind the door and followed her son outside.

'We'll be a while,' he told Norman and Phyllis.

Norman's turmoil had reached its peak, and now, as he heard the door being closed, he found himself unable to speak.

'You said in your letter that you wanted to talk to me about something,' said Phyllis.

'Aye.' Norman's mouth was dry and he picked up his cup to find it empty.

'Would you like more tea?' Phyllis picked up the teapot.

'Yes, er, please.'

'I've never known you so quiet.'

'No.' It was as if an unseen force, a malevolent goblin, had taken possession of him and paralysed his vocal chords.

'The cat's got your tongue, hasn't it?' Phyllis emptied the dregs and then refilled his cup. 'You were so keen to talk to me, and now you seem to have forgotten what you wanted to say.' She got up and joined him on the sofa. 'It wouldn't have anything to do with Ronnie Emerson, would it?'

'Aye, well....'

'Hutch says you're not keen on the idea of Ronnie and me spending time together.'

Norman knew he was blushing, and there was nothing he could do about it. He forced himself to speak. 'He's... he's not right for you, Phyllis.'

'Oh? What makes you say that?'

Norman had known Phyllis for more than seventeen years, and now he was struggling to speak to her about the thing that mattered most to him. Suddenly, the words tumbled out. 'You could do a lot better.'

'Do you have somebody in mind, then?' She seemed to be teasing, as if she knew what was on his mind.

'Aye.' The goblin tightened its grip.

'Are you going to share the secret with me? After all, I've a right to know.'

It was now or never; at least, it seemed so to Norman. In a hoarse voice he barely recognised as his own, he managed to say,

'Phyllis, I've had a soft spot for you since we were kids, and now it's more than that, a lot more. Don't throw yourself away. I can offer you a good life.' He paused, shocked by his own frankness. He'd said it, he'd beaten the goblin, and now he had to make his proposal. Fondly and without the awful croak that had bedevilled him from the outset, he said, 'Let me take care of you, Phyllis.'

'Are you proposing marriage to me?' Her expression suggested that the news was no surprise, but no less welcome for that.

'Yes, I am. That's just what I'm trying to say.'

'Well, then.' She appeared to consider his proposal. Suddenly, she smiled and said, 'In that case, I'd be daft to turn you down.'

Norman's face was burning. 'Do you mean you accept?'

'Yes, I accept.' She took his hands in hers, at least, as far as she was able, his being considerably larger than hers. 'Mind you, it's a funny sort of proposal, isn't it?'

His relief turned to alarm. 'Why do you say that?'

'Well, I'm still waiting for you to kiss me. That's what people do, you know, when they get engaged to be married.' She moved a little closer, but waited for him to seize the moment.

'Phyllis,' he said, taking her in his arms, 'I hardly dared hope for this.' He'd only ever kissed her very diffidently, always on the cheek, and only when the occasion called for it, but now he could kiss her as the film stars did in the pictures. The only difference was that it meant very much more than it ever did on a cinema screen.

'I love you, Phyllis, and that's a fact.'

'Well, that's a coincidence, Norman, because I love you, and that's in spite of your funny ways.'

'What funny ways?'

As if the answer should have been obvious, she said, 'Keeping me waiting like this.'

'It didn't seem right, not until I talked about it with Hutch.'

'I know.' She stroked his hand, as if reassuring a child. 'Hutch told me in his letter.'

'You knew, then?'

She nodded. 'I wanted to hear it from you. A girl likes to be courted, you know.'

Norman liked her stroking his hand. It was a new experience, and the fact it was she who was doing it made it all the more special. One lingering question had to be asked. 'Phyllis,' he said, 'if I hadn't proposed to you, would you have married Ronnie Emerson?'

'Oh, that's a difficult question. You see, Ronnie hadn't got round to asking me either.'

'But, if he had?'

'Well, I'm not getting any younger. I'm twenty-three, and opportunities don't come along every day.' She smiled at his awkwardness. 'No, Norman, if you hadn't proposed when you did, I'd have had it out with you sooner or later. This was meant to happen.'

'Aye, it was.' The fair-haired, blue-eyed object of Norman's longing was there in his arms and, even now, he could scarcely believe it.

They spent a further half-hour or so in secluded bliss before Hutch and his mother returned.

Hutch maintained an air of amicable innocence, but his mother was less skilled in deception. As her son emptied the shopping bag, she looked first at Phyllis and then at Norman, as if she expected an announcement.

'We'd better put you both out of your misery,' said Phyllis. 'Norman and I just got engaged.'

'Oh!' Mrs Hutchins's exclamation was more out of relief than surprise. 'Engaged! I'm that happy for both of you.' For a woman not normally given to displays of affection, she surprised everyone by hugging her daughter and accepting a kiss from Norman. Hutch simply shook Norman's hand and hugged Phyllis as soon as her mother released her.

'We'll go shopping tomorrow,' said Norman, evidently relishing the prospect. 'I'm going to put a ring on your finger before I go back to London, Phyllis.'

'I hope you're not going to spend silly money,' said Mrs Hutchins, always quick to curb excessive spending. 'You could give her your mother's old ring. That's what a lot of young men do.'

'I know what I can afford, Ma, and I've been saving up for this. Anyroad, my dad pawned the wedding and engagement rings when we were hard up. He never did manage to redeem them.'

'No, he wasn't often in work, poor man.'

'He'd have been as happy as Larry if he'd been here today,' said Hutch, 'and so would your mother.'

'I don't suppose you remember much about her,' said Phyllis.

'No, we didn't get to spend a lot of time together.'

Perhaps realising that his reference to Norman's deceased mother had cast a shadow over the proceedings, Hutch introduced a different topic. 'Here's something else to celebrate,' he said. 'The band's going to do a broadcast on the National Programme's late spot. It's a week on Thursday, and I'm going to make sure Rosie Turner knows about it.'

Mrs Hutchins shifted uncomfortably. 'You're not still holding the torch for her, are you, Jack? She's spoken for, you know.'

'I know. I just want her to know, because she poured scorn on me when I said I was going to London. She said I had big ideas.'

'That's two things to tell her about,' said Phyllis, standing up. 'In fact, I'll go to the telephone kiosk now and see if I can catch her.'

'I'll come with you,' said Norman.

———◆►◄———

It seemed to Norman that the jewellers in Bradford would offer a much wider range of rings than those in Cullington, so he and Phyllis took the bus there the next morning. Phyllis was already resigned to having to wait, maybe a week, while a ring was altered to her size, and she was delighted when, having shown her a number of rings, a jeweller produced what for her was the perfect setting of a sapphire surrounded by tiny diamonds. It had been altered for someone, who had found it necessary to cancel the transaction, and it was Phyllis's size. It was also within Norman's budget, although Phyllis still considered it a huge sum.

On their return, they showed it to Mrs Hutchins, who was speechless, and to Hutch, who thought it was the perfect ring for his sister. Her telephone call to Rosie Turner had occasioned an impromptu gathering at the Turner household on Saturday evening. Obligingly, Mr and Mrs Turner were at a Ladies' Night at Mr Turner's lodge.

Rosie met them at the door with lavish congratulations. She took their hats and coats and waited pointedly for Phyllis to remove her gloves. When she did, it prompted an exclamation that, had he been able, Hutch would have preserved for all time.

'Phyllis, what a *beautiful* ring! *Where* did you get it?'

'Taylor and Jackson in Sunbridge Road.'

'My goodness. They're terribly exclusive.'

It amused Hutch to hear her still finding opportunities to use 'exclusive.'

'I always said there was something going on between you and Phyllis, Norman.'

'You did, Rosie, and there wasn't, but there is now.'

'And you and Hutch are doing so well. I got your picture postcard, Hutch.'

'Good. I wondered.'

'Come and dance with me. Someone, put a slow foxtrot on, will you?'

'Where's Mr Rushworth tonight?'

'He's at a family gathering. He couldn't get out of it.'

'What a shame.'

'Ronnie Emerson isn't here either, and that's maybe a good thing.'

'Aye, he won't be too pleased when he hears the news.'

The gramophone was playing 'It's Easy to Remember' by Rodgers and Hart, and Hutch couldn't resist saying, 'We play this sometimes,' as he led Rosie on to the floor.

'Your new club looks very fashionable, Hutch.'

'So it should, Rosie. It's brand new. Carl, our bandleader, brought a lot of new ideas with him from America.'

'How wonderful.'

'But we don't use the word "fashionable" nowadays.'

'No?'

'No, it's considered old hat. We talk about things being modish or *chic*.'

He was conscious that Rosie's foxtrot was lacking something. Either, he'd grown used to better things, or dancing with Mr Rushworth was doing her no good at all. Whatever the reason, he found Penny a better partner.

'It must be wonderful to be at the centre of things in London. I mean, everything at the height of fash... so *chic*.'

'It is, and I'll tell you something else, Rosie.'

'What?'

He couldn't remember when she'd been so attentive. 'On Thursday week, you can hear us on the National Programme late-night spot.'

'Really? How wonderful.' She was stunned into silence, or so it seemed, until she asked, 'What does "Thursday week" mean?'

'It's what they say in London instead of "a week on Thursday".'

'It's more modish, I suppose.'

'You've got it, Rosie.'

As they saw out the dance, he asked, 'Isn't Eleanor at home tonight?'

'No, she's out with friends.'

'Good for her.'

The music ended, and Rosie raised her voice to make an announcement. 'Listen, everybody. Hutch has just told me that his band.... What's it called, Hutch?'

'The Carl Duverne Dance Orchestra.'

'Yes, The Carl Duverne Dance Orchestra are going to broadcast from.... Where, Hutch?'

'The Golden Slipper in Mayfair.'

'They're going to broadcast from The Golden Slipper in Soho on the National Programme's late night spot on Thursday week.' She looked around for puzzled faces, and said, 'That's a week on Thursday.'

Hutch couldn't think what the attraction had been for him all those months earlier.

16

Norman and Phyllis took their leave of each other on Tuesday morning, sad to be parted but happy withal. During this time, Hutch, who had already said his farewells, stood discreetly outside, watching the threadbare population go about its business. It was difficult not to feel a trace of guilt.

Eventually, Norman joined him and they walked to the station. Again, Norman was unusually quiet, and Hutch respected his feelings.

Presently, Norman broke his silence by saying, 'I'm fair suited, Hutch.'

'I know, Norm. It shows.'

'Does it?'

'You could only make it more obvious if you walked around in sandwich boards, telling everybody about it.'

'That's just it, Hutch. I feel like telling everybody about it.' He gave his friend a lop-sided look and said, 'And that's not the kind of thing I'd have let on about before this weekend.'

'No, it's not,' agreed Hutch, showing his return ticket.

They carried their cases on to the platform and waited.

'I'll tell you what, Hutch,' said Norman, 'I wish I'd had a camera handy when Rosie Turner saw the ring. I thought her eyelids were going to disappear.'

'It's given her something to gossip about,' said Hutch. 'That's when she's not trying to fit "*chic*" and "modish" into everyday conversation.'

On their arrival at Rumbold Street, Hutch lost no time in

informing Mrs Wheeler of Norman's news, and she insisted on inviting them into her sitting room for a glass of sherry. It was the first time either of them had tasted sherry, and they were unimpressed, but they appreciated the gesture nonetheless.

Norman prevailed on Hutch not to mention the engagement to anyone in the band. It was clear that he was fearful of embarrassment, and Hutch naturally agreed, but not without some leg-pulling.

'I can't believe it, Norm,' he said. 'You're downright brussen in most respects, but you were terrified of proposing to our Phyllis, and now you're scared of what your workmates will say.'

'Everybody's allowed one weakness, Hutch. Remember that.'

'All right. Your secret's safe with me.'

They arrived at the club that night for an early band call, to learn that the band had a new clarinettist. His name was Vernon Waterhouse and he also hailed from the West Riding.

'We'll be taking over the band before long,' said Hutch. 'That's three of us out of twelve, no, thirteen.'

'Two-and-a-half,' corrected Norman. 'He's not the size of two penn'orth of copper. He doesn't look as if he has a good blow in him.'

'Keep your voice down,' said Hutch. 'Carl can hear you.'

'Right,' said Carl, giving Norman a mischievous look, ' "Limehouse Blues". I've put it into tonight's programme. Are you ready, Vernon?'

'Yes, sir.'

'Carl.'

'Yes, Carl.'

'A-one, a-two, a-one, two, three, four.' The number began in its characteristic, breathless way and the momentum grew until it reached the clarinet solo, when Vernon drew himself up to his modest full height and launched into a brilliant, glittering solo that took the rest of the band completely by surprise.

The number reached its end, and Carl gave Norman a knowing look.

'Well,' said Norman, 'it just shows, you can't always go by appearances.'

They had a break of thirty minutes before the club was due to open, and Hutch and Norman used it to become acquainted with their new colleague.

Norman asked him, 'Where are you from, exactly?'

'Littletown, Liversedge. Do you know it?'

'Aye. We're from Cullington.'

'Well, I'll be blowed.'

Norman could contain his mischief no longer. He asked, 'Is everybody as little as you in Littletown?'

'No, they're not, and I bet they're not all as daft as thee in Cullington, either.'

'You asked for that,' said Hutch, laughing immoderately.

'Aye well, you're a good clarinettist. I'll grant you that,' said Norman.

Carl, who had heard the conversation, came to join them. 'I'm glad you guys are getting along,' he said. 'There's no room for bad feeling in this band.'

'It was just a bit of friendly banter,' Norman told him.

'Good.' Raising his voice, he called the musicians to take their places. Before long, they were playing the music that had brought Hutch, Norman, and now Vernon, two hundred miles from their homes. It was the perfect way to earn a living.

As members drifted in, Hutch noticed one man who looked familiar but who was difficult to place. The woman who accompanied him was unremarkable; in fact, they seemed an unexceptional pair, except that the staff were immediately at their elbows, and it was that obsequious attendance that alerted Hutch to his identity. With a sense of shock, he realised that the man he'd been staring at was King Edward the Eighth. He'd only ever seen him in the newspapers and newsreel films, and they were in black and white, but now he was convinced he'd recognised the monarch. He'd no idea who the woman was, but that was of no importance.

His cue was coming up, and he gave the music his full concentration.

When the band took its break, it became apparent that other musicians had identified the King, because the conversation was all about him.

'I don't know what he's doing here,' said one of them. 'Ciro's is his usual haunt.'

'He does the rounds,' said another. 'I think he's easily bored.'

'I get the impression he's not very popular,' said Hutch.

'Not among musicians,' said Bob Wiley, the bass player. 'Not after what he did to poor old Bill Cotton.'

Norman joined in the conversation, asking, 'What did he do?'

'He was a bloody nuisance,' said Bob. 'He kept going on to the stand and trying to play the drums.'

'What did the drummer do?'

'He got out of the way. I expect he didn't want to upset the management. Bill wasn't so careful. He let it be known he wasn't pleased.'

'That's right,' said Jim Fulford, First Trombonist. 'The Prince was forever making requests as well. He seemed to think the club was there for his personal use. In the end, he complained to the management that Bill was being obstructive, and they moved him and his band to their club in Paris.'

Someone said, 'That doesn't sound so bad.'

'It was for Bill. He didn't speak a word of the lingo, and he couldn't get jellied eels or pie and mash for love nor money.'

There was good-natured laughter, and the conversation moved on. For his part, Hutch would have something to tell Rosie Turner when he saw her again, because he'd already ascertained that the King was a very unremarkable dancer.

They resumed their places on the stand, and Carl was about to count them into 'I Only Have Eyes for You', when the King came forward to speak to him. Hutch heard him say, 'I have a request, Mr Duverne. Will you play "Cavatina"?'

Carl frowned and asked, 'Will I play what?'

' "Cavatina". It's from *Cavalleria Rusticana*. You must know it. I want you to play it.'

'I'm afraid we can't, Your Majesty. It's not in the band's repertoire.'

The King raised his voice. 'But, damn it, all I'm asking you to do is to play it.'

'And I'm telling you, Your Majesty, that the number you want to hear is not in the band's repertoire.'

'We'll see about that.' The King returned to his table and snapped his fingers to a passing steward. Meanwhile, Carl counted the band into the number from 42nd Street.

During an eight-bar *tacet*, Hutch saw a man in evening dress approach the King's table, but he had to look away as his cue came up.

It wasn't until closing time that he heard the full story. It seemed that the King had complained to Fred Normanton, who had simply informed him that if Carl Duverne had said that the number was not in the band's repertoire, then that was obviously the case and there was nothing to be done about it. The affronted monarch and the lady accompanying him then left the premises, vowing never to return.

Hutch really did have something to tell Rosie. Meanwhile, he had Penny's company. She was less inclined than Rosie to gossip and was a good deal more fun.

———◆◆———

When Fred Normanton called everyone to a meeting the next day, rumour and conjecture abounded. News of the King's petulant departure had circulated with predictable swiftness, the main suspicion being that some government official must have ordered the club's closure. It was therefore a nervous gathering that waited for Fred to arrive.

When he did, he seemed reassuringly unperturbed.

'Good afternoon, everyone,' he said. 'To put you all out of your misery, let me tell you straight away that everything's fine, so you can stop worrying. I brought you here partly to set your minds at rest, but otherwise to explain my action last night. Before I do that, I must tell you that there was no disrespect, either on my part, or on Carl's, but His Majesty does have something of a reputation in the West End.' His observation was greeted by knowing laughter, and he waited for it to die down.

'I will not have this club monopolised by one member, whoever he is, and therefore Carl was right to refuse his request.' With an impish smile, he told them, 'Members of some clubs have been known to endure three, and sometimes four, performances of the Cavatina from *Cavalleria Rusticana*. Apparently, it's His Majesty's favourite number.'

There was unbridled laughter, during which Hutch decided that not even Rosie would believe what he'd just heard.

'The club will continue to function as normal, and you can all look forward to the band's first broadcast on the National Programme.'

17

It was an odd sort of time, or so Hutch thought, when the Italians were massacring Abyssinian tribesmen, Hitler's army was treating the Rhineland as its own, and the band at the Golden Slipper was getting excited about its first wireless broadcast. He said as much during the break to Norman, who had a ready answer, as usual.

'It's time Hitler and Mussolini had their ear'oles brayed,' he said.

'But who's going to do the braying?'

'We saw the Hun off in nineteen-eighteen. The Italians were on our side then, but I'm told they were as much use as a chocolate toasting fork.'

'We've been doing nothing but disarm since then. I don't think we have the strength, Norm.'

Norman gave the matter brief consideration and said, 'All the more reason why they should act now, before Germany gets any stronger.'

As he tightened the ligature against his reed, Hutch wondered what, if anything, the government was going to do. It seemed to him that diplomacy was the answer, but they knew more about it than he did. It was best left to them to find a solution.

The band took its place on the stand and, as the first members arrived, Carl counted the musicians in to 'Blue Moon' by Rodgers and Hart. It was one of Hutch's favourites, and he got a special buzz when Penny came on to sing the vocal refrain.

Time seemed to pass quickly, as it always did when they were on the stand, and before long it was almost time for the broadcast. The BBC's engineers had been in earlier, fixing up the microphones and various pieces of equipment. It seemed odd to Hutch, that they should be called engineers, when they never got their hands dirty, but he was having to get used to a great many new things, and he accepted the inconsistency along with the rest.

They reached the end of the current number and someone motioned the members to be quiet. Next, a man in evening dress came to the microphone. It seemed he was the BBC's presenter. He waited for a signal from the engineers, and spoke to the nation at large.

'Good evening, listeners. This is the BBC Regional Programme coming to you from the Golden Slipper in Mayfair, and bringing you the Carl Duverne Dance Orchestra.' He spoke the band's name with a flourish and then disappeared from the stand.

Carl smiled round at everyone and counted them in to 'Cheek to Cheek' featuring Penny and him. It gave Hutch extra pleasure to know that Phyllis and his mother had stayed up to listen, and he knew that Norman was feeling the same glow.

The presenter reappeared at the end of the number to tell everyone, quite unnecessarily, what it was that the band had just played, and to announce the next, which was 'All I Do is Dream of You'.

Before long, it was Penny's turn again to sing the vocal refrain, which she did remarkably well, considering it was her first broadcast too.

Two numbers later, they played 'Stay As Sweet As You Are', with Carl providing the vocals.

They played 'The Continental' as an instrumental number to give the singers a rest, but then Penny was back with 'It's Only a Paper Moon.'

Midnight came far too quickly, the presenter 'signed off', as he called it, for the BBC, and the engineers removed their equipment, still without getting their hands even grimy.

Eventually, they broke for the night, and Penny came to find Hutch.

'Come back with me,' she said. 'I'm so excited, I shan't be able to sleep, anyway.'

'All right, but I'll have to leave early in the morning.'

'I know.' It was understood that Hutch had to be back at Rumbold Street before Norman was about. He would have been horribly embarrassed if his friend knew what he'd been doing.

Norman asked, 'Are you coming, Hutch?'

'No, I'm taking Penny home. I'll see you in the morning.' They left the club and took a taxi to Penny's flat.

She chattered all the way, still excited about the broadcast. Her family and friends, including everyone at the stud factory, had been listening, she told Hutch.

He paid off the taxi and followed her up the stairs to her flat, where she lost no time in disrobing. Hutch wondered if every girl undressed as quickly. It must be a skill known only to women, he decided, like folding shirts and darning socks.

'Come on,' she urged, 'get in, quick. It's too cold to stand around.'

It was certainly cold in the flat, and standing on linoleum with bare feet while he removed his trousers was exquisite torture. However, once between the sheets, he forgot the austerity of the unheated room, and gloried in the welcome of Penny's warm embrace.

Between kisses, she relived the broadcast in detail, so that Hutch wondered if his attendance were completely necessary, but persuasion won in the end, and the excitement of the broadcast gave way to a thrill of a different kind.

With some difficulty, Hutch roused himself. He had no idea of the time, but the first vestige of sunlight was visible over the London skyline. He rubbed his eyes and peered at the luminous dial of his wristwatch. It was almost five-thirty, time to go home.

He eased himself out of bed, his reluctance to disturb Penny being only partly out of consideration, but also the knowledge that if she were awake, she would almost certainly try to persuade him to stay. Her immediate need always had to come before any other consideration.

He dressed quietly, finally letting himself out with infinite caution, even avoiding the middle of each stair in case he caused it to creak.

Once outside, he relaxed, and walked the short distance to the tube station, where he boarded an early train to Leicester Square.

He arrived at number 26 shortly after six o' clock, and opened the front door to see Norman in his newly-purchased dressing gown and with Mrs Wheeler. They were at the foot of the stairs. If Norman were surprised to see him up and about, he showed no sign of it, but simply said, 'Give us a hand, Hutch. Mr Wheeler's in a bad way.'

Hutch could only imagine that, in view of recent events, Mrs Wheeler had gone to find him and had to fall back on Norman.

He followed them into the bedroom, where Mr Wheeler was gasping for his life. Mrs Wheeler pulled out the chamber pot, as before. It already contained a quantity of urine but that couldn't be helped. As Norman lifted Mr Wheeler, Hutch laid two pillows on the bed to give him elevation.

'Pull the bedclothes back, Hutch,' said Norman. 'He's got his feet caught up in 'em.'

Hutch hauled back the sheet, counterpane and blankets so that Norman could heave Mr Wheeler into position.

'Now then, Mr Wheeler,' said Norman with gruff kindness, 'let's get some of that stuff off your chest.' Both men set to work, Norman massaging and Hutch patting the area between Mr Wheeler's shoulder blades.

'I don't know what I'd do without you both,' said Mrs Wheeler as her husband began to expectorate.

'It's no trouble,' Norman assured her.

She continued to watch the process until, overtaken by curiosity, she asked, 'Why are you in evening dress at this time of the morning, Mr Hutchins?'

'I fell asleep in somebody's armchair, Mrs Wheeler. I woke up with a blanket over me and a stiff neck.'

'Oh, dear.'

Norman gave him a grown-up look and continued to work on Mr Wheeler's lungs.

After a while, Hutch said, 'I think that's enough for now, don't you, Norm?' The process was highly necessary but it was nevertheless an ordeal for Mr Wheeler.

'I think so. Are you ready for a rest, Mr Wheeler?'

'Yes... I think so. Thank... you.'

Norman lifted him clear of the pillows while Hutch pulled them out and rearranged them. Then, together, they turned him and lowered him on to them.

'Thank you... very... much.' Mr Wheeler was even more breathless than usual.

'Yes,' said Mrs Wheeler. 'Thank you, both.'

'No trouble, Mrs Wheeler.'

'No trouble at all.'

As they made their way upstairs, Norman said, 'That must have been a hefty dose of gas. His chest's even worse than my dad's was.'

'I was just thinking that,' said Hutch.

'I mean, what kind of life is it for him, stuck in that room and coughing his lungs up all the time?'

'It's not all that good for Mrs Wheeler either.'

———————

Neither was surprised when Mrs Wheeler called on them again a few days later. They performed the same service as before, but it was clear that the congestion in Mr Wheeler's lungs was more critical than ever. As he fought for breath while Hutch and Norman did what they could, it seemed that they were making no headway.

'You'd better telephone for an ambulance, Mrs Wheeler,' advised Norman. 'He needs oxygen.'

They continued to massage and encourage, sounding a great deal more optimistic than they felt, and Mr Wheeler choked, spat and gasped for breath, until the ambulance arrived and they were able to hand him over to expert hands.

Mrs Wheeler went with her husband in the ambulance, so there was nothing Hutch and Norman could do. In any case, they had to leave for the club in half-an-hour.

———————

When Hutch telephoned Mrs Wheeler at the break, she took a long time to answer, and he was about to hang up, believing her to be still at the hospital, when she picked up the telephone. Not surprisingly in the circumstances, her voice sounded strained.

'Hello, Mrs Wheeler, it's Jack Hutchins. How's Mr Wheeler?'

'Oh hello, Mr Hutchins.' There was a moment's silence, and then she gathered herself sufficiently to give him the news, but it came as a choked whisper. 'He died,' she said, 'shortly after we reached the hospital.'

With his lungs in that state, it was going to happen before long, but it was still a shock. 'Oh, Mrs Wheeler,' he said, 'I'm sorry.' He wondered what else he could say. There wasn't much he could say, except, 'Norman and I will be back tonight.' He told her lamely, 'We'll help you with anything that needs to be done.' He had no idea what might need to be done, but it was a genuine offer, and besides, he felt sorry for her. If there were only some way he could help her, then he would do it gladly.

Norman's response, when Hutch told him, was as practical as he'd come to expect.

'I'm sorry for her, right enough, Hutch, but it's a blessing for him not to go on living the way he had been.'

At the end of the evening, Penny made no effort to hide her disappointment when Hutch turned down her invitation.

'It was so good last night,' she said, 'I thought you'd want to do it again.'

'I would, Penny, but I might be needed at Rumbold Street.' He was disappointed, too, more by Penny's reaction than at being unable to join her.

'What can you do for her? You can't bring her husband back.'

'Put yourself in her position, Penny. She's just lost her husband, she's in an awful state, and she'll have loads of things to do.'

'At this time of the bleedin' night?'

'I don't know. When somebody's in that position, time doesn't mean a thing.' He was losing patience with her. It wasn't the first time she'd shown herself to be self-centred, but her attitude was downright callous.

'Suit yourself, Hutch. I'm going home.' She gave him a last look of disapproval and left the club.

At that stage, Norman considered it safe to emerge from the shadows.

'Just had words, have you?'

'Just a few, but never mind. Let's find a taxi.'

———— ►◄ ————

They could hear movement inside Mrs Wheeler's sitting room, so Hutch tapped gently on the door. A few moments later, Mrs Wheeler opened it, red-eyed and desolate.

'Hello, Mrs Wheeler,' said Hutch. 'We've come to see if we can do anything for you.'

She looked at him wearily before answering. 'No, there's nothing you can do. Thank you all the same.'

Norman asked, 'When did you last have a meal, Mrs Wheeler?'

She shook her head hopelessly. 'I don't know.'

Hutch said quietly, 'Breakfast time, most likely.'

'That's no good,' said Norman. 'Will you let me get you something to eat?'

Seemingly disoriented, she half-shook her head. 'I don't know.'

'Is it all right if I use your kitchen?'

'Yes.' Her answer seemed to come with little or no thought.

'Right, I'll see what I can find.'

'Come and sit down,' said Hutch. 'You're not yourself tonight.'

'No, I'm not.'

'Well, who can blame you?' He steered her to the Victorian chaise longue and sat with her. Beside her, on a fireside table, was the wedding photograph that Hutch had noticed when he first came to the house. She looked at it, apparently without it registering, but then she murmured, 'We had no proper life together.'

'What's that, Mrs Wheeler?'

'I'm saying Bernard and I had no married life; at least, not as people think of it. He re-joined his regiment the day after we were married, and the next time I saw him, he was in hospital.' She closed her eyes, causing a tear to roll. 'I'm sorry,' she said.

'There's no need to be sorry.' Hutch had never spent time in the company of an older woman in those circumstances, but the least service he could offer was to provide the handkerchief from his breast pocket. It occurred to him to ask, 'Have you any family or friends you want notified?'

'No.'

'None at all?'

'None. War has a way of taking friends and relations.'

'That's true.' In her case, it was also extremely sad.

After a while, she asked, 'What's the time?'

Hutch looked at his wristwatch. 'Five-past-one,' he told her.

'It's time you were both in bed instead of fussing over me.'

'It's time you were in bed, Mrs Wheeler, but you need to eat first.'

'But you need your sleep,' she insisted.

'So do you, and we don't have to be up in the morning.'

'Even so, Mr Hutchins....' The argument might have continued, had Providence not intervened in the unlikely shape of Norman, who stood in the doorway and announced, 'It's ready and on the table.'

'Come on, Mrs Wheeler,' said Hutch. 'It's snap time.'

Obediently, she stood up and followed Hutch to the dining room, from which the appetising aroma of fried bacon was making Hutch yearn for breakfast. The occasional fry-up had become a regular treat since the day of his audition at the theatre.

'Bacon and eggs,' announced Norman. 'I don't know how you feel about fried bread, so I've done you some toast.'

'Thank you, Mr Barraclough. Suddenly, I'm quite hungry.' Turning to Hutch, she asked, 'What is "snap time"?'

' "Snap" was the sandwiches, usually bread and dripping, that we used to take into work. We had ten minutes for breakfast at eight o' clock and another break at one o' clock, and they were called "snap time".'

'I'd no idea.'

'Do you want tea or coffee?' Norman stood, poised for action, like an unlikely butler.

'Oh, tea, please. Coffee keeps me awake.'

Hutch asked, 'What do you have to do in the morning, Mrs Wheeler?'

She had to think. 'What day is it?'

'Tomorrow? It's Friday.'

'Oh, in that case, there's only the laundryman to see to.'

'Let me do that.'

'I couldn't.'

'Of course you can. It's easy enough, and you need to sleep, Mrs Wheeler.'

'Thank you, Mr Hutchins. I'm truly grateful.'

18

During the next few weeks, Hutch and Norman supported Mrs Wheeler in what practical ways they could, which included accompanying her to her husband's funeral at St Anne's Church in Soho.

The last funeral they had attended was Norman's father's, but the two occasions were sadly different. Mr Barraclough's funeral had drawn old comrades from the West Yorkshire Regiment as well as neighbours, occasional workmates, and veterans of various regiments and corps. Apart from Hutch and Norman, Mr Wheeler's was attended only by the three other lodgers at 26 Rumbold Street, none of whom had known anything of the deceased's illness and incapacity until they heard the vicar read the eulogy.

It seemed a cold and impersonal process, and more than anything else, Hutch felt tremendous compassion for Mrs Wheeler, who deserved none of it. Unfortunately, there was nothing he could do.

After the Final Commendation, those present followed the coffin to the graveside. In the absence of any real comfort he could give, Hutch lent Mrs Wheeler his arm the way he'd seen it done, and he was pleased when she accepted the gesture quite naturally.

At the end, she withdrew her hand so that she could drop a handful of earth on to the coffin. Having done that, however, she sought once more the support of his arm, and, having taken their leave of the vicar, they walked up the path together. At Mrs Wheeler's request, there was no limousine, so they walked back to Rumbold Street.

Once inside, Mrs Wheeler looked around her and asked, 'Who's here? I must put the kettle on.'

'I've seen to that,' Norman told her. 'Just you sit yourself down and take it easy.'

There were just three of them, the other lodgers having awkwardly made their excuses and left.

———————

That night, Hutch and Norman arrived at the club to find that the programme for the evening had been changed.

'I'll do all the vocals,' Carl told the band. 'Penny's gone. She found a better offer at the Blue Lagoon.'

'How did that come about?' Hutch thought Penny had been behaving a little strangely, but he'd imagined she was sulking after he'd refused to go home with her. She'd barely spoken to him for two weeks or so.

'Come and see me afterwards, Hutch,' was all Carl would say.

The meeting finally dispersed, and Hutch waited to speak with him before the club opened.

'It's bad news for you, Hutch,' said Carl after checking that no one else was about. 'She's sharing an apartment with Danny Fitzroy, the drummer at the Blue Lagoon.'

Hutch managed to say, 'Thanks, Carl.' He was completely stunned. Penny had been petulant at not getting her way, but he'd grown to accept that. There'd never been any suggestion of a break-up, and now she'd taken up with Danny Fitzroy without a word.

He had to work hard to concentrate during the next few hours, but he managed it, and the time eventually came for Norman and him to get a taxi home. Norman made no mention of Penny, and Hutch was grateful to him for that.

They arrived at number 26 and let themselves in quietly and went up to their rooms.

Having arrived at his room, Hutch decided to check that the laundry was ready for collection the next morning, Mrs Wheeler having been somewhat vague about it during the past two weeks. As he passed her sitting room, he thought he heard a noise. He stopped to listen in case she needed help, and then he realised that what he could hear was the sound of her sobbing. She should have been in bed, but she was still in her sitting room, struggling to cope with her grief. She'd behaved with great dignity in public, and he realised she'd been holding back her emotions until she was alone. The thought of her, lonely, bereft and heartbroken, gave him an unfamiliar, hollow feeling deep in his stomach, because there was no way he could help her.

—————▸◄—————

The new excitement for the band was a series of recording sessions at Abbey Road in St John's Wood. Following a recent merger with Columbia, the company was now called Electrical and Musical Industries, or EMI, but musicians still referred to it as The Gramophone Company, a name that carried enormous prestige in the music business.

The musicians were paid an extra pound per hour for recording, and Hutch sent that along with his usual weekly contribution to his mother, who always protested that she had no need of so much money, but that she would 'put it by for a rainy day'.

For his part, Norman was saving up for his single goal, which was to get married.

19

OCTOBER

As the band met to rehearse, all the conversation was about the so-called Battle of Cable Street, when anti-fascist demonstrators had clashed with Moseley's Blackshirts.

'In a way, I'm sorry I missed that,' said Norman.

'And I'm relieved that you did,' Hutch told him.

'I said, "In a way". I haven't forgotten I'm bound over.'

'Good. Keep it in mind, Norm.'

There was other news, too. A delegation of more than 200 unemployed had set off on foot from Jarrow, en route for London, to protest against unemployment and poverty.

Norman asked, 'How far is Jarrow from here?'

'Search me. Happen Vernon knows. Have you a minute, Vernon?'

The clarinettist put down his instrument and asked, 'What's up?'

'Do you know where Jarrow is?'

'Yes, it's on Tyneside, where they build ships.'

Norman asked, 'How far is that from here?'

'Oh, three hundred miles or so.'

'They'll never make it on foot.'

'If they do,' said Hutch thoughtfully, 'they'll wear out some boot leather.' After some thought, he said, 'I was just thinking about the Welsh miners we met last winter. Do you remember?'

'Aye, poor buggers. It's a reminder of how lucky we are.'

A further reminder came a few seconds later from Carl, who was ready to begin the rehearsal. Hutch had noticed a new face, an attractive girl with dark, bobbed hair, and he imagined she must be the new vocalist Carl had told them about.

'Good morning, everyone. Let me introduce Jessie Dean, our new singer. She's come to us from the Blue Lagoon, so it's a step up for her.'

His last remark earned a good-natured laugh, but he waved it aside.

'Let's start with "Smoke Gets in Your Eyes". A-one, a-two, a-one, two, three, four.'

It was ironic that Jessie should have left the Blue Lagoon, and Hutch wondered what had happened to Penny in the meantime. He put the thought from his mind and counted the sixteen bars up to his entry.

Jessie's voice appealed to him immediately. It had a classical quality, and yet it radiated warmth despite the sadness of the song. She was pretty, too, although not in the same way as Penny was pretty, or 'cute', to use Carl's terminology. Jessie's appeal was difficult for Hutch to describe, at least at first sight, but he intended to see much more of her.

'Stop.' Carl held up his stick to the band. 'Hutch, that's not like you. You missed your cue.'

'I'm sorry, Carl. I lost count.'

Carl grinned. 'We're all human, Hutch. Bar thirty-four, then.' He counted them in again, and Hutch played to the end of the number, ashamed that he'd allowed himself to be distracted.

When they broke for coffee, he found Jessie talking to Norman, who greeted him in his usual deadpan way.

'This is Hutch,' he said. 'He's all right as long as he doesn't have to count bars.'

'Thanks, Norm. It was my first offence.' He took Jessie's hand. 'How do you do, Jessie. It was your singing that distracted me.'

'Was it so bad?' Her clear brown eyes betrayed her amusement.

Norman picked up his tea to leave them. 'I'll let you dig yourself out of this one, Hutch,' he said.

'It was beautiful,' said Hutch. 'That was the distraction.'

'Thank you.'

'I've been wondering,' he said. 'You came from the Blue Lagoon, didn't you?'

'Yes.'

'The girl who used to sing with this band went there about six months ago.'

'Penny?'

'That's right. Whatever happened to her?'

'She left with a problem.'

'Oh?'

'To be fair, it was Danny Fitzroy's problem, too. He's the drummer there.'

'Ah.' Realisation dawned.

'I'd just come down from the College and I was looking for work. Jack, the bandleader, gave me a break when Penny left the band three months ago.'

'Was that the Royal College of Music?'

'Yes, they'd be horrified there if they knew what I was doing.'

'It's honest work, Jessie.'

'I know, but they're very unworldly.'

Hutch decided to act before someone else did. 'Are you seeing anyone just now, Jessie?'

It was clear that his question surprised her, because her eyes opened wide. 'No, I'm not.'

'Will you let me take you to lunch after the rehearsal?'

She looked as if she were considering his invitation. 'Do you want to tell me how things are done in this band?'

'No.' He imagined Carl would have done that already.

'Are you going to tell me things I should know about the nightclub scene, because I'm an innocent newcomer?'

'No, I just decided I like you enough to ask you out to lunch.'

She seemed to crumple. 'Oh, Hutch, I'm sorry. You must think I'm awful. Of course I'll join you for lunch.'

'Good. I mean, if you want to know any of those things, I'm happy to oblige, but that's not why I asked you.'

———◄►———

They had lunch at the Corner House. Hutch's finances had improved since the previous occasion, so the bill caused him no anxiety. On the other hand, Jessie was still recovering from her gaffe.

'I've had so many insincere propositions since I came into the business, I'm afraid I've come to expect them.'

'Don't give it another thought,' Hutch assured her. 'As a matter of fact, I'd no idea what you were talking about at first.'

'I know. I should have realised you were genuine.'

'You didn't know me. Anyway, let's draw a line under it and start a new page.' It wasn't the kind of thing any of Gary Cooper's characters would have said, but he wasn't Gary Cooper. He was Hutch Hutchins, and he'd decided since the episode with Penny that he was content to be himself. He was even working on the centre hair parting favoured by a few of his more self-possessed colleagues.

She smiled gratefully. 'I've been trying to place your accent. Are you from Lancashire?'

'No, Yorkshire. There are three of us in the band. Norman and I are from Cullington, near Bradford, and Vernon's from Liversedge, not far away.'

'Isn't he the virtuoso clarinettist?'

'That's right.'

'You see, no one in the world of opera has any idea what talent there is in the dance bands.'

'I daresay we're just as ignorant about them.'

'You're very modest, Hutch.' As an afterthought, she said, ' "Hutch" is an unusual name, isn't it?'

'My real name's Jack Hutchins. Only my mother calls me "Jack".'

'I should have realised it was a nickname.'

Now more settled, she looked prettier, he decided. A smile made a big difference. He asked her, 'Have you seen *Swing Time?*'

'No, but I'd like to. Fred Astaire and Ginger Rogers are unbeatable.'

'I've always thought so. They're showing it at the Regent Street Cinema. Would you like to go?'

'You really are a fast worker, Hutch, but yes, I think I should.'

———◆◄———

They both enjoyed *Swing Time*, but they agreed that the story wasn't the best they'd seen.

'The music made up for an awful lot,' said Hutch, 'but you expect that from Jerome Kern.'

'Yes, the music was lovely.' They were standing outside the cinema.

'I have to go back to Soho to do some shopping,' said Hutch. 'Do you want to come?'

'I won't. I have a few things to do at home.'

Hutch hailed a taxi. 'Where do you live?'

'In Greek Street, above a restaurant.'

'That's handy.' He opened the door for her and climbed in after her. 'Greek Street, Soho, please,' he told the driver.

'What are you shopping for?'

'A tenor sax.' He'd been saving for it since he got the job at the Golden Slipper. It was a big occasion.

'How exciting.'

It seemed to Hutch that she and Penny were completely different.

The taxi driver dropped them in Greek Street.

'That's where I live,' said Jessie, pointing to a first-floor window.

Hutch made a mental note of it for later.

'Thank you. I really enjoyed lunch and the film.' She inclined her cheek.

'Maybe we can do something soon,' he suggested, giving her a chaste peck.

'Yes, I'll see you at the club and we'll arrange something. 'Bye for now.'

''Bye.' He went on his way, happier than he'd been for some time, and the prospect of owning a new tenor saxophone made him happier still.

———— ►◄ ————

Hutch and Jessie saw a great deal of each other when they weren't performing at the club. It was a blissful scene, unlike the one Hutch and Norman witnessed at the end of the month.

The miners from Jarrow arrived in Marble Arch on the thirty-first. Some wore coats tied with string and all of them had boots that seemed about to fall apart. They were ragged, footsore and weary, but still proud.

Hutch had filled a brown paper carrier bag with bread, cheese and fruit, and he handed it to one of the marchers.

'Thank you very much, sir.' The man took it gratefully.

'Don't call me "sir",' Hutch told him, remembering how he'd said something very similar to the Welsh miners they'd found singing in the street. 'We're working men, like you. We're just luckier.'

It seemed that Norman was of a similar mind. 'We can't take this lot to Lee Kwan Yan's restaurant,' he said soberly. Instead, he called out, 'Good luck, lads.'

They greeted his message with a cheer that was unintelligible because of their strange dialect, but there could be no mistaking the sentiment.

'If we hadn't had music to fall back on,' said Hutch, 'we could have been in their situation.'

It made them appreciate their way of life all the more.

20

Hutch and Jessie saw each other regularly. She came from a background about which he knew nothing, and she was similarly uninformed about his, so they had a great deal to talk about.

One new experience for Hutch occurred when Jessie took him to the Sadler's Wells Theatre for a performance of Verdi's opera *La Traviata*. He had only ever played in the orchestra, and that was when the D'Oyly Carte and Carl Rosa companies came touring, so to enjoy the whole performance from his seat in the auditorium was a new excitement, and one he intended to repeat.

His relationship with Jessie was close and affectionate but not ultimately physical, such was her fear of pregnancy. After his highly physical relationship with Penny, Hutch felt occasionally frustrated, but not in a way that impeded his feelings for Jessie.

From time to time, there were distractions, the most dramatic being the King's abdication that December. It naturally provoked discussion everywhere, that Friday, including the band room of the Golden Slipper during the break.

'I don't see what the fuss is about,' said Norman. 'We don't know anything about her, fair enough, but what difference could she make to anything? He was the King, when all's said and done.'

Jessie was inclined to agree. 'I think it's a shame,' she said, 'treating her like that just because she's a foreigner and she's been divorced.'

'I still say he was too selfish to be King,' said Vernon. 'Remember how he behaved that night he came here? It were all about what he wanted, and when he couldn't have it all his own way, he took his bat home like a spoilt brat.'

'He's selfish, all right,' said Bob Wiley. 'He's so used to partying and carousing, I doubt if he'd ever have given a thought to affairs of state.'

'They never gave him a chance,' objected Norman. 'He were King for less than a year.'

'You're missing the point,' said Hutch, who had been following the conversation but had kept silent until then. 'When the war came, Norm, your dad and mine both enlisted, didn't they?'

'What's that got to do with it?'

'Hear me out, Norm. They did their duty, and so did a hell of a lot more, and if the King couldn't choose duty over his private life, then he wasn't fit to be a king. I think he's done the right thing in handing the job over.'

'It's going to be hard work for the new King,' said Jessie. 'He never expected this to happen, and now it's all fallen on his doorstep.'

'Aye,' said Vernon, 'what do we know about the new King?'

'I've always felt sorry for him with that awful stammer,' said Jessie.

Bob nodded in sympathy. 'I suppose it'll take him a bit longer than most to get his point across,' he said, 'but I still have more time for him than I have for his brother.'

'The Duchess is nice,' said Jessie.

'The Duchess is dead,' Vernon corrected her. 'Long live the Queen.'

'Of course. It'll take time for us all to get used to a new King and Queen.'

'It will, Jessie,' agreed Vernon, 'but I can't see things changing at the Golden Slipper because of it.'

'Things might,' said Bob, looking at his watch, 'if we don't get back to work. They don't have kings and queens where Carl comes from, and he's not bound to make allowances for all the excitement.'

Carl was as understanding as ever and the abdication was not mentioned again until the club closed its doors.

———◆►◄———

Hutch and Norman were looking forward to going home for Christmas, but the band still had work to do. To begin with, they had another recording session at the EMI studios.

The producer, an amiable, talkative man, was waiting for them when they arrived.

'I was here yesterday,' he said, 'and Ambrose and his orchestra were here.'

Norman asked, 'Did you tell them we were coming today?'

'No.' Unused to Norman's dry wit, the producer looked puzzled.

'You should have. They can't have all that much excitement in their lives.'

The session was soon in progress. It was the band's third visit to Abbey Road, and Hutch and the others were now much more relaxed than they'd been on the first occasion. For Jessie, however, the session was her first, and she was understandably nervous.

'Just concentrate on the music,' Hutch had told her, remembering the time he'd given Penny the same advice, and it still seemed to be good advice, because Jessie's vocal refrains came out as warm and appealing as ever. After the session, she made a point of thanking him for his encouragement.

'It really worked,' she said. 'I couldn't have done it without you.'

'You'd have been fine,' he assured her. 'Everybody's nervous to some extent. You're not alone.'

Carl joined them to register his approval. 'Well done, Jessie,' he said. 'You're a natural recording artist.'

'Thanks, Carl. I was just saying that I was terribly nervous, but Hutch gave me some advice that really helped.'

'Oh? What advice was that, Hutch?'

'Nothing clever. I just think that the secret is concentration. Most of these songs are special, and they deserve to be played and sung well, and for that you have to concentrate.'

'That makes perfect sense, Hutch.' Carl patted him on the shoulder. 'Thanks for helping our new nightingale through her first session.'

'It was no trouble, Carl.'

Later, when they were alone, Hutch said, 'If other bosses were more like Carl, the world would be a happier place.'

'It would,' agreed Jessie, 'and it would be happier still if more people took a leaf out of your book and shared their wisdom as generously.'

'It was just something that worked for me, Jessie.'

'Hutch,' she said patiently, 'you gave me much more than "just something". I looked at the microphone and I was terrified. Then I remembered what you'd told me, and it worked.'

Hutch was unimpressed. 'We're all in this together, you, me and the rest of the band. Why shouldn't we help each other?'

'All right,' she said, kissing him, 'but I'll always remember your advice and I'll pass it on whenever anyone needs it.'

'That's the spirit.' He glanced at his watch and said, 'If we don't get to the club soon, we'll test Carl's good nature to its limit.'

———◆◆———

Norman was preoccupied, but very much with the present, or more correctly, a present, in this case, for Phyllis. As far as he was aware, she had never owned a wristwatch, and it was hardly surprising, as the Hutchins family had always regarded such an item as a frivolous luxury. Both Hutch and he had watches now; their busy lifestyle demanded it, but Phyllis's wrist remained unadorned, and Norman intended to remedy that situation at Christmas.

It was with boyish excitement that he called at the shop in Pentonville Road. The windows, filled with brooches, necklaces, earrings, cufflinks, tie pins, shirt studs, engagement rings, signet rings, napkin rings, clocks and watches, were a reminder of his Easter visit to a jeweller with Phyllis, and they added to the excitement of the occasion.

He opened the door and stepped inside, momentarily surprised by the thick pile carpet that told him he was entering a world of luxury and discernment. He walked up to the counter and rang the bell.

A young man wearing an immaculate suit appeared from the back of the shop. 'Good morning, sir,' he said. 'How may I be of assistance?'

'I'm looking for a wristwatch,' said Norman. 'It's for a lady.'

'Of course, sir. We have a wide range of wristwatches. Perhaps you could give me an idea of the kind of price you have in mind?'

Norman had anticipated the question, having been asked the same thing when he'd bought Phyllis's engagement ring. 'No,' he said, 'will you just show me a selection, and then I'll have time to think about it?'

'Certainly, sir.' The assistant went to the back of the shop and returned with several watches, disappearing again to fetch several more, until Norman was confronted with a bemusing array.

After some elimination, he narrowed the choice to three watches, all of which appealed to him, but there was one in particular that he could see Phyllis wearing. He moved it away from the rest so that he could see it on its own.

'That watch, sir,' said the assistant would cost you five pounds, seventeen shillings and sixpence.'

Norman considered the price, which represented more than a weeks' wages for many. However, Phyllis was priceless, and therefore price was meaningless. 'Fine,' he said. 'This is the one I'll take.'

'Would you like it gift-wrapped, sir?'

Again, Norman stopped to think. What would Phyllis want? At Rimmington's she would see perfumes and other gifts wrapped extravagantly for customers, and he was pretty sure she would prefer a more personal presentation. 'No, thank you,' he said. 'Will you just put it in its box, please?'

'Of course, sir.' The assistant obliged, finally placing the box in a brown-paper bag that bore the shop's name. 'That will be five pounds, seventeen shillings and sixpence, please, sir.'

Norman handed him six pounds in notes and took the half-crown change. After a moment's thought, he dropped the half-crown piece into the collecting box at the end of the counter. It would help to keep lifeboats afloat, and that was highly necessary at any time of the year.

————◆◆————

Hutch had also been shopping, although at a more modest end of the market.

He'd decided on suitable presents for his mother and Phyllis, he'd already sent money to Phyllis so that she could buy the turkey and everything that went with it, and now he had to find a copy of the book Jessie wanted. His search took him inevitably to Charing Cross Road, where at last he found a shop that sold books about music. The contents of the window looked promising, so he went inside and found an austerely-dressed woman with an equally severe expression. She observed him over rimless glasses.

'Good morning, sir,' she said. 'How can I help you?'

'I'm looking for a book....' He had the title written on a piece of paper. It was in his inside pocket, and he searched for it, wishing he'd done it earlier.

'I should hope you're looking for a book, otherwise you're in the wrong shop.' There was no lightness in her tone.

He found the piece of paper. 'It's called.... Here,' he said, handing it to her, 'I can't pronounce this man's name. I think it might be French.'

'Oh,' she said, reading it aloud, '*Kobbé's Opera Book*. It's to be hoped you can pronounce the names of the composers, not to mention the characters and the titles in it.'

Hutch's patience was nearing its limit. He'd heard of the two million surplus women and he sympathised with them, but he failed to see why they should vent their frustration on innocent shoppers. 'Have you got a copy,' he asked shortly, 'or do I need to go to another shop?'

'Oh, I think we have a copy.' She disappeared to look for it, reappearing shortly afterwards with the required volume. 'It's rather expensive,' she warned.

'Very likely.'

'It's one pound two shillings and sixpence.'

'I daresay I'll manage that.'

She peered at him over her glasses to ask, 'Are you buying it for someone else?'

'Yes. Does that alter the price?'

'No, I was simply wondering why you want it.'

He leaned forward, looked both ways to ensure privacy, and said softly, 'I'm five foot ten-and-a-half inches tall. When I stand on tiptoe, my maximum reach is seven foot four inches, but the top shelf in my kitchen is seven foot six inches off the floor.' He tapped the book on the counter. 'As you know, I can't pronounce this bloke's name, but if I stand on his book, I'll be able to reach everything on the shelf. Then, when I've emptied it, I'll most likely use the book as a doorstop.'

'Really!'

'Yes, really.' He handed her a one-pound note, a florin and a sixpenny piece, thankful that he had no reason to return. He could also look forward to the Christmas holiday at home, where shopkeepers spoke only one language, but were generally courteous and well-mannered.

21

Hutch and Norman arrived home in the middle of the afternoon on Christmas Eve to find the house decorated with paper chains and a Christmas tree by the stairs. Phyllis and Mrs Hutchins were naturally delighted to see them again.

'It's a wonder they let you have Christmas Eve off,' said Mrs Hutchins, momentarily out of breath after hurrying downstairs. 'Everybody else has to work right up to pegging-out time.'

'That's if they have work,' said Phyllis, handing tea to the home-comers.

Mrs Hutchins asked, 'Is unemployment a problem in London?'

'Not so as you'd notice,' said Hutch. 'The south seems to have escaped the worst of it.'

'That Mr Chamberlain was on the newsreel, boasting about how clever he's been,' said Phyllis. 'He should come up here and learn the truth.'

'Better still,' said Norman, 'he should do another clever thing and make himself disappear up his own... flue pipe.'

Hutch looked at the time and announced, 'When we've had this cup of tea, Mother, we need to go shopping.'

'Whatever for?'

'Your Christmas present, that's what for. I've been looking forward to this.'

'Well, I don't know what you mean, and the town'll be busy now with Christmas shoppers.' She added, 'I'm glad I did all mine in good time.' Looking up at the clock, she asked, 'Where are you thinking of going at this time in the afternoon?'

'Arnold Wilson's. I think they'll have what I'm looking for.' He'd consulted Phyllis on the subject, and she'd advised him.

'Well, I never.' His mother was as flustered as ever when the attention was on her.

'Na then, Mother, get your hat and coat on and we'll catch the five-and-twenty-past bus.'

'Nay, Jack, it's a waste o' bus fare. We can walk down there.'

'The sky's looking black, Mother. I don't trust it to stay fine.' In truth, Hutch was concerned about his mother's health. Her breathlessness had increased since Easter, when they were last home.

'I think you've picked up some extravagant ways in London,' she said, fastening her coat. 'I hope you haven't been spending silly money this Christmas.'

———————

'I've been nagging her to see the doctor,' Phyllis told Norman, 'and she finally agreed and saw him last week.'

'What did he say?'

'It's her heart. It was obvious, really. He gave her something for it, but it's not going to make the trouble go away.'

'I can hear her struggling,' said Norman. 'I wish she'd take things easier.'

'She means a lot to you, doesn't she, Norman?'

'Right enough, She always has. She did plenty for me when my dad was alive.'

'Well, you needed looking after, and so did your dad.'

As one thought led to another, Norman said, 'Our landlady's husband was in a bad way after being gassed. If anything, he was worse than my dad.'

'Did you meet him?'

'Yes, a few times. Mrs Wheeler came to Hutch and me when he was struggling to breathe. She couldn't lift him, you see, and he was helpless.'

She squeezed Norman's hand, as if he were the one needing comfort. 'I'm glad you could help him,' she said, 'and her, of course.'

'It wasn't for long. The last time, he had to go into hospital. He died there.'

'Oh, his poor wife.'

'I know. She told Hutch they'd had no married life. They'd got married, and then the next day, he re-joined his regiment. The next she knew, he was helpless in hospital.' He reflected soberly, 'There a limit to the services a man can provide when he's fighting for breath.'

'Trust a man to think of that. Anyway, how do you know about that sort of thing?'

'It stands to reason. I know what my dad was like, and there were times when he couldn't eat or drink, never mind owt else.'

Satisfied that Norman had been speaking purely from theoretical knowledge, she asked, 'What are we going to do about getting married, Norman?'

'How do you mean?'

'I mean, when are we going to do it, and how are we going to manage it, living as we do, so many miles apart?'

'Well, I could get a job with a band up here, say in Leeds or Bradford. It wouldn't pay as well as the job I've got now, but that wouldn't matter, because we'd be together.'

'And the cost of living up here is less than it is in London, so I'm told.'

'I wouldn't know about that, Phyllis.'

'No, you wouldn't,' she laughed, squeezing his hand harder. 'Sometimes, I think you're not fit to be out on your own.' Then, by loose association, she said, 'I hope you two are behaving yourselves down yonder, and not getting into fights with Blackshirts all the time.'

'I'm a reformed man, Phyllis. I don't do that sort of thing nowadays, and Hutch doesn't either.' He decided against telling her about his brush with the law. In his slender experience, women tended to over-react to that kind of news.

'I hope so.'

'Anyway, the Blackshirts haven't been a problem since they got their backsides tanned in Cable Street.'

Phyllis was about to say something, when the door opened and Hutch and his mother came in.

'Give me your hat and coat, Mother,' said Hutch, and then you can sit yourself down and get your breath back.'

'Nay,' she said, 'if I'm breathless, it's because of seeing you pay out silly money on a coat for me. There were no need for it.'

'There was. This old thing's ready for t' rag-and-bone man.' It was surprising how easily Hutch reverted to the vernacular when he came home.

'Just enjoy it, Mother,' said Phyllis, 'and enjoy the fact that Hutch thought enough of you to buy it.' By way of encouragement, she added, 'We're all looking forward to seeing you wear it tomorrow.'

Outnumbered, Mrs Hutchins accepted defeat. 'Well, I'll put t' kettle on an' we can all have a cup of tea.'

'Don't you dare, Mother. Just sit there and take it easy.' Phyllis picked up the kettle and filled it at the sink. There was a tap on the range, that they used for washing and cleaning, but drinking water had to be drawn from the sink tap.

'You're all ganging up on me,' she complained.

'It's for your own good.'

Mrs Hutchins remained silent while Phyllis brewed tea. When she spoke again, it was to say, 'I suppose you'll all be going round to Turners' on Boxing Day.'

'Not this Christmas,' said Phyllis, 'nor any Christmas, if it comes to that. Crawley's closed down last June, and the Turner family moved out of the mill house. I don't know where they're living now. I suppose he'd be old enough to retire, but they'd still need a smaller house.'

'No wonder Rosie never replied to my letter,' said Hutch.

Mrs Hutchins closed her eyes wearily. 'You're not still fancying your chances with her, are you, Jack?'

'Not in the slightest. Anyway, the last I heard, she was engaged to be married. I remember meeting the unlucky man, although it's probably fair to say they deserve each other.'

Mrs Hutchins's curiosity was unabated. 'Why did you write to her, then?'

'It was to tell her about King Edward and Mrs Simpson coming to the club. You know what a snob Rosie is. I thought it might interest her, especially as the King made such a fool of himself.'

'Jack,' said his mother sharply, 'that is disrespectful, talking about the King like that.'

'That'll be the day when he shows any respect for anybody else.'

'Even so, he was King until not long ago.' She thought momentarily and said, 'I still don't know what to make of that business.'

Tactfully changing the subject, Phyllis said, 'Neville and Rosie Rushworth, as they are now that they're married, went to live somewhere the other side of Bradford. It seems Mr Rushworth has come down in the world, and he's had to start working for a living. Mind you,' she added, 'it'll be no hardship. He's working as a teacher at one of them posh schools where they have to pay to send their kids.'

'I wonder if he teaches them Greek as well as Latin,' said Hutch, remembering his conversation with Rosie.

Norman, who had been silent so far, said, 'There was another daughter, wasn't there, the one you danced with last Christmas, Hutch? If I recall, you kissed under the mistletoe when you thought none of us were looking.'

Hutch said uncomfortably, 'Well, I always felt sorry for her, and it's the sort of thing you do at Christmas, isn't it?'

Phyllis saved his embarrassment by saying, 'I believe Eleanor got a job as a secretary somewhere. At least she got away from Rosie's controlling influence.'

'Well,' said Hutch, 'I wish her well. She deserves it.'

Mrs Hutchins looked up at the mantlepiece clock and said, 'It's ten-past four. Schools should be losing by now.'

'They broke up on Wednesday,' Phyllis told her.

'Na then, we can expect carol singers anytime now.'

'I've got mince pies and ginger beer waiting for them.' Before her mother could object, Phyllis said, 'Hutch sent me the money to pay for it all.' She smiled sweetly at her brother, who nodded in confirmation, established as he now was in his role as family spendthrift.

Phyllis poured tea for everyone, and matters of finance were forgotten, at least for ten minutes, until Mrs Hutchins's prophesy was fulfilled by a juvenile rendering of 'See Amid the Winter's Snow.' It was unclear at first, whether there were two or three singers, and when Hutch opened the door at the end of the carol, he saw the reason why. A girl and a boy of around ten years old accompanied a girl who might have been five at a pinch.

'Come inside and get warm,' he told them.

They came into the house, and the little girl stared at the Christmas tree, which must have been an exotic novelty in her eyes.

'Come to t' fire,' urged Mrs Hutchins. 'You must be frozen silly. Come and stand here an' take your coats off or won't feel the benefit when you go outside again.'

'This'll warm them up,' said Phyllis, bringing a plate with three mince pies on it. 'There you are. Now, what would you like to drink? Is ginger beer all right? It had better be, 'cause that's all we've got.'

Blinking in the glow of the fire, the bemused children each accepted a mince pie and a glass of ginger beer.

Phyllis said, 'It's nice, isn't it? I spent ages making that ginger beer.'

'Don't believe her,' said Norman. 'She has a ginger beer well round the back and she just lowers the bucket into it when she wants some.'

'And you can stop telling these kiddies silly things,' said Mrs Hutchins. 'You'll have 'em believing you if you're not careful.'

When the mince pies were gone, Hutch asked, 'Are you going to sing for us again before you go?'

His question was greeted with nods.

'What are you going to sing?'

The two older children held a whispered conference, after which the girl said tentatively, ' "O Little Town of Bethlehem".'

'Go on, then.'

The performance began as a duet, such was the fascination of the Christmas tree for the smallest of the children, but a nudge from her older sister served as a reminder of her duties, and the trio was once more up to strength.

At the end of the carol, Phyllis warmed their coats in front of the fire and then handed the older girl a paper bag. 'Here,' she said, 'there's some more mince pies to take home with you. Well sung, and I hope you all have a lovely Christmas.'

The girl conquered her shyness and said, 'Thanks, miss.'

'Just a minute.' Hutch stood in front of them, barring their way. 'You haven't had your wages yet.' He took some money from his trouser pocket. 'Hold out your hands,' he told them, giving each of them a shilling piece.

The boy found his voice for the first time and asked, 'Are you sure, mister?'

'You'd better put it in your pocket before I change my mind,' Hutch warned him. 'Now, have a really happy Christmas, all of you.'

'And don't let them mince pies spoil your tea,' cautioned Mrs Hutchins.

The children left with a flurry of Christmas greetings.

As Hutch closed the door, his mother asked, 'How much did you give 'em, Jack?'

'A bob apiece.'

'Three bob? Are you made of money?'

'Compared with what those waifs are used to, I must seem to be,' he said, 'but it was little enough, considering what they gave us.'

———◆◄◆———

Christmas morning and the opening of presents brought forth further protestations of extravagance, but as Hutch said, they were better off than they'd ever been, so they might as well enjoy it.

Mrs Hutchins wore her new coat, still maintaining that its purchase had been unnecessary, but unable to deny that it was much warmer than her old one.

When nearly all the presents had been opened, Norman beckoned to Phyllis to join him in the yard. Bemused, she followed him, and when the back door was closed, he gave her a small parcel.

'I don't know why it has to be a secret,' she said, untying the string that bound it.

'I don't want you to make a fuss in there,' he explained.

'Me make a fuss?' She opened the wrapping paper and saw the box and its label. 'Norman, what are you giving me?' She gasped as she took the lid off and saw the watch for the first time. 'It's beautiful, but it must have cost a fortune. Thank you, Norman.' She kissed him. 'You shouldn't have, you know.'

'Everybody wants to talk about money,' he said, 'and I wish they wouldn't.'

'Even so.'

'No, Phyllis, I buy you nice things because that's how I feel about you. I'd buy you the best if I could.'

———▸◂———

Inside, Mrs Hutchins realised that her daughter and Norman were missing.

'Where have they got to?' She asked the question of no one in particular and carried out her own search. Eventually, she opened the back door and closed it again hurriedly. 'I wish they wouldn't do that in public, where folk can see them,' she said.

22

New Year's Eve celebrations at the Golden Slipper were boisterous in the extreme. It was a time for optimism, at least on the part of those cushioned against recession, and the club's members made merry, as they always had.

New Year had never meant a great deal to Hutch and Norman beyond the usual superstition, but it pleased them, nevertheless, to see the members enjoy the occasion.

The next morning, Hutch was recovering from the late night, when Mrs Wheeler knocked on his door.

'Mr Hutchins,' she said, 'you're wanted on the telephone.'

Half-awake though he was, Hutch caught a note of alarm in her voice, and he pulled his dressing gown on to open the door.

'It's your sister, Mr Hutchins.'

'Thank you, Mrs Wheeler. I'll come.' As he followed her downstairs, he knew that Phyllis could only be calling him for one of two reasons. Either his mother was ill or it was the worst news of all.

Steadying himself, he picked up the telephone and the earpiece and said, 'Hello, Phyllis.'

'Oh, Hutch.' She sounded terrible. 'It's mother. She took ill this morning. I sent for the doctor, but by the time he arrived, it was too late to do anything for her.' Almost in a whisper, she said, 'She's dead.'

Although he'd half expected it, he felt suddenly cold. He wanted to sit down, but there was no seat in the hallway. Instead, he leaned against the wall to speak to his sister. 'I'll come up as soon as I can find a deputy,' he told her. 'In the meantime, will you get an undertaker? I can't remember any of their names.'

'I can. I'll get the Co-op to come, anyway.' Her voice was tremulous, so that two hundred miles away, he wanted to reach out and touch her to reassure her.

'I'll be with you as soon as I can,' he promised.

As he hung up the earpiece, Mrs Wheeler came out of her kitchen with an unspoken question on her face.

'My mother died this morning,' he told her.

'Oh, you poor boy.' She'd never called him that, and there'd never been any physical contact between them, but she clasped his hands with hers as if it were the most natural thing to do. 'I'm so sorry,' she said. 'Can I get you anything? A cup of tea?'

'No, thanks, Mrs Wheeler. I have to tell Norman, and then I need to find a deputy to take my place in the band.' As he spoke, he felt as if he were functioning automatically, rather than as a thinking person.

'Let me know if you need anything.'

'I will, Mrs Wheeler. Thank you.' He climbed the stairs again and knocked on Norman's door. After a second knock, he was rewarded with an incoherent mumbling from within. He knocked again. 'Norm, it's Hutch.'

The door opened, and Norman stood before him with his eyes still closed.

'I'm sorry, Norm. Phyllis phoned me just now to tell me my mother's died.'

Norman's eyes opened and he blinked. 'How?'

'I don't know. Listen, I have to go to Archer Street and get a deputy.'

'No, Hutch.' By this time, Norman was awake. 'We both have to, because I'm coming with you.'

'I'll see you downstairs.'

———— ◆►◄ ————

After enlisting the services of two deputies and leaving explanatory notes at the club for Carl and Jessie, they caught the twelve-fifteen train from King's Cross to Leeds. Only when the train had been in motion for some time, did they realise that neither of them had eaten since the previous night. Accordingly, Hutch got out of the train at the first opportunity, and bought sandwiches and tea for them both. For the remainder of the journey, they travelled largely in silence.

On the short walk from Cullington Station, Hutch voiced the regret that had occupied his thoughts ever since Phyllis's telephone call.

'I feel bad, Norm.'

'Of course you do, mate.'

'I mean, that I wasn't there. I couldn't be with my mother and our Phyllis at the end.'

'It wasn't your fault, Hutch. You're not to blame for anything.'

The exchange continued until they reached the house, where Phyllis greeted them red-eyed but no less relieved to see them. For some time, she clung to Hutch while he spoke what soothing words he could muster. Finally, he whispered in her ear, 'Are you going to welcome Norm home while I put the kettle on?'

Without a word, she detached herself from him and went to Norman's waiting arms.

Later, as they sat drinking tea, Phyllis told them how she'd got up as usual to get ready for work, and had taken a cup of tea to her mother.

'She was lying there, fast asleep, I thought, but I couldn't rouse her, so I went to the telephone kiosk by the butcher's and called the doctor.' She fell silent for a moment, remembering. 'He said she'd most likely died of heart failure in her sleep. I've to collect the certificate from the surgery tomorrow.'

'If she went quietly in her sleep,' said Norman, looking pointedly at Hutch, 'it was a blessing.'

'If she'd made any noise at all, she'd have woken me,' confirmed Phyllis. 'I've been sleeping with one eye open for... I don't know how long.'

'You've borne it all, ever since I went away,' said Hutch.

'I was glad to, Hutch, so don't start feeling guilty about it.'

'Keep telling him,' said Norman.

Something suddenly occurred to Hutch, and he asked, 'Where is she now?'

'She's still upstairs, if you want to go up and see her. The Co-op sent a woman this afternoon, to wash her and lay her out in a clean nightdress. They're coming back after five o' clock to take her to the Chapel of Rest, I think they called it, and someone will stay behind to help us make the funeral arrangements.'

———▸◂———

Mr Goldthorpe, the funeral arranger, a grey-haired man with an appropriately solemn expression, accepted a cup of tea from Phyllis and consulted his notes. ' "Mary Elizabeth Hutchins",' he read, ' "Aged forty-four years and seven months." '

'That's all she was,' said Hutch. 'She seemed a lot older.'

'Where would you like the funeral to take place?'

'That's a hard one,' said Phyllis. 'She was brought up a Methodist, but she fell out with the minister after the war over something he said about war graves.'

Hutch asked, 'What was that?'

'He made a careless remark about nobody knowing whose was whose. He was young and new to the job, but Mother took offence.' Turning to Mr Goldthorpe, she said, 'It was only a few years after our dad was killed at the Battle of Jutland. His grave is at the bottom of the North Sea.'

'That was unfortunate and it must have been very hurtful,' Mr Goldthorpe reminded them, 'but we need to decide where to have the funeral.'

'If the Reverend Forster's still at St Martin's,' suggested Norman, 'I know he'd do it.'

'The Reverend Forster is still the incumbent,' confirmed Mr Goldthorpe. 'I'll be happy to ask him.'

'Thank you.'

'Would you like the organist to attend?'

'Yes, please.' Hutch answered for Phyllis as well as himself.

'And the choir? They have an excellent choir at St Martin's.'

Hutch looked towards Phyllis and saw her shake her head. 'No,' he said, 'She disliked a lot of fuss. I think the organ will be enough. Can we discuss the hymns with the vicar?'

'Of course.' Turning to the next page, he asked, 'Burial in the church graveyard?'

Both Hutch and Phyllis said, 'Yes.'

'Would you like us to provide a car to take you to the church?'

'No, thank you,' said Phyllis. 'We can find our own way there.'

'What about a reception, a wake, after the funeral?'

'I'll see to that,' she assured him. 'There won't be many there.'

'We need to arrange a date and a time for the funeral.'

———◆◆———

Afterwards, Hutch looked about him and said, 'I don't know if she ever made a will. At all events, she'd hardly anything to call her own.'

'There is a will,' said Phyllis. 'It's a home-made one on one of those forms they sell at the Post Office, but it's signed by her and two witnesses. She named you and me as executors.'

'Oh, hell. What does that involve?'

'Don't worry. I did it for Auntie Edna, so I know what to do. All you have to do is agree with me.'

For the first time that day, Hutch smiled. 'I've been doing that all my life,' he said.

'It'll be straightforward. She had some cash that you sent her, and she put it by for a rainy day.'

'I remember. How much is there?'

'Nearly two hundred pounds. It'll cover her funeral expenses, and she didn't owe anybody so much as a farthing.'

It seemed right to Hutch. 'That's how she lived her life,' he said, 'and she'll go out not owing a farthing.'

———◆◆———

While Hutch was at the doctor's surgery in the morning, collecting the Medical Cause of Death Certificate, Phyllis and Norman discussed arrangements of a different kind.

'I know I suggested that I could get a job up here,' said Norman, 'but that would leave Hutch out on a limb.'

159

'You're right, it would.'

'How would you feel about joining us in London? You'd soon get a job down there.'

'Do you think so?'

'They don't know there's a slump,' he confirmed. 'Nobody's told 'em, least of all, that daft article Chamberlain.'

'Well, as I see it, you two are all I have left in the world, so it makes sense for me to join you and make sure you both behave yourselves.'

23

The funeral took place as planned, with Hutch, Phyllis and Norman in the front pew. The only other mourners were neighbours who had known Mrs Hutchins for some years. They declined Phyllis's invitation to go back to the house after the funeral, as they were reluctant to intrude.

As Phyllis poured the tea, she said, 'I've given mother's new coat to Mrs Horsfall. I hope you don't mind, Hutch, but her husband's out of work and she's down on her uppers.'

'You did the right thing, Phyllis.'

'Mother's bound to turn in her grave at the recklessness of it, but I really can't be bothered with selling the furniture. It's not worth much anyway, and the estate will still be in funds when I've discharged the outstanding expenses.'

Hutch asked, 'What will you do with it?'

'I'll get the Salvation Army to take it away. They'll know folk who'll be glad of it.'

Norman considered the situation and asked, 'What notice do you have to give Rimmington's?'

'One week. It's the same with the landlord.'

'I'll leave you money for your train fare and expenses,' said Hutch, 'and there's a room waiting for you at Rumbold Street.' Mrs Wheeler had promised that.

'Thanks, Hutch. I only hope it's true that jobs are easier to come by in London.' After a few seconds' thought, she said, 'I'm like Dick Whittington setting out to seek his fortune.'

'In that case, we'll have to see if Mrs Wheeler takes cats in.'

———◆◀———

Hutch and Norman returned to London, where Carl welcomed them. The deputies had been adequate, but not, as Carl put it, 'Like the guys who usually occupy those seats.'

Meanwhile, Hutch regularly scanned the jobs page of the *Evening Standard* for Phyllis's benefit.

Eventually, the time came to collect her from King's Cross Station, and as the train pulled in, they waited outside the ticket barrier.

The cloud of smoke cleared to reveal a large number of passengers, but, eventually, Hutch spotted her and nudged Norman.

'There she is,' he said, pointing. She looked unsure, having travelled by train for the first time, but then she saw them waving, and came forward to the exit, where she surrendered her ticket.

'Oh,' she said, accepting a kiss from each of them, 'I'm glad to see you two. I've never done anything like this before.'

'You'll get used to it,' Hutch told her. 'Let's have your cases.'

'How lucky I am,' she said, 'with two men to carry my luggage.'

'It beats me how you can fill two suitcases,' said Norman.

'Ah, well,' she said knowingly, 'women have to pack things that men have never even heard of.'

'I'll take your word for it.'

They led her to the taxi rank and took their place in the queue, which looked daunting, but which shortened surprisingly quickly, so that before long, Hutch was able to lift Phyllis's cases into a taxi and say to the driver, 'Rumbold Street, Soho, please.'

Phyllis looked around her in disbelief. She asked, 'Is this the only way to get to where we're going?'

'No,' Hutch told her. 'We could get a tube train or a bus, or we could walk. It's not very far. In fact,' he said, looking through the window, 'We're nearly there.'

'Well, why are we travelling in a taxi?'

'It's your first day in London,' said Norman. 'We thought we'd push the boat out, so to speak, and ride in comfort.'

As the taxi neared Rumbold Street, the driver asked, 'Whereabouts in Rumbold Street, guv'nor?'

'Number twenty-six,' Hutch told him.

'Number twenty-six. Right you are, guv'nor.' The driver took them to the door, and Hutch picked up the cases while Norman paid the fare.

'This is unbelievable,' said Phyllis. 'By the way, why did the driver call you "guv'nor"?'

'They call everybody that. It just means "boss".' He put the cases down to unlock the front door.

'This is very posh,' said Phyllis, looking along the hallway.

'We don't use that word,' Hutch reminded her. 'Remember Rosie Turner?'

'Oh, yes. "Exclusive", wasn't it?'

'That's right. Anyway,' he said as Mrs Wheeler entered the hallway, 'let me introduce you to our landlady. Mrs Wheeler, may I introduce my sister and Norman's *fiancée*? Mrs Wheeler is right at the top of my list of favourite landladies, Phyllis.'

'I'm the only one he knows,' said Mrs Wheeler, smiling at the introduction, 'but I'm pleased to meet you, Miss Hutchins.'

Mrs Wheeler showed Phyllis to her room on the ground floor, leaving the men to talk.

'It won't be long before Phyllis and I have to find somewhere else,' said Norman.'

'Why?' It made no sense to Hutch.

'Can you see Phyllis settling for the cooking facilities here? No, I have it in mind to find a two-bedroom flat somewhere, just until we're married.'

'Oh, well, good luck with that, Norm. I reckon I'll stay here awhile. Now that you've taught me to cook and sew, I should be all right.'

Norman grinned. 'If I know you,' he said, 'you'll be bringing your mending over for Phyllis to do.'

'It's what you used to do.'

'Right enough.' There was no point in denying it.

Mrs Wheeler brought Phyllis downstairs and left her to join the men.

'I still can't believe it,' said Phyllis. 'Indoor toilets, hot-water geysers and electric lights everywhere.' Thoughtful for a moment, she said, 'It's rather expensive when you add in the extras, but it's lovely all the same.'

———▸◄———

Within three weeks, Phyllis was offered a job in the accounts office of Bourne and Hollingsworth's department store in Oxford Street, which she naturally accepted. After the worst possible start, the new year seemed to be looking up, although life was less than ideal for Hutch when Jessie next spoke to him.

It was at the end of a Saturday night stand at the club. He was putting his tenor saxophone back into its case when she asked if she might have a word with him. She seemed concerned about something.

'Of course. What's the problem?'

She hesitated. 'The thing is, this is my last night with the band.'

'Is it?' It was news to Hutch.

She nodded. 'I've been given the part of Santuzza in *Cavalleria Rusticana* with the Carl Rosa Opera. It's a marvellous opportunity, because most singers have to spend some time in the chorus before they get a principal part.'

'Of course.' He was beginning to consider the implications.

'No, listen, Hutch. We're going on tour. We'll be in Wales next month.'

'Well, it's not the end of the earth. I mean, surely you'll be coming back.'

Her look of concern changed to one of apology. 'You don't understand,' she said, 'From Wales we go on to Manchester and then Liverpool and Leeds. It's a long tour. The thing is, it wouldn't be fair of me to keep you waiting.'

'I don't know. How long is the tour?'

'five weeks.'

'That's not very long. I don't mind waiting until you get back.'

'Are you sure?'

'Positive, but keep in touch.'

'Of course I will.' She kissed him and left the building.

———▸◄———

Three weeks later, he received a letter postmarked *Liverpool.* Pleased to hear from Jessie again, he opened it, expecting the usual kind of news. Instead, he read something rather less pleasing.

Dear Hutch,

It grieves me to be writing this letter, because the last thing I want to do is hurt your feelings.

The fact is, I shan't be seeing you again, because I'm involved with someone else. He's the baritone who sings the part of Alfio in the opera. I don't expect you to understand this, but when singers and actors play intense scenes, the drama sometimes spills over into real life, and that's basically what happened between James and me.

I hope you're not terribly hurt and that you find someone more reliable than me. You deserve that.

Take care of yourself.

Yours affectionately,

Jessie.

It was a familiar story and it seemed to be Hutch's destiny. At least, that was how it felt for a while.

24

MAY

The investiture in March of the title of Duke of Windsor on Prince Edward, and then the coronation of King George VI and Queen Elizabeth eclipsed the controversy surrounding the abdication, prompting a nationwide round of parades, street parties and celebrations. One such event took place, quite naturally, at the Golden Slipper, although the event did not receive unanimous approval, as the musicians discovered at the band call, when Brian Elliot, the guitarist, aired his republican views.

'I don't see why we should be doing this,' he said.

'We're rehearsing to make tonight's party a success,' Carl told him gently.

'I know that. I just don't hold with all this bowing, scraping and forelock tugging. We've just got rid of one expensive sponger, and now we have to welcome another.'

There were murmurs of, 'Be quiet, Brian,' and 'Sit down and let's get on with the rehearsal,' but Carl was inclined towards a diplomatic response.

'However you feel about royalty, Brian,' he said, 'try looking at it this way. It's a gig. Be thankful for it.'

'So we now have to be thankful because an unelected aristocrat has graciously given us an excuse to hold a party.'

'That's right, Brian, but for your colleagues' sakes, perhaps we should continue this discussion after the rehearsal.'

It was evident that the disaffected guitarist disagreed, because he proceeded to place his instrument in its case.

'If you go now,' Carl told him equably, 'there'll be no coming back.'

Without a word, Brian fastened the catches on his guitar case and left his desk.

'Call at the office and they'll give you your wages,' said Carl. He waited until Brian was out of the room before saying, 'That was unfortunate, but don't worry. We'll have a guitarist by tonight.' It was a well-known fact that there were more musicians than there were jobs. The message would go to Archer Street, and within twenty minutes, at least one guitarist would arrive at the club, ready to audition. Some things were certain, even if employment was not one of them.

———◆◆———

The band had a new vocalist, a pretty, fair-haired girl called Vera, whose off-duty interest was Jim Fulford, the band's First Trombonist. Hutch didn't mind. He was realistic enough to accept that he couldn't win every time.

Vera was singing 'Moon Over Miami'. It seemed an odd choice for Coronation Night, but the members were happy to fill the dance floor whatever number was being played.

Jim started his trombone solo, and Hutch thought, as he often did, that Norman made a much better sound, but that was a matter for Carl.

The next number was 'The Very Thought of You', an important one for Hutch, not only because the tenor sax played a prominent part in the arrangement, but because the number meant so much to him. It was a magnificent song written by a master of the craft, and what was more, it had clinched Hutch's job with Carl's band.

Taking over the theme from the piano, he played it with his usual sensitivity, earning a smile and a wink from Carl, who knew how he felt about the song. Then the violins took over, preparing the way for Carl's vocal refrain. Hutch was *tacet* for sixteen bars, and he used them to bask in the glorious sound the band and its leader were making.

At the end of the number, he looked down at the dance floor, where couples were making their way back to their tables, possibly having shared something of the bliss he'd experienced. As one couple left the floor, the girl turned towards the band, and it was as if she were looking straight at him. He thought he recognised her, but her identity eluded him for the moment, and then her partner led her away, and it was time for Hutch to concentrate on the next song.

The band played several more numbers, some classics among the rest, so that enjoyment was never far away. Soon, however, it was time for the band to take a break, and they did so gratefully.

Hutch was enjoying his first drink of the night, when Carl called him to the door of the band room.

'Two visitors for you, Hutch,' he said, holding the door for him.

'Thanks, Carl.' He was surprised to see the girl who'd looked at him from the dance floor, and her partner, a young man with an immaculate pencil moustache. He couldn't imagine why they'd come to see him, until the girl smiled in recognition and said, 'Hello, Hutch. Don't you remember me?'

Her gown and make-up had fooled him, but her voice gave him the prompt he needed. 'Eleanor,' he said, surprise having relieved him temporarily of the appropriate words.

'This is a bit different from one of Rosie's Thursday nights at home, isn't it?'

'Yes, but it's still great to see you. What are you doing in London?'

'I live here. I work at Pettifer estate agents in The Strand. This is Ewan Broadmead, by the way. He's a member here, and when he told me we were coming to this club, I remembered that you worked here.' Continuing with the introductions, she said, 'Ewan, this is Hutch Hutchins. We're both from Cullington.'

Mr Broadmead took Hutch's hand and viewed him as if handling a curiosity. 'Such a coincidence,' he said, 'that Ellie should know one of the musician chappies here.'

Hutch saw Eleanor wince. 'That's what I am,' he confirmed, 'a musician, and I must be getting along for the second half. I'm glad to have met you, Mr Broadbent.'

'Broad*mead*.'

'Of course, and it's been really good to see you again, Eleanor. Thank you for taking the trouble to come and find me.'

'Not at all. It's been lovely to see you again. Goodnight, Hutch.'

'Goodnight, Eleanor. Goodnight, Mr Broadbean.'

'Broad*mead*.' But it didn't matter, because they were on their way to their table, and Hutch was required again on the bandstand.

He was glad Eleanor had escaped the dying town that had been Cullington, and found a good job, even if she had developed questionable taste in men. Still, as a good 'musician chappie', he had work to do, and he put the matter behind him as he took his place in the reed section.

———◆◆◆———

Hutch had been genuinely delighted to see Eleanor again. He remembered fondly the two occasions when he'd danced with her, when she seemed to lead a Cinderella existence, at least where Rosie was concerned, and he'd enjoyed seeing her enjoy those brief moments of pleasure. Unfortunately, however, young girls had a way of growing up and making their own decisions, and it was an awful shame to find her in the company of a superficial waste of time. Mr Broadloom, or whatever his name was, might possibly have hidden qualities, but as far as Hutch was concerned, he seemed to be cast in the same mould as Rosie's husband. The Turners really knew how to pick them.

With that thought, he dismissed the matter and occupied himself with the more practical concerns of everyday life. He was therefore surprised, the next day, when Carl handed him an envelope.

'It's not scented,' he said, 'but it's addressed in a woman's handwriting.'

'Thanks, Carl.' Hutch placed the envelope in his inside pocket. The mystery would keep until the break.

For the next hour or so, Hutch forgot about the mysterious letter and concentrated on his playing, but during the first break, when he picked up his drink, he heard something crackle inside his jacket, and he remembered the unopened envelope.

Taking it out, he opened it and unfolded the letter. To his complete surprise, it was from Eleanor, or 'Ellie', as she signed herself.

Dear Hutch,

It was lovely, seeing you again last night, but I feel I have to apologise for Ewan's attitude. I say, I have to, because, he would never dream of apologising, as he sees nothing wrong with his rude and patronising behaviour. I was cross that he'd spoiled what for me was a happy reunion, and I told him so. I thought you should know.

I've written my office telephone number at the top of this note in case you feel that you'd like to catch up on things since Christmas 1935.

Fondest regards,

Ellie.

Hutch read it again, resolved to telephone her in the morning.

25

Pettifer's telephonist answered briskly but cheerfully, 'Good morning. Pettifer Estate Agents and Surveyors.'

'Good morning. May I speak to Miss Eleanor Turner, please?'

'Miss Turner. Who shall I say is calling?'

'Jack Hutchins.'

'Please hold the line for a moment, Mr Hutchins.' There was silence for maybe a minute, and then the telephonist spoke again. 'Miss Turner's not answering her telephone, Mr Hutchins. The likelihood is that she's with Mr Pettifer. Would you like her to return your call when she's free?'

'Oh, yes, please.' He gave her Mrs Wheeler's number. 'I'll be here for the rest of the morning,' he told her.

He'd hardly been upstairs ten minutes, when the telephone rang, and Mrs Wheeler called him.

'It's a Miss Turner,' she said innocently.

Hutch picked up the telephone and the earpiece and said, 'Eleanor? Hutch here.'

'Hello, Hutch. I'm sorry I missed your call. I was taking dictation.'

'Don't worry. Thank you for your note. You mustn't worry about Mr Broadbottom. I've forgotten the incident already.'

She laughed. 'It's Broad*mead*.'

'Is it? I'm really calling to ask you if you'd like us to meet for a chat. You mentioned it in your note.'

'Yes, I'd like that. When do you suggest?'

'Are you working all day today?'

'No, only until noon.'

'Good. How about lunch? We could meet at the Strand and Craven Street Corner House.' He'd become rather fond of the Lyons' Corner Houses and their cheerful waitresses that people called 'nippies'.

'Wonderful. I can be there by a quarter past twelve, if that's all right.'

'I'll look forward to it.'

———— ▸◂ ————

It was no surprise that, eighteen months on and freed from family constraints, Eleanor had not been immediately recognisable when she visited the club. With her dark hair cut in the ever-fashionable bob, half-hidden by a fedora that matched the blue in her patterned dress, the application of a little discreet make-up had effected a transformation.

She asked, 'Is something the matter?'

'Nothing at all. I didn't mean to stare, but you look so nice I couldn't help it.'

'And in my workaday garb. Thank you, Hutch,' she said, opening the menu. 'You know, I still can't believe this is happening.'

'You took me completely by surprise when you came to the club.'

'Yes, I couldn't believe it when Ewan told me he was taking me to the Golden Slipper. I still have the postcard you sent me,' she said, 'when you were celebrating the opening.'

'Have you?' Hutch remembered sending separate postcards to Eleanor and Rosie, knowing that Rosie would never share hers with her younger sister, but he'd never imagined that it would have so much importance for Eleanor.

'Of course. When I was living in Cullington and constantly in the background at home, it was nice to remember that the man who'd danced with me twice was a musician at a fashionable West End nightclub.'

'You make me sound very important, Eleanor.'

'You work in a glamorous world. Anyway,' she said, tapping her menu, 'we should decide what we're going to eat.'

'Of course.' Hutch peered at the menu and said, 'Someone needs to go back to school and learn to spell. Look at the way they've spelt "rabbit".' He pointed to the offending word.

'That's not "rabbit",' said Eleanor, 'it's "rarebit". Have you never tried Welsh rarebit?'

'No,' and now he wished he hadn't mentioned it. He'd been with her only a few minutes and already he'd revealed his ignorance.

'You should. It's lovely. I only found out about it, oh, two years ago, when my mother took me to Lingard's in Bradford.' She finished perusing the menu and said, 'You know, if I may, I'd rather like the Welsh rarebit.'

'Of course.' He decided to be honest. 'I'm going to show my ignorance again,' he said, 'but what is Welsh rarebit?'

'It's melted cheese with lots of good things in it, poured on to toasted bread and then grilled.'

'I think I'll have that too.'

'Good.'

'It'll be a new experience for me,' he said humbly.

'Oh, Hutch, don't be like that. As I said, I only learned about it fairly recently, and no-one's expected to know everything.'

It seemed to Hutch that, beneath the new sophistication, Eleanor was as he remembered her: artless, innocent and appealing. It really was a voyage of discovery, though, because he'd just learned something else, that, as well as being all those things, she was kind-hearted. He should have realised that, even after meeting her only twice, and then very briefly. Still feeling a little awkward, he changed the subject and said, 'I noticed that you signed the note "Ellie". Do you like to be called that?'

'Yes, it's a break with the past, but you don't have to call me that if you don't like it.'

'But I do like it.'

'I'm glad you do. Actually,' she confided, 'the only people who call me "Eleanor" are my family. It's not so bad when my parents call me that, but Rosie has a way of saying it that reminds me of the ugly sisters summoning Cinderella.'

Hutch could imagine that very easily, but he kept it to himself. Also, the nippy had arrived to take their order, so he dealt with that.

When she'd gone, Ellie said, 'You'll have heard about Rosie and Neville, I imagine?'

'About them getting married?'

'Yes, and he's now Classics Master at Highfield Lodge Prep School. It's one of those places parents choose when they want prestige they can afford. You know, bargain boasting rights.'

'Forgive my ignorance again, but what is a prep school?'

'It's for boys between the ages of eight and twelve. It's supposed to prepare them for public school.'

It sounded like the right job for Neville. He was reminded of the night Rosie introduced them, and he asked, 'Does he teach them Greek as well as Latin?'

'No, only Latin, apparently. Only the more expensive schools offer Greek.' Then, clearly trying not to laugh, she said, 'You'll never guess what Rosie's doing.'

'I can't imagine.'

'She's Assistant Matron. That means she organises the laundry and runs the tuckshop.'

'I don't believe it.' He couldn't imagine Rosie collecting dirty washing and dispensing bulls' eyes and peppermint drops.

'It's true, but I don't know how much longer it'll last. I mean, she's capable of turning the place into Dotheboys Hall in no time at all.'

'So you've all gone your separate ways,' he said, also trying not to laugh. Fortunately, he'd read Nicholas Nickleby at school, so he knew about Dotheboys Hall and was spared further embarrassment.

'Yes, when the mill closed, it caused widespread hardship, as you can imagine, but the least deserving came out of it unscathed. My father retired, he and my mother took a smaller house, Rosie and Neville took to the cloisters, and I escaped and found a better job.'

'How do your parents feel about you being alone in the big city?'

'I'm staying at the Christian Women's Lodge, so they reckon I'm safe and respectable. In any case, they're far more concerned about Rosie's welfare. Some things never change.'

'I wouldn't call you undeserving,' said Hutch.

'Well, you know what I mean.'

'I felt that you deserved better, that time Rosie wouldn't let you into the drawing room.'

'And you rode to my rescue, like a knight to a damsel in distress.'

'Not really.' He shifted self-consciously. 'I just thought it was a shame.'

'Oh, Hutch, I really meant that. I've never forgotten that night, nor the Boxing Day when you danced with me in the hall. They were two acts of generosity in a place where kindness was a stranger.'

It was uncanny, how she could read his discomfiture when he thought he'd concealed it so well. 'I can see, now,' he said, 'why it meant so much to you, and I'm glad I did it.' Changing the subject, because he was conscious of being under the spotlight, he asked, 'Won't Mr Broadmead mind about us meeting today?' He thought he should get the ridiculous man's name right, if only for once.

She laughed. 'I thought it was funny, the way you kept changing his name. I suppose it was to show him you weren't as impressed as he wanted you to be.'

'That's right.'

'Well done. Anyway, to answer your question, it's none of his business.'

'Isn't it?' Now he was very confused.

She gave him a puzzled look that turned quickly into one of realisation. 'Did you think I was seeing him regularly?'

'Well, yes. He was with you at the club, so I naturally thought....'

She laughed again. 'That was an isolated occasion, never to be repeated, especially after he behaved so badly.'

'I suppose he can't help the way he's been brought up.' His mother used to say that about ill-mannered children, and it seemed freshly appropriate.

'Whether or not, he's seen the last of me.'

'Just because of what he said to me?'

'Yes, I'm loyal to my friends.' She leaned forward to ask, 'I can call you a friend, can't I?'

'I should hope so.' It seemed a good moment to ask an important question. 'Ellie, are you seeing someone regularly?'

'No, I'm Cinderella, remember?' She smiled at his look of disbelief. 'Seriously, I haven't been here very long. I suppose I haven't had time to meet all that many people. It's just as well, really, because I'm going to be away for a while.'

'Where are you going?'

He had to wait for her answer, because just then, the nippy returned with their order. When she had deposited two plates of Welsh rarebit in front of them and checked that they had everything they wanted, they thanked her, and Ellie said, 'My boss is sending me to the Brighton Branch.'

'Why is he doing that? You're his secretary, aren't you?' It seemed very strange.

'No, I was only standing in for his secretary this morning. She'll be back on Monday. I'm going to Brighton to work as a temporary replacement for the Manager's secretary there, just until they find the right person to fill the job.'

He was uncomfortably reminded of Jessie telling him about her long absence with the Carl Rosa, but he dismissed it from his mind. 'That doesn't sound too bad,' he said.

'It could take a month, or maybe two.'

'When are you leaving?'

'In a week's time. That's when the present secretary will have worked her notice.'

He could put it off no longer. 'Look,' he said, 'Sunday is my night off, and I wondered if you and I could go somewhere together.'

'I couldn't possibly monopolise you on your only night off.'

He suspected she was being less than serious. 'Yes, you could,' he insisted, 'tomorrow, if you're free.'

'What do you have in mind?'

He'd been thinking about that. 'The Carlton Hotel in Victoria,' he said.

'Can you recommend it?'

'I've never been,' he admitted, 'but Sydney Kyte and his band have just taken up residence there, so the music's bound to be good.'

She nodded approvingly. 'But I'm still going away in two weeks' time,' she reminded him.

'But not for ever.'

'All right. I'll be honest and say that I'd like to spend some more time with you.'

'That's settled, then. I'll telephone the Carlton and book a table.'

———◆◦◆———

When he reached Rumbold Street, he met Phyllis and Norman, who were also returning from lunch.

'You missed a good meal, Hutch,' said Norman. 'We were going to ask if you wanted to come, but we couldn't find you.'

'Sorry, I had things to do.'

'Things?'

'Yes, just... things.' He would tell them at some stage.

With the kind of insight that comes naturally to a woman, Phyllis asked, 'What's her name?'

He was rumbled. 'Ellie,' he told her. 'Eleanor Turner. She's called "Ellie" nowadays.'

'I'd heard she was in London,' said Phyllis. 'Come upstairs and tell us about her.'

'All right.' Now that his secret was out, he was happy to talk about his lunchtime tryst. That way, he could enjoy it all over again.

26

When Ellie left her hat and coat with the cloakroom assistant, Hutch found himself staring again. Her dress was French navy with a 'V' neck, a flared skirt and a matching bolero top. In all, she looked exquisite.

'Ellie,' he said, 'you look... lovely.' It was a word he'd heard used often at the club, and he'd thought it sounded soft, but now he'd used it, and it seemed the only word to describe her.

'Thank you, Hutch.'

At Hutch's suggestion, they allowed the head waiter to show them to their table so that they could hear the band, now playing 'Lovely to Look At', a number Hutch remembered from one of their BBC broadcasts.

'Oh, Hutch,' said Ellie, 'let's dance.'

The head waiter said to Hutch, 'I'll bring the menu to you later, sir.'

'Thank you.' He led Ellie on to the floor and they joined the line of dance.

'If my sister ever got anything right, Hutch, it was that you danced the best slow foxtrot in Cullington.'

'That must have been before she met Mr Rushworth and developed her passion for the quickstep. The slow foxtrot didn't get a look-in after that. Anyway, thanks, Ellie.'

'Credit where it's due, Hutch.' She closed her eyes blissfully and let him lead her through the rest of the number, during which Hutch was surprised to receive a smile of something akin to recognition from Sydney Kyte. He wondered for a moment if the elegant bandleader had mistaken him for someone else, but he quickly dismissed the matter, being concerned for the moment with the dance and Ellie's company.

The number ended, and they returned to their table. Two minutes later, the waiter arrived with the menu and the wine list. Hutch was still a relative novice in such matters, but he managed the occasion without embarrassment. With the memory of lunch at the Corner House and his unfortunate gaffe distressingly fresh in his mind, he was considerably relieved.

The waiter finished taking their order as the band began 'The Night is Young and You're so Beautiful'. Hutch saw again the dreamy look in Ellie's eyes. He'd noticed it first when he danced with her at Rosie's gathering.

'Do you like this one?'

'Mm, it's lovely.'

Fascinated by her childlike pleasure, he asked, 'Would you like to dance?'

'Oh, please.' As he took her in hold, she said, 'It feels so good to be allowed to do this.'

For a moment, he wondered what she meant, and then he realised that only a relatively short time had passed since the regular gatherings at the Turners' home. 'Of course,' he said, 'Rosie.'

'It made her feel important. When my parents left her in charge of me, she took the responsibility seriously.'

Hutch said nothing. Instead, he wondered how he could ever have been interested in someone as vacuous, silly and callous as Rosie.

As the number went on, it was clear that music and dancing meant a great deal to Ellie, and for all her exclusion from Rosie's Thursday night parties, she danced exceptionally well, a fact that Hutch felt obliged to point out.

'I have the feel for it,' she said, 'and I think that's very important.'

'You certainly have that,' he agreed.

They returned to their table and, with expert timing, the wine waiter arrived with the wine.

Hutch had seen club members perform strange rites when tasting wine, but he simply inhaled the bouquet and took a sip before giving his approval. The waiter poured the wine and left them.

'I'm glad you don't make a performance of it, like some men do,' said Ellie. 'Neville is quite embarrassing, especially when he complains.'

'You don't surprise me, Ellie.'

'I know. Isn't he awful?'

He decided to be completely honest. 'The reason I don't go through all the motions,' he said, 'is that before I came to London I was a mill maintenance engineer. I lived in a terrace house in Alma Street and I'd never tasted wine or even seen a waiter.' Looking around the restaurant at the elaborate plaster work and crystal chandeliers, he said, 'I'd seen places like this in films, but I never thought I'd eat and drink in one. So, you see, it's no wonder I made that silly mistake yesterday with the Welsh rarebit.'

'I wish you'd forget about the Welsh rarebit, Hutch. I think you're adjusting remarkably well to your new life, and I hope you don't imagine that I've always frequented this kind of place. I'm Cinderella, remember?'

Her smile helped to ease his awkwardness, but he was still conscious of the difference between them. 'But your family have always been—'

'They've always been very good at keeping their younger daughter in her place. Believe me, Hutch, since I arrived in London, I've had to learn things that Rosie took completely for granted.'

The arrival of their first course interrupted their conversation, but when the waiter was gone, Hutch said, 'There's something I don't understand.'

'You're lucky, Hutch. There are lots of things that baffle me.'

'Me too, but there was something you said yesterday that made me wonder.'

'Go on, spill the beans.'

'You said something about kindness being in short supply at home.'

'It was,' she confirmed. 'Life *chez* Turner was all about creating the right impression. You'd think a mill manager was placed pretty high in the usual order of things, wouldn't you?'

'As I recall, it was always a good idea to keep out of the manager's way, just in case he was feeling the wrong way out,' he agreed. 'He wielded a lot of power.'

She smiled at the image. 'Well, powerful though a manager

is, there's a world of difference between him and the mill owner, and my parents made every effort to behave as if that difference didn't exist.'

'Why?' It seemed incredible to Hutch, who'd always regarded Ellie's father as one of the ruling class.

'You find social climbers in every walk of life, Hutch, and my parents worked at it full-time. Actually, now I think of it, they're probably struggling like mad to adjust to their reduced circumstances.' She smiled mischievously. 'I imagine Rosie's doing her share of struggling as well, under all that laundry.'

'Very likely. You see, the reason I mentioned it is, well, you strike me as a kind person.'

'Thank you, Hutch.'

'Well, you are, and I can't help wondering how you learned kindness in a house where there was so little.'

Ellie put down her knife and fork and pushed her plate to one side. 'There was Mrs Holroyd, our cook,' she said, folding her hands on the table, 'and Agnes, the maid.'

'Seriously?'

'Seriously.' Ellie nodded in confirmation. 'When I was little, and life seemed impossibly cruel, Mrs Holroyd would take me into her arms and hold me tight so that I felt protected against the whole world and its injustice. Then, when I stopped crying, she would teach me one of life's lessons and help me understand why things were as they seemed. She was both cook and philosopher, although not everyone knew that. My family saw her simply as a cook, but as far as I was concerned, she was just wonderful and I loved her.'

It was a different world from anything Hutch had known, and he was fascinated. He asked, 'What about the maid?'

'Agnes was fun. She had tremendous spirit – she needed it in that place – and she was like a kindly, loving, older sister. Also, she was forever covering up for me when I'd done something silly.'

The band created an interruption with 'Love is the Sweetest Thing', and Ellie said, 'We danced to this the first time. Do you remember?'

Hutch was already on his feet and offering her his hand.

'It's a beautiful song,' she said.

'Yes.' Hutch was still thinking about Mrs Holroyd and Agnes. It hurt when he thought about Ellie being so unhappy, and he was more than ever glad that he'd been able to show her some kindness on those two brief occasions.

The band took a break after the number, but instead of joining them immediately in the band room, the leader walked over to speak to Hutch.

'Hello,' he said. 'I hope you're both enjoying the evening. Please don't get up.'

'Yes, thank you, Mr Kyte.'

Ellie added her response, apparently sharing Hutch's surprise.

'Didn't I see you playing with the Carl Duverne band at the Golden Slipper?'

'Very likely, Mr Kyte. I play tenor sax there. My name's Hutch Hutchins, by the way, and this is Miss Turner.'

'I'm delighted to meet you both,' he said, shaking hands with them. 'I thought I recognised you. I was there for the opening. That's a fine band Carl's put together.'

'Thank you, Mr Kyte. We're certainly enjoying yours.'

'That's very civil of you. Now, Miss Turner,' he said, transferring his attention completely to Ellie, 'is there anything you'd like us to play?'

'How very kind,' said Ellie, recovering from her surprise.

'It's what they pay us for,' he assured her.

'Of course. I'd love to hear "For You, Just You, my Baby", if that's possible.'

'Not only is it possible, but you may depend on it.'

When Sydney Kyte left them to re-join his band, Hutch said, 'He does it so easily.'

'What does he do so easily?'

'Just being as suave as he is. I mean, he's a nice bloke and he seems genuine, but I think you have to be born like that.'

'It doesn't mean a thing, Hutch. All right, he's a nice chap, as you say, but so are you.'

Before Hutch could say anything, the waiter arrived with the main course.

'Ewan Broadmead is what I think you'd call suave,' said Ellie when they were alone again, 'but we both know the truth about him, don't we?'

'I see what you mean.'

'Good, because I don't care about a man's background or his class. It's what's inside that matters, and how he behaves.'

With that out of the way, they chatted easily through the main course, so that Sydney Kyte's next announcement surprised them both.

'This is a request, ladies and gentlemen. It's "For You, Just You, My Baby".'

Hutch led Ellie on to the floor.

'I always wanted to dance to this one,' she said, 'but I was never allowed.'

'Well, they're playing it just for you,' said Hutch, 'and no one's going to push you out ever again.'

'Cinderella's welcome to her Prince Charming,' said Ellie. 'I prefer to dance with my knight, who dances the best slow foxtrot, not only in Cullington, but probably in London as well.'

'Thanks, Ellie, but I doubt it, although you'll have to tell Rosie about this. I'm sure she'd love to know what you're getting up to while she's up to her ears in dirty laundry.'

They were able to thank Sydney Kyte again before the end of the evening, which came all too soon, as Ellie had to be at the Lodge before locking-up time.

———◆◆◆———

As they stood in the porch, Ellie said, 'Thank you for a truly lovely evening, Hutch.'

'Thank you for coming.' Hurriedly, he asked, 'Where will you be staying in Brighton?'

'At the YWCA, at least to begin with.'

'If I write to you there, will you let me come down to see you?'

'Of course, if you really want to. It takes about an hour on the train.'

'That's nothing.' He felt that time was slipping away. She would have to go inside soon. 'Ellie?'

'Yes?'

'Is it all right if I kiss you?'

'Oh, I think I can allow that.' Her eyes were full of fun.

It wasn't as if kissing a girl was a new experience; he'd done far more than that with Penny, and there'd been Jessie as well, but he was suddenly nervous. Slowly, he bent to touch her lips with his, gathering confidence and then drawing her into a prolonged and sensuous kiss that ended when they heard the doorknob being turned from the inside.

'I'll write to you, Ellie.'

'Yes, please write. Goodnight, Hutch.'

'Goodnight, Ellie.' He watched her enter the building, and then the door was closed by the invisible guardian. He headed for the underground, elated beyond reason and already looking forward to his first visit to Brighton.

27

D ear Hutch,
Thank you for your letter and for your kindness in asking about the new, well, temporary, job.

Things are more relaxed here than at Head Office, so I've been able to get to know everyone and find my way around quite easily. Brighton is a remarkable town and very popular at this time of the year. If you've never been here, I'll look forward to showing you around. If you have, maybe you can show me some of the sights!

I feel terribly flattered that you want to visit me here, and you're naturally very welcome to do that. Just let me know when you're coming.

How are things at the Golden Slipper? I'm ever so glad we were able to meet again.

I look forward to hearing from you. Take care of yourself.
Fondest regards,
Ellie.

Hutch read the letter twice before putting it into his pocket. He would probably read it again later and he would certainly reply to it as soon as he could, but first, he had to put his laundry and Norman's out for collection.

When he reached the hallway, he noticed that Phyllis had already left hers before leaving for work. He wasn't surprised. Neither was he surprised that she was already making noises about finding somewhere else to live. As Norman had prophesied, she was finding the cooking facilities very limiting. She'd also calculated that the extra rent payable for a small flat would be partly offset by not having to pay for 'extras', such as baths and laundry. She intended to do the washing and ironing herself, as she always had.

With the laundry out of the way, he returned to his room to reply to Ellie's letter. He'd recently bought a fountain pen, the first he'd ever owned, and he intended to put it to good use. He took out his writing pad, also an improvement on his previous notepaper, and began,

Dear Ellie,

Thank you for your letter, I'm glad you're finding things more relaxed at the Brighton office. To be honest, I don't know much about office work, but it must be better when everybody is friendly and not stuffy.

I've never been to Brighton or anywhere else that's by the sea, so I'm looking forward to my first visit.

I'd like to come down on Sunday, if it's all right with you. The train gets into Brighton at five-past ten on Sunday morning.

Things are going well at the club. Since you left London, we've done a BBC broadcast and made some recordings as well. Carl was right when he said that the band was 'going places'.

Let me know if Sunday is all right, and take care of yourself.

He wondered, for a moment, how to sign off. He'd ended his last letter with *Yours sincerely*, but Ellie had written *Fondest regards*, which sounded much friendlier. Recalling a recent conversation, he made his decision.

Always at My Lady's service,
Hutch.

He hoped it wouldn't sound silly, and he was relieved when he read Ellie's reply.

Dear Sir Knight,
Thank you for your letter. Sunday will be perfect. I'm looking forward to it already. I'll meet you at the station.
Fondest regards,
Ellie X.

He saw her as soon as he stepped off the train. Even in a purple, cotton-print shirt dress and floppy-brimmed sun hat, she was instantly recognisable. She smiled broadly when she saw him, and inclined her face for the chaste peck that was deemed respectable in public.

'Hello, Hutch,' she said. 'Did you have a good journey?'

'I'd hardly call it a journey,' he said, 'but yes, thank you. A chap on the train told me it was less than fifty miles. It's not all that far from London.'

'Do you think of London as your home?' She walked with him to the turnstile, where he showed his ticket. The ticket collector punched it and handed it back to him for the return journey.

'I suppose I do now. Don't you?'

'I believe I do,' she said. 'Yorkshire was all I'd ever known, so it was properly home, but I began to enjoy life so much more when I started work in London. Brighton's very pleasant too.'

He gave her his arm and they walked along the straight road from the station. Suddenly he stopped.

'What's the matter?'

'That's the sea, isn't it?'

'Yes.' She seemed amused at first, but quickly checked herself. 'Of course, you've never seen it, have you?'

'Only at the pictures,' he said, 'and then it was in black and white.' Entranced, he continued along the road, and the great, blue, shimmering expanse grew ever wider. 'I can't believe it.'

'You've got all day to get used to it,' she assured him.

'I don't think I'll ever get used to it.' He walked on, mesmerised, until a thought from the past occurred to him. 'My dad was killed at sea,' he said.

'I'm sorry, Hutch.'

'I never knew him. I was only two years old at the time. I was just thinking, though, how beautiful the sea looks today, and what horrors there are out there.'

'It's true,' she agreed. 'Shall we find somewhere where we can have coffee?'

'That's a good idea.'

'You've had breakfast, haven't you?'

'Yes. Have you?'

She assured him that she had and led him to a tea room on the sea front. 'We can have coffee in there,' she told him, 'and you can stare at the sea to your heart's content.'

They found a table by the window and sat down.

'I don't know what you must think,' he said.

'About what?'

'Me, behaving like a little lad, seeing the sea for the first time.'

'You know what I think about you.' She touched his hand with hers, and the feel of her white cotton glove seemed to emphasise the difference he felt in spite of what she said.

A waitress came, and they ordered coffee.

'I'd never tasted coffee until I came down to London,' he said.

'But you'd tasted chocolate. In our kitchen,' she reminded him.

'What made you remember that?'

'I've never forgotten it, but I mentioned it then because I've decided that, whenever you feel awkward about experiencing new things, I'm going to remind you of the person you are and what I like most about you.'

Caught unawares, Hutch was silent for a moment. Eventually, he said, 'There's nothing special about me, Ellie. I did what I did because I felt sorry for you. In the few minutes I'd known you, I knew you were a really nice girl and you didn't deserve to be left out. I suppose I just wanted to... well, I wanted to take care of you and... you know, make things right, even if it was just for one dance.' As he said it, he felt ridiculous.

Ellie blinked rapidly and turned away. Presently, she gripped his hand and said, 'Don't ever tell me you're not special, Hutch, because it's not true.'

Happily, the waitress provided a distraction by bringing their coffee, and Ellie concentrated on pouring it for them.

'Would you like to see the Royal Pavilion? It's one of the big attractions in Brighton.'

'Have you seen it?'

'No, I thought it was something we could do together.'

'Right,' he agreed, 'I'm game if you are.'

Suddenly, Ellie remembered something and said, 'I had a

letter from my mother this week. It seems that Rosie's given up her job as Assistant Matron. I knew it couldn't last.'

'I wonder what caused that.'

'I'll tell you. It's not really a subject for the table, so I'll just say that she wasn't exactly in her element dealing with the laundry.'

Hutch could find little sympathy for her. 'Was it the hard work that put her off?'

'No.' Ellie lowered her voice to say, 'Bedwetting.'

'They're a bit old for that, aren't they?' In Hutch's experience, babies wet their nappies, but they soon grew out of it.

'Don't you believe it. Many of those children are frightened and insecure, especially the youngest, the ones who've only just arrived and are sleeping away from home for the first time. When they're eight years old and in a strange place, they need love and certainty, and they were never going to get that from Rosie.' Then, after a little more thought, she added, 'Of course, some of them are already unhappy before they arrive.'

'You've surprised me, Ellie.'

'That children of the well-to-do can lead unhappy lives?'

'I suppose so. I'd never really thought about it.'

She squeezed his hand again. 'Privilege is a funny thing, Hutch.'

He was inclined to agree. 'I still can't get over the difference between you and Rosie,' he said.

'Can't you? If you remember, Rosie was groomed for society by ambitious parents. I was nurtured by loving servants, except I didn't think of them as servants. They were my family.'

'Where are they now?'

'Mrs Holroyd went to work for another family, and Agnes is still working for my parents. I'm looking forward to seeing her when I go home.'

————◆►◄————

The Royal Pavilion was another surprise for Hutch. They agreed that the interior was beautiful, but couldn't help finding it extravagant.

'It's a funny thing about the Princes of Wales,' said Hutch.

'Not all of them, surely?'

'No, but did you hear about King Edward coming to the club?'

'No, Rosie mentioned it, but as usual, she kept the details to herself.'

'Okay.' Hutch told her about the King's visit and his petulant behaviour when he couldn't have his own way.

When he'd finished, Ellie nodded and said, 'I think I know why Rosie was so secretive about your letter. It was sufficient for her that the King was there. She wouldn't want to think about anything that wasn't nice.'

'I wasn't impressed by him.'

'No, and for all the new King is younger than he is, he's a lot more grown up.'

'Maybe it's because one was groomed by an ambitious family to be King,' suggested Hutch. 'I don't know who was responsible for King George's upbringing. I shouldn't think it was the servants.'

'They'd both have a nanny, of course, and maybe Queen Mary had something to do with it, and I'm sure Queen Elizabeth has been good for him. They always look very happy together.'

———◆�># ———

They spent the afternoon on the pier and then had dinner at a restaurant with a conveniently good band.

Eventually, the YWCA and Hutch's train beckoned, and it was necessary for them to leave.

As they stood on the steps of the YWCA, Ellie said, 'You will come again, won't you?'

'Of course I will.'

She looked thoughtful for a brief spell, and then said, 'I know what will bring you back.'

'What's that?' As far as Hutch was concerned, his return was guaranteed.

'In Medieval times,' she explained, 'a lady gave a knight her favour, an article of clothing or something special, so that he would return from slaying dragons or whatever he was going to get up to, and bring it back to her. The superstition was that the responsibility of returning the favour would ensure his survival.' She fished in her bag for a minute and took out a lady's handkerchief with the letter 'E' and some tiny roses embroidered on it. 'There,' she said, pushing it into his breast pocket, 'you're my knight, and that's my favour. One day, I may ask for it back, but what I really want is you to keep coming back.'

'Do you really?'

'Hutch, do you think embroidered Irish lawn handkerchiefs grow on rose bushes? Of course I do. You do want to come back, don't you?'

'Yes, I do.' Only the residual shyness he felt in her company prevented him from telling her how much he wanted that. Instead, he held her close and, as many a knight and his lady must have done in centuries gone by, they kissed with much feeling.

28

Hutch made two further visits to Brighton before the secretarial post was filled and Ellie could return to London. When he met her off the train, that Saturday, however, it was clear that something was troubling her, and she explained as they made for the turnstile.

'I wrote to the Lodge, asking if I could have a room there again, and they were full up.' With a helpless expression, she said, 'I've nowhere to live.'

'We'll find somewhere,' he said, stopping at the exit. 'Don't you worry.'

'Why have we stopped?'

'I'm waiting for a telephone kiosk to come free.'

Eventually, someone stepped out of one of the kiosks, and Hutch claimed it, leaving Ellie to guard her luggage. He picked up the receiver and dialled Mrs Wheeler's number.

The telephone rang several times, and then Mrs Wheeler answered. Hutch pushed the button to release his two pennies and said, 'Mrs Wheeler? It's Hutch.'

'Hello, Mr Hutchins. Did you meet the young lady?'

'Yes, I did. I'm wondering if you have a room available to rent.'

'As of this morning, yes, I have two. Mr Barraclough and Miss Hutchins have moved out. I've no doubt they've told you where they're going.'

It was news to Hutch, although he knew Norman and Phyllis had been flat hunting. 'No, but I'll soon find out.' He would see Norman that evening at the club.

'There was a call for Mr Barraclough this morning. I believe it was about a flat. Then they packed and left.'

'Oh well, I'll hear all about it tonight. In the meantime, Mrs Wheeler, my friend Miss Turner needs accommodation. She was staying at the Christian Women's Lodge, but now that she's returned from Brighton, it seems they're full up.' He thought that mentioning the Lodge was probably as good as a testimonial.

'By all means bring her along, Mr Hutchins.'

'Thank you, Mrs Wheeler.' Opening the door of the kiosk, he spoke to Ellie. 'Mrs Wheeler has a room. When can you come over?'

With a look of relief, Ellie said, 'Straight away.' She looked at her watch and said, 'The office is closed now, anyway, so I'm free for the rest of the weekend.'

'Okay.' He relayed the message to Mrs Wheeler, who said she would be happy to show Ellie the room when they arrived.

'I pay twelve bob a week and feed myself,' Hutch told her. 'I couldn't afford full board when I arrived, and then Norman came down and took over the cooking. I've learned quite a lot from him.' He turned the key and opened the front door to number twenty-six.

'I could cook for both of us,' said Ellie.

'Can you cook?' It was a total surprise.

'Yes, I can. It's one of the things Mrs Holroyd taught me,' she explained.

'I'm getting to like Mrs Holroyd more and more.'

The kitchen door opened, and Mrs Wheeler came into the hall.

'Mrs Wheeler, this is Miss Turner.'

They shook hands, and Mrs Wheeler said, 'Miss Hutchins' old room is ready. You can have that if you decide to stay. It's just here.' She pointed to the ground floor room that Phyllis had vacated only that morning.

Knowing that Mrs Wheeler liked to keep men and women on different floors, Hutch said, 'Miss Turner and I will have our meals together, Mrs Wheeler.'

'That's quite all right.' Mrs Wheeler nodded, leaving the rest unsaid.

'Thank you. I'll go up to my room while you go through

everything with Miss Turner.' He wanted to be out of the way when she mentioned the embarrassing bit. Arriving home as he did after midnight, he was unlikely to be found in Ellie's room after ten o' clock, but Mrs Wheeler had to make the rule known. She kept a respectable house.

He came down to find that Ellie had moved into the room. Everything was settled. 'I'd have carried your bags in,' he said.

'Thank you, Hutch, but I'm not helpless.' Taking advantage of Mrs Wheeler's absence, she kissed him and said, 'Thank you for arranging this for me.'

'Oh, it was the obvious thing to do. Would you like to go to the Corner House for lunch to celebrate?'

'Yes, please, that's a lovely idea. Just give me a few minutes and I'll join you.'

———◆◆◆———

As they waited for their order, Ellie said, 'It'll be a luxury, not having to be back by locking-up time. Mrs Wheeler's given me a front door key. She's very trusting.'

'She's nice,' agreed Hutch.

'She told me how you and Norman helped her with her husband and looked after her when he died.'

'I hope she didn't go into too much detail,' said Hutch.

'She didn't mention the ins and outs of it, but she did say it was a blessing to have two strong men around when she needed someone to lift him.'

'Yes, poor bloke.' Hutch's mind returned to Mr Wheeler's last days. 'Poor Mrs Wheeler, too.'

'She said you were a great support at the funeral.' It seemed that Mrs Wheeler had told Ellie rather a lot, because then, she said, 'I didn't know you'd lost your mother recently, Hutch. I'm ever so sorry.'

'Thanks, Ellie.' He was spared having to say more, as the waitress arrived at that moment with their order.

'You're quite fond of Welsh rarebit now,' said Ellie when she'd left them.

'It's a kind of apology. I got its name wrong, so the least I can do is enjoy it.'

'You're the only man I know who's apologised to a Welsh rarebit,' said Ellie, 'and that alone makes you special.'

'I'm glad you think so.'

'I haven't known many men,' she announced, 'but I've known some horrors.' It was clear that she had someone in particular on her mind, because she went on to say quietly, 'I had news from home just before I left Brighton. It wasn't good news.'

Hutch waited for her to continue.

'Neville has lost his job at the school. They paid him up for the term and told him not to return.'

'How on earth did he manage that?' Hutch had always believed that schoolteachers, unlike millworkers, were set up for life.

Ellie lowered her voice further and said, 'He lost his temper with a boy and flogged him quite horribly. They're allowed to use the cane, but he went too far. Another boy brought Matron to the dormitory, and she saw the awful weals on the boy's... you know... *behind*, and reported the matter to the headmaster.'

'In that case, I've no sympathy with him.'

'Neither have I, Hutch. He has an awful temper, but so has his father, apparently.'

'That's no excuse.' Hutch considered the news and said, 'I wasn't impressed when I met him, but I thought he was just a fool. I'd no idea he was such a nasty piece of work. '

'He and Rosie are living apart.'

'Already?'

'I told you he has a terrible temper. He gave her an awful bruise on her eye, and she walked out on him. She's living with my parents now.'

'I don't blame her.' Hutch knew as well as anyone that Rosie could be irritating, but she didn't deserve that kind of treatment. 'I'm old-fashioned,' he said. 'I'd never hit a woman, or a girl, for that matter.'

'I'm glad you mentioned the girl. I shan't be twenty-one until July, nineteen thirty-nine.'

That surprised Hutch. 'So you're not nineteen yet.'

'Not until the eighteenth of next month.'

'I'd never have guessed it, not that it matters.'

She gave him a coy smile and said, 'Aren't you worried about being seen with a babe in arms?'

'Don't be silly. I'm happy to be seen with you. In fact, not just happy, but proud.'

'Oh, Hutch.' She reached across the table to squeeze his hand. 'That's a lovely thing to say.'

Having defied his shyness to make his feelings known, he was determined to justify them. 'Some people,' he said, 'are taken with the silly, artificial ways they see in others. Rosie took to Mr Rushworth because she thought he was glamorous and exciting. That was what impressed her, and now she's learned her lesson the hard way.'

'I hope so for her sake.'

'So do I.'

'What do you look for, Hutch?'

He had no need to consider his answer. He'd been honest with her, so there was no going back. 'I don't really look for anything,' he said. 'A bloke would need to wear a blindfold not to see that you're pretty. In fact, you're a lovely-looking girl, but that's not the whole picture. You're all kinds of things that are important to me. You're honest, innocent, kind-hearted, and there isn't an ounce of guile in you. Those things mean much more to me than something as false as glamour.'

Ellie blinked repeatedly, as she had in the tea room in Brighton. 'Hutch,' she said, 'you say the loveliest things.'

'I couldn't if I didn't mean them.'

'You're the very soul of chivalry.'

'You know,' said Hutch, smiling, 'I've thought about that knight business and I reckon it must have been hard work in olden times.'

'What makes you say that?'

'It was an honour for a man to be a knight, so I think he'd be very committed to his work, forever looking at his sun dial and wondering if he could manage another noble deed before sunset.'

'Perhaps you're right. If so, I hope his sun dial was more

reliable than my silly wristwatch.' She screwed her eyes up with embarrassment. 'It would be, of course,' she said. 'Sun dials are never wrong.'

'Does your watch need cleaning?'

'No, I've tried that. It's a cheap one that'll never be any better.'

'They had the right idea all those years ago, didn't they? They couldn't beat the old sun dial.'

'Unless the sun went behind a cloud.'

Hutch agreed, although, for him, there wasn't a cloud in sight. He also knew what to give Ellie on her birthday.

29

I t turned out that Phyllis and Norman were only a short distance away, in Wingate Street, where they'd been fortunate enough to find a small flat with two tiny bedrooms and a kitchen that was more to Phyllis's liking. The rent was rather more than their combined rents had been at Rumbold Street, but it was still within their budget. The opportunity had come via a member of the band, and at short notice, hence their quick departure from Rumbold Street.

It was sheer good fortune that Ellie's birthday fell on a Sunday, so that it could be celebrated properly. Hutch had visited the shop in Pentonville Road, where Norman had bought Phyllis's wristwatch, and his next job was to reserve a table at the *Café Anglais* in Leicester Square.

At a respectable hour of the morning, when Ellie would be dressed and ready to receive him, he went downstairs and tapped on her door.

There was a muffled noise from within, and as the door opened, he saw the reason for the unintelligible utterance. Ellie was eating toast.

'Happy birthday.'

She swallowed. 'Thank you. Would you like some toast?'

'Please, if you're making some.'

Ellie cut two slices of bread and placed them in the electric toaster, a recent purchase by Hutch.

'Now, are your hands clean?'

'They will be in a minute.' She washed them quickly at the sink and dried them. 'Right.'

'Here's your card.' He handed it to her with a flourish, and while she was removing it from its envelope, he took a small package from his pocket. 'As we're going somewhere special tonight,' he said, 'I thought you might like to wear this.'

Mystified, she undid the gift wrapping, which Hutch took from her with one hand whilst rescuing two slices of toast with the other.

'That was clever,' she said, still finding her way into the box. 'How can you handle hot toast like that?'

'It's not too hot for the toughened hands of the manual worker,' he told her.

She finally opened the box and gasped. 'Hutch, this is lovely! It must have cost you a fortune.'

'Not quite, and it was worth it. Happy birthday.'

'Mm. Come here.'

Hutch obliged, and received a lavish kiss of gratitude.

'Thank you, Hutch. It's beautiful,' she said, taking off her old watch and replacing it with the new one.

'It looks good on you. Where's the butter?'

'I'll do it.' She buttered the toast for him, looking at the same time at the card. 'It's a lovely card, too,' she said. 'I think it's what the Americans call "custom made".' She pointed with the butter knife to where Hutch had added a digit, changing the message from *Today You Are 9* to one befitting a person ten years older.

'You'd think in a city of this size, I'd be able to find a card for a nineteen-year-old, but no, I had to adapt.'

'It's lovely, and so are you.' She kissed him again. 'Where are we going tonight?'

'We're going to the *Café Anglais* in Leicester Square. I had to ask around, how to pronounce it,' he admitted.

'And you pronounced it perfectly. Who's playing there?'

'Bert Firman and his Band.'

'They broadcast sometimes, don't they?'

'Oh, yes, he's a well-known bandleader.'

'I'm looking forward to it already, and I shan't be late now I have a beautiful wristwatch that keeps proper time.'

Reading the time upside-down, Hutch said, 'You'll need to set it.'

'Give me a chance. I've only just got it.' She set the time by Hutch's and wound the watch up. Finally, with it back on her wrist, she said, 'You really are a lovely man. Let me kiss you again.'

———◆�► ◄———

The band was playing 'When Did You Leave Heaven?'

The waiter had shown them to their table, but instead of taking his seat, Hutch asked, 'Shall we?'

Ellie joined him and they took to the floor. The waiter tactfully retreated.

'This is the best birthday I've ever had,' said Ellie.

'Why is it the best?' Hutch was still learning to appreciate her somewhat unique values.

'Because I'm spending it with you. Also, I'd rather dance the foxtrot with you than with anyone else.'

Hutch tried to think of an appropriate response, but all he could think of was, 'I feel the same way.' As he spoke, he felt awkward and inept.

'About the foxtrot?'

'Any dance.' He felt clumsier still as he said, 'I'd rather dance with you than anyone.'

'Oh, Hutch.' The two words were loaded with feeling, but neither Ellie nor Hutch spoke again until the end of the number.

When they returned to their table, Ellie said, 'When you say lovely things to me, I go all squidgy inside.'

'I'm not very good at saying the right things.'

'Oh, but you are.'

Further argument was avoided when the waiter returned with the menu.

'Unfortunately, sir,' he said, 'the turbot proved highly popular and is no longer available.'

'I see.' He might have been disappointed had he known what turbot was, but he was spared that setback.

Ellie said, 'Turbot is popular, but I think halibut is every bit as nice. You do like fish, don't you?'

'Yes, I do.'

'I prefer the meaty kind, like halibut. In fact, it rather appeals tonight.'

Realising that Ellie had thrown him a line, Hutch said, 'Yes, I'd like to try it.'

'Good.' She turned back a page and said, 'Now let's decide what to have first. Do you like puff pastry?'

'Yes.' He'd come across it once and found it fragile but agreeable.

'They have prawn *vol-au-vents*. The prawns are in mayonnaise, so they'll be peeled, which is good, and they're served in puff pastry cases.'

'That sounds nice.' Hutch had once wrestled with whole prawns, and the idea of having them ready-peeled was enticing.

'Two minds with but a single thought,' said Ellie.

Hutch said nothing, realising that he'd been led, kindly and sensitively, through a grown-up maze. Besides, he had plenty to think about. Ellie's remark about feeling squidgy inside had sounded a similar but previously-unknown note within him as well. His careful upbringing and apprenticeship as an engineer had made him a stranger to fanciful ideas, but now he was undergoing a new and unsettling experience that was anything but matter-of-fact. It was surprising enough that Ellie was affected by his naïve compliments, but he had only to look at her and his heart seemed to melt so that he felt a kind of helplessness to which he was a stranger, but which was no less exciting for that.

'Have you made your choice, sir?' The waiter's voice brought him back to earth.

'I think so.' He looked at Ellie, who nodded. 'We'd both like the prawn *vol-au-vents* and the halibut, please.'

'An excellent choice, if I may say so, sir. Would you like me to send the wine waiter to your table?'

'Yes, please.' It was becoming easier all the time.

'Well done, Hutch,' said Ellie when they were alone again.. 'I studied French, and I couldn't have pronounced "*vol-au-vents*" better myself.'

'Thank you. I think it must be the musical ear. I listened to you and copied you.' He shook his head and said, 'I've a lot to learn, as you know.'

'And you're learning quickly.' She looked over his shoulder and said, 'Here comes the wine waiter.'

'I believe you'd like to see the wine list, sir,' said the waiter, opening it and placing it before Hutch.

'Yes. What do you recommend with the halibut?'

'With the halibut, sir, I have no hesitation in recommending the Chablis.' He pointed elegantly with his little finger to the wine in question. It was quite expensive, a 1931 vintage, but Hutch was determined to celebrate Ellie's birthday properly.

'Thank you. We'll have the Chablis, then.'

'Certainly, sir.' The wine waiter closed the wine list and left them.

'Hutch,' said Ellie, 'that was masterly.'

'Not really. I've heard members do it that way at the club.'

'I'd never have known.'

The band was approaching the end of the number, and Hutch said, 'Will you excuse me? I need to speak to the bandleader.'

Surprised once more, Ellie said, 'Of course.'

Hutch waited for the end and then approached the rostrum. The bandleader saw him and smiled his greeting.

'Good evening, sir. How can I help?'

'Good evening, Mr Firman. This is an excellent band.'

'Thank you.'

'I play with the Carl Duverne Orchestra at the Golden Slipper. My name's Hutchins.'

'I'm delighted to meet you, Mr Hutchins, and I congratulate you, also, on having found an excellent band.'

'Thank you, Mr Firman. Would it be possible to hear "Love is the Sweetest Thing"?'

'It will be a pleasure to play it for a fellow musician.'

'Thank you very much.'

When he re-joined Ellie, she asked, 'What was that about?'

'A sort of musical birthday card.'

She was left wondering for the moment, because the wine waiter arrived with the wine, a bucket of ice and a stand. Elaborately, he cut the seal, drew the cork and poured some for Hutch to taste.

'That's good,' said Hutch, leaving him to fill their glasses.

'Thank you, sir.' With a flourish, the wine waiter departed.

'It's funny,' said Hutch, 'but since I came south, I've been called "sir" by waiters, waitresses and even a Welsh miner.'

'How did you meet a Welsh miner?'

'Some of them had come to London to busk,' he told her. 'There was no work for them at home.' He told her about the sorry line of miners in their threadbare clothes, and the achingly beautiful sound they made. 'I'm not kidding, Ellie, it was tragic, and not only that, but they were being treated as vagrants. They had to walk in the gutter.'

'Horrid,' she agreed, 'but you spoke to them?'

'Norman and I took them to Lee Kwan Yan's restaurant in Chinatown for fish and chips.'

Ellie was blinking.

'I'm sorry. I didn't mean to upset you.'

'You haven't. I was just thinking about you and Norman.' She dabbed the corners of her eyes with her napkin. 'Two latter-day knights.'

'No, just two blokes who hadn't forgotten what it was like to be hungry.'

During their conversation, band parts had been discreetly given out, and now Bert Firman looked across at Hutch, who nodded.

'A request, ladies and gentlemen. It's a Ray Noble classic: "Love is the Sweetest Thing".'

Hutch stood and offered his hand to Ellie, who took it readily.

'This was the first number we ever danced to,' she said.

'I know. That's why I requested it.'

'Oh, Hutch.'

It seemed that only Ellie could inflect so much meaning into those two words. That and other thoughts occurred to Hutch as they danced to the classic that meant so much to both of them.

———————

Mindful of the ten o' clock rule, they had to say goodnight on Mrs Wheeler's doorstep.

Big Ideas

Ellie said, 'I've had a wonderful birthday, Hutch. Thank you.'

As Hutch bent to kiss her, he felt strangely disinhibited. Maybe it was the special nature of the evening, or maybe he was simply feeling more at ease with her by then but, almost without thinking, he said, 'I love you, Ellie.'

Her eyes opened wide. She asked, 'Do you mean it?'

'Of course I do. I just didn't have the nerve to tell you until now.'

'Oh, Hutch!'

It was enough that he knew what she meant.

30

A s they met before band call two weeks later, it was clear to Hutch that Norman had something on his mind. Knowing him as he did, however, he waited for his friend to speak, which he did at the coffee break.

'Hutch,' he said, 'I've been meaning to have a word.'

'I'd never have known.'

The irony was lost on Norman, preoccupied as he was. 'Aye, well, I feel awkward, and I want to clear the air about Phyllis and me moving out.'

'What's bothering you, Norm?'

'Just, well, how it looks.'

'It looks to me as if Phyllis has found herself a kitchen with hot and cold water and a cooker.'

'Aye.' Norman was clearly still at a loss for the right words.

'My mother would have been up in arms, as you know, at you two being under one roof without a chaperone, but times change, and it doesn't bother me.'

'Doesn't it? I mean, there's nowt going on, and Phyllis wouldn't stand for it, anyway. Not that I....'

'Relax, Norm. I know you're both on your best behaviour, an' you're looking to get wed, anyway.'

For the first time, Norman looked relieved. 'Yes, we are. I just wondered, when I saw you looking a bit thoughtful, that maybe it was on your mind.'

'No, not that. It's something else altogether, but I think we're wanted again. I'll see you after band call.'

The band was preparing for another recording session, so they rehearsed some new numbers and brushed up some older ones. The next session was going to feature Vernon Waterhouse, and, joking apart, Hutch and Norman were both pleased for him.

At the end of band call, they headed for the coffee house close by and took their usual table.

'Right, Hutch,' said Norman with characteristic directness, 'what's on your mind?' With his problem dealt with, he saw no reason why Hutch shouldn't unburden himself readily.

After some consideration, Hutch said, 'It's about Ellie and me.'

'Isn't it going well, Hutch?'

'It's going very well. Things couldn't be better,' he said, adding, 'as they stand.'

'Aye?'

'We haven't discussed it yet, but we both know we want it to be permanent.'

Norman's face registered pleasant surprise. 'Well,' he said, 'I can recommend it.'

'There's only one problem.'

'Well, go on, then. Let's hear it.'

It was perhaps as well on that occasion that Norman's grasp of tact erred on the blunt side, in that it left little scope for hedging or delay. 'We could be waiting two years,' Hutch explained.

'Whatever for?'

'Ellie was nineteen last month. Unless her father gives his consent for her to be married, we'll have to wait for her to be twenty-one.'

Norman studied the bottom of his teacup. Whilst Hutch had long since developed the taste for coffee, Norman remained loyal to tea. 'Why wouldn't he give his consent? She's a bit young, but they get wed at nineteen nowadays, and even younger.'

'Think about it, Norm.' Hutch had been thinking about little else for some time. 'The difference between Mr Turner and me is....' He was at a loss for a description.

'Right enough,' agreed Norman, 'As I remember him, he's not short of wind and bluster, but I'd like to see him get a tune out of a saxophone.'

'He's a mill manager, and if he remembers me at all, it's as a maintenance engineer.'

'That's a load of bunkum, Hutch, and that's putting it mildly. He was manager at Crawley's, but they've closed, and he's out of work. You were an engineer at Atkinson's, but they've closed, and you're a successful musician now, in a fashionable Mayfair club. What's holding you back? Go and talk to him, and tell him it's his best chance of getting his daughter married off to a bloke with summat about him, an' not a dead loss, like that daft bugger that married their Rosie. You never know, we might have a double wedding on our hands. That's if you frame yourself and play your cards right instead of dithering around like a curate at his first christening.'

———▶◀———

That evening, before going to the club, Hutch sat on Ellie's bed, watching her sew a button on to one of his dress shirts. She made it look as easy as winking, and she hadn't stabbed herself once. It was good of her to do it, as well, as she'd only just come in from work.

'Ellie,' he said, 'I know this is very sudden, but....' He wondered quite how to put it. 'You know that Phyllis and Norman are planning to get married, don't you?'

'Yes, isn't it lovely?'

'You see, Norman and I were talking this morning, and he suggested... well, it's just an idea at this stage, but how do you fancy joining them?'

She looked puzzled. 'Going to their wedding? Of course, that would be lovely.' She cut the thread and handed the shirt to him. 'When's it to be?'

'We don't know yet.'

'Oh.'

'But that's not what I meant. I really meant to ask you if you'd like to be married on the same day as them, at the same church and everything.'

She stared at him until realisation overtook her, and she asked, 'Are you asking me to marry you?'

'Yes.' He was surprised she hadn't gathered that already. He thought he'd made it quite obvious.

'Oh, Hutch!' She left her chair and joined him on the bed. 'Of course I will!' She joined him in a hug. 'I want that more than anything!'

They held each other for several minutes, simply enjoying the moment, and then Hutch asked, 'Could you get a weekend off, a Saturday morning, or, better still, a Friday as well?'

'Yes,' she said, kissing him by way of celebration, 'I have some holiday to come.'

'Good. I'll arrange a deputy, and then we can go and see your parents.'

'Yes, we'll need their consent.' Then, a thought occurred to her. 'I hope you're not going to be terribly in awe of my father, Hutch.'

'Not even a little bit.'

'Good, because he'll intimidate you if he can. My mother will be quietly superior, but he's bound to play the big boss.'

'He's not my boss, Ellie. The worst he can do is withhold his consent, and if he does that, we'll just wait until you're twenty-one and then get married, whether he likes it or not.'

'You've really thought about it, haven't you?'

'Of course I have.' There was no need to tell her about Norman's blunt advice that morning. Instead, he told her of his own resolve. 'I love you, Ellie. I don't even want to think about life without you, and I'm going to marry you, come what may.'

————◆┝◀————

Preparations had to be made. First, Ellie telephoned her parents and told them of her planned visit. They were understandably curious, as they hadn't expected her until Christmas, but she was carefully vague about her reason for going home.

Hutch spent some time in Archer Street, finding a suitable deputy; he wanted to provide Carl with a top quality musician, and he finally succeeded in finding a saxophonist who had played, at one time, with Jack Payne and his orchestra until illness intervened.

After some reflection, he decided to book a hotel room in Bradford. He wasn't convinced he would receive a warm welcome at the Turner household, and he needed somewhere he could take Ellie if things failed to go the way they wanted. He also intended to visit the shop in Bradford where Norman had bought Phyllis's engagement ring, and that would happen with or without Mr Turner's consent. Whether it was down to Norman's encouragement or simply his own determination, Hutch felt more resolute than ever, so that he was almost looking forward to the meeting. It would be interesting, as well, to see Rosie again in her changed circumstances. The events of the past two years might have had a steadying effect on her, but he wasn't inclined to bet on it.

He would also no doubt pass his old address at some time, and that would be an occasion for nostalgia as well as a reminder of how far he'd travelled in pursuit of his ambition.

With those thoughts and a new and unassailable sense of purpose, he and Ellie finally caught the nine-fifty train from King's Cross to Leeds.

31

The Turners' house was on the outskirts of Cullington, distant enough from the terraced cottages and boarded-up mills that the only embarrassment Ellie's parents had to suffer was the memory of the mill's closure and their reduced circumstances.

As they stepped off the bus, Ellie took Hutch's arm, as she always did. 'No one does this in Cullington,' she observed.

'They've had the niceties of life knocked out of 'em, Ellie. It's as much as they can do now to survive.'

'Yes, it's too awful for words.' She opened the gate, and they walked down the path to the door.

'If anyone had told me two years ago that this was a step downwards, I'd have thought they were joking,' said Hutch. 'It's less than they had, right enough, but it's a far cry from where I used to live.'

Ellie rang the doorbell, and less than ten seconds later, it was opened by a servant, whose unremarkable features were suddenly transformed into a picture of joy.

'Miss Ellie!' She drew Ellie into a rapturous hug. 'My little girl!'

'Oh, Agnes, it's wonderful to see you again.' Then, mindful of Hutch's presence, she said, 'This is Agnes, Hutch. Agnes, this is Mr Hutchins.'

Hutch extended his hand, but Agnes hesitated.

'It's all right, Agnes,' Ellie told her.

Agnes accepted his hand. 'How d' you do, sir? I'm pleased to make your acquaintance.'

'How d' you do, Agnes. Ellie's told me a lot about you, and I'm very pleased to meet you.'

'I'll tell Mrs Turner you're here.' Agnes took their hats, coats and gloves, and disappeared down the hallway.

Hutch asked, 'Why didn't she want to shake hands with me?'

'She wanted to, but you're a visitor, and visitors only shake hands with their equals.'

'What a lot of bunkum.' He'd wanted to use the word ever since his conversation with Norman, and it now seemed quite appropriate.

'I'm inclined to agree. Let's go through.' Ellie led him along the hall to the sitting room, where Agnes opened the door for them to enter.

Hutch had met Mrs Turner on only one occasion, but he had no difficulty in recognising her. Her figure had broadened a little in the intervening years, but she seemed no less dignified than he remembered.

'Hello, Mother.' Ellie kissed her dutifully. 'I don't know if you've met Mr Hutchins.'

To avoid Mrs Turner's embarrassment, he prompted her. 'We met once, Mrs Turner. It was only a brief visit, so I don't expect you'll remember it.'

'I do remember it, Mr Hutchins,' she said, taking his hand. 'You're one of my daughter Rosemary's friends, I believe. At all events, I'm happy to meet you again.'

'Likewise, Mrs Turner.'

'I trust you had a pleasant journey.'

'Very pleasant, thank you.'

Returning her attention to Ellie, she said, 'Your father should be joining us soon. I don't know what's keeping him. Please take a seat, Mr Hutchins.'

'Thank you, Mrs Turner.' Hutch joined Ellie on one of the sofas, unable to believe the Turners' insistence on living in the grand manner despite their enforced adjustment.

'Where are you staying, Mr Hutchins?'

'At the Midland Hotel in Bradford.'

'I see, but you'll join us for lunch, presumably?'

'Thank you, Mrs Turner. If it's quite convenient.'

'Of course.' She pushed a button beside her chair to summon Agnes, who appeared at the door promptly.

'Yes, ma'am?'

'There are two extra for lunch, Agnes.'

'Yes, ma'am, and dinner?'

Hutch shook his head. 'I don't want to trouble you further, Mrs Turner.'

'Very well. We'll have coffee, I think, Agnes. You'll take coffee with us, won't you, Mr Hutchins?'

'Thank you, Mrs Turner.'

'Mr Turner and Mrs Rushworth are here, ma'am.'

'Thank you, Agnes.'

First to enter the room was Rosie, who acknowledged her sister briefly before forsaking her for Hutch.

'Hutch! I didn't expect to see you,' she said, inclining her face theatrically for a kiss. 'What are you doing here?'

'Just visiting, Rosie.'

'Father,' said Ellie, as her parent came into the room.

'Eleanor.' He kissed her.

'Father, this is Mr Hutchins.'

'Mr Hutchins is joining us for lunch, Joseph.'

'How d' you do, Mr Turner.' Hutch offered his hand. 'We have met briefly, but it was some time ago.'

'Hutch used to come on Thursdays, father,' said Rosie. 'He dances a divine foxtrot.'

'Well, Mr 'Utchins, you're welcome to stay to lunch as you're hevidently a friend of both Rosemary and Heleanor.'

'Thank you, Mr Turner.' Hutch was reminded of his host's haphazard distribution of the initial 'h'. He imagined it must be a perpetual embarrassment for Mrs Turner.

Agnes arrived with the coffee, and meaningful conversation was shelved for the moment.

———◆◆———

At lunch, Hutch was conscious of being under scrutiny, especially by Mrs Turner, but he was confident, nevertheless, that his conduct at the table had offended no one. His attention had been largely on Ellie, who appeared to grow increasingly nervous throughout the meal. From time to time, he tried to reassure her by touching her hand beneath the table, knowing that, if it did no more good, she would appreciate the gesture.

After dinner, Mr Turner, who had been looking at Hutch and Ellie from time to time with a degree of speculation, took him aside.

'I imagine you've come 'ere for a purpose, young man.'

Hutch nodded. 'That's right, Mr Turner.'

'Na then.' As Agnes was clearing the dishes, he said, 'Mr 'Utchins and I will have coffee in my den, Hagnes.'

'Very good, sir.'

By this time, Ellie was clearly nervous, so Hutch gave her a quick smile and squeezed her hand surreptitiously before following his host to the mysterious location.

'I call it my "den",' said Mr Turner, opening the door and ushering Hutch inside, 'because it's where I like to come when I want a bit of peace and quiet.'

Hutch looked around him at the bare walls and wondered what his host did when he was enjoying his retreat from the noise and distraction of family life.

'Some chaps prefer to call it a "study", but I don't 'old with that nonsense. I gave up studying a long time ago, when I'd learned all I needed to know about dyein' and finishin'.' He gestured towards a Windsor chair and said, 'Sit yourself down.' Taking his seat behind a large but apparently superfluous desk, he said, 'Rosemary tells me you were at Hatkinson's.'

'That's right, until the mill closed.'

'That were a sorry business an' all. It were t' same with Crawley's.'

Hutch could only nod in agreement. Privately, he was amused by the way Mr Turner's accent had broadened since his earlier attempts to impress his guest.

Agnes brought in a tray of coffee things, which she placed on the desk.

'All right, Hagnes, we'll see to it.'

'Very good, sir.' She left the room, favouring Hutch with a smile that made him wonder if maybe Ellie had been indiscreet.

As Mr Turner poured the coffee, he asked, 'You're not on the Square, are you?'

'I beg your pardon?'

'The Freemasons,' he translated.

'No, I'm not.'

'I thought not. Do you take milk?'

'No, thank you. I have it black and without sugar.'

'Oh, na then.' He handed Hutch's coffee to him and poured milk into his own. 'Well, young man,' he said, 'what is the purpose of your visit?'

'My purpose, Mr Turner, is to ask you for your daughter Eleanor's hand in marriage.' He thought it wise to use Ellie's full Christian name, as he was making a formal request.

Mr Turner appeared stunned, and Hutch wondered quite what he'd been expecting.

'Did I 'ear you right, young man?'

'I hope so. Ellie and I want to get married, but first we need your consent because Ellie's not yet reached her majority.'

There was an ominous silence, and then Mr Turner asked, 'What exactly was your job at Atkinson's?' The initial 'h' now seemed to have retired altogether.

'I was a maintenance engineer, but that's all in the past.'

'If it's all in the past, what 'ave you been doing since Atkinson's closed, might I ask?' His manner had changed completely, and he was now openly displeased.

Hutch found himself wondering if his task might have been easier had he been a Freemason. 'I've been working as a professional musician. I play tenor saxophone in the Carl Duverne Dance Orchestra at one of the most fashionable clubs in London.'

'Do you call that *work*?'

'Work is what it is, Mr Turner, and what's more, it's honest work, it calls for skill, and it's well paid.'

In his agitation, the irate parent rose to his feet to say, 'You come to me as an unemployed maintenance mechanic who plays a bit of music on the side, and you expect me to let you marry my daughter? Let me tell you something, young feller. You've got a nerve!'

'I'm not unemployed, Mr Turner. I have stamps on my insurance cards to prove it, I have receipts from the Inland Revenue, I have a healthy bank account, and I'm more than capable of supporting Ellie as well as myself.' He realised that his voice had also risen during the last sentence, but he didn't care. Joseph Turner had revealed himself just as he'd expected, as an overbearing, narrow-minded bully.

'You've got all that, 'ave you? What are your earnings? Come on, let's 'ear some 'ard facts an' figures.'

'I'm paid twelve pounds a week plus a pound an hour extra for recording and broadcasting.'

''Ow much?' Clearly, he found the sum outrageous.

'I just told you, and it doesn't end there. We get regular pay rises, and we'll be paid handsomely when we travel abroad.' It wasn't exactly on the cards, but Turner wasn't to know that, and it wasn't beyond the limits of possibility either.

Mr Turner sat down again, almost in a daze. 'Twelve quid a week,' he said. 'Twelve quid a week for playin' music.'

'And extra for recording sessions and broadcasts,' Hutch reminded him.

It seemed that Mr Turner hadn't heard him. 'Twelve quid a week,' he said.

'It could easily go up to fifteen by Christmas.'

'What?'

For a moment, Hutch feared that his host might succumb to a fit of apoplexy. 'Don't upset yourself, Mr Turner,' he said. 'Look at it this way. People wanted worsted cloth, so Crawley's paid you to manage their mill for as long as they could sell it. On the other hand, people want entertainment, and I'm paid to supply that. When you think about it, there isn't that much difference, except that there's still a demand for entertainment, and the worsted cloth industry isn't what it was, let's be honest.' He was hitting below the belt, but he was, after all, dealing with a bully.

After a brooding silence, Mr Turner said quietly, 'So you intend marryin' my daughter?'

'Ellie.' Hutch didn't want him to get the wrong idea. He was welcome to Rosie. Anyone was.

'Listen, lad. 'Rosemary's weddin' cost us a small fortune.'

'It would. Neville Rushworth did things with style, I believe.'

'Don't mention 'is name in this 'ouse.'

'Sorry. I'm not carried away with him myself.'

''E brought Rosemary to ruin, you know.'

Hutch couldn't really follow the logic of that assertion, but he was happy to agree. 'That's true, but I only have Ellie's happiness and wellbeing at heart. I'm sure you can see that.'

'No, listen, young man. You're missin' the point. Rosemary's weddin' cost us that much, that we can't possibly afford another. Do you follow what I'm gettin' at now?'

'Yes, but I can set your mind at rest on that score. It won't cost you a brass farthing.'

'What?' This time there was no anger. It was simply an expression of incredulity.

'No, I'll pay for the wedding.'

'Good Lord.'

'That's right. Make no mistake, Mr Turner. Ellie and I want to get married, and if you don't give us your consent now, we'll just wait two years until Ellie's twenty-one, and we'll do it then.'

'Well....' Mr Turner was clearly flummoxed. He looked around the bare room, and the coffee pot seemed to give him inspiration. 'Do you fancy some more coffee?'

'Why not? It beats arguing, and particularly when we both want the same thing.'

'The same thing?'

'Ellie's happiness. That's black, with no sugar, please.'

They sat and drank coffee together, Mr Turner talking about the old days and asking questions from time to time about life in London, and Hutch trying to sound interested in a world he'd been happy to leave behind.

Eventually, they emerged and joined the rest of the family in the sitting room, where Mrs Turner's obvious displeasure and Ellie's tearful countenance suggested that proceedings had been equally dramatic. When Ellie saw Hutch in the doorway, she came to him immediately.

'It's all right, Ellie,' he told her, taking her hands in his. 'Everything's fine.'

Mrs Turner gave him a thunderous look before turning to her husband and demanding, 'Well, Joseph, have you set him straight?'

'No, Isabella. I think it's fair to say that 'e's set me straight, and before I tell you the 'ole story, you'd better tell Hagnes to lay another place for dinner.'

———◆◀———

After dinner, Hutch got up to catch his bus. 'I'll be back in the morning,' he said. 'I'm taking Ellie shopping.'

'What for?' Petulant though she was at finding her younger sister in the spotlight, Rosie would never remain in ignorance for want of a direct question.

'To buy an engagement ring. I think we'll probably try Taylor and Jackson in Sunbridge Road.'

'Taylor and Jackson? Isn't that where Norman bought Phyllis's ring? They're very exclusive.'

'No one says "exclusive" nowadays, Rosie. The prevailing phrase is "*the* place to go".'

Ellie allowed herself a smile, but said nothing. It seemed she was still unable to believe the events of the day.

Mrs Turner asked soberly, 'Have you given any thought to the kind of wedding you both have in mind?'

Hutch looked at Ellie, who nodded, but was clearly happy for him to speak for them both.

'My sister Phyllis is marrying my best friend Norman Barraclough,' he said. 'We're thinking of joining them and making it a double wedding.'

'A *double wedding*,' said Rosie, now recovered from her initial sulk. 'How grand.'

'Well, Rosie,' said Hutch, 'you know me. I always did have big ideas.'

THE END

Lightning Source UK Ltd.
Milton Keynes UK
UKHW010705250321
380963UK00001B/35